The Bomb in the Attic

The Bomb in the Attic

JACOB HAY

WILDSIDE PRESS

The Bomb in the Attic

It was Dr. Chernowith who suggested this.

Hogarth, the guard on the afternoon shift, had led me into the bare, gray-walled, high-ceilinged little chamber which serves the prison's visiting psychiatrists as a consulting room, bade me be seated, and then left. I sat on a chipped white metal stool beside a chipped white metal table and waited. There was another chipped white metal chair on the other side of the table. Table and chairs were bolted to the floor. There was a door opposite the one by which I had entered, and set into this door at eye level was a peephole. Through the peephole stared a bloodshot eye. I stared at the eye for several minutes during which it did not blink, and finally I had to look away. Then Dr. Chernowith came in.

"Ah, yes, yes, yes," he said happily, carefully closing the door behind him. The eye was still there, fixed and malignant. "I see you have observed my eye," he went on, sitting down on the other white chair and laying a thin Manila folder on the table. "Gives the boys something to think about when I'm held up. Glass, of course. Now then, Lazenby, let's get right down to this sex problem of yours."

I opened my mouth to reply, but he abruptly held up his hand to silence me as he flipped open the folder and peered through his thick-lensed spectacles at the contents of what I assume was my medical record. This he studied for some time, and I was thus enabled to observe his appearance more closely. He was short, portly, pale and bearded like a Tudor. His eyes, even behind those heavy glasses, were soft, black and melancholy.

"Lazenby," he read from the first page of my record, the sound of his voice slightly blurred as it filtered through his mustache.

"Frederick William, white, male, born Dexter, Pennsylvania, six-six-twenty-four, five feet eleven, one-seventy pounds, eyes brown, hair brown, no scars, mole on sole of left foot. Occupation, journalist and editor. Married; no children. Any insanity in your family, Lazenby?"

"None," I replied instantly and heartily. Too heartily?

"Ever had a nervous breakdown? Dizzy spells? Urge to go down on all fours and howl at the moon? Anything unusual?"

"Look," I begged. "Do I look like a loony?"

"Ever seen anybody who doesn't?" he riposted cleverly, and taking the first page of my record, he began folding it rapidly into what I perceived was going to be a cocked hat. "Now about this thing with sex that's put you in here—ever read any Krafft-Ebing? Come, come, of course you have. In that case, you'll realize that you have all the makings of a classic case."

"You mean like 'X, a young man of good family employed as a broker's clerk in Leipzig'?" I asked. Dr. Chernowith nodded, pleased, and with a few deft manipulations transformed my medical record from a cocked hat into a bird's head which opened and shut its beak as he moved his fingers.

"That's it exactly. Frankly, Lazenby, I'd like to see your case written up for the *Journal*; a real clinical run-down, with footnotes and all. Given a few breaks, Lazenby, you could become a milestone. Not many fellows get that kind of chance."

"Just call me Lucky Pierre," I muttered bitterly. "You are aware, Doctor, that I would be within my rights in refusing to say anything until my—" I stopped. Chernowith was not listening; instead he had whipped out a pencil and was scribbling a note on the second page of my record. "Now what?" I asked.

"You said 'Lucky Pierre,'" he answered brightly. "I suppose you're aware of the association? Very interesting. Go ahead."

"Until my lawyer is present," I resumed bleakly. "I have not been convicted of anything; I am awaiting trial on a ridiculous charge that will undoubtedly be dropped when all the information is available to the authorities, and the fact that I am forced to remain in jail at all is purely and simply a matter of principle on my part, and can be laid to the sheer, puritanical malevolence on the part of the judge in refusing to allow me a reasonable bail. I am innocent as the day is long, despite the outrageous allegations of the police and press."

"Deuced lucid," cried Dr. Chernowith, laughing merrily and slapping his pudgy thigh in amusement at this sally. "I like you, Lazenby; as sex maniacs go, you're a decent chap. Not your usual, bleary-eyed, whimpering sort, with their furtive giggles and unspeakably crude *double-entendres*. Give this thing a little effort, and you'll do wonders getting rid of it. Ever want to kill your father?"

"I am not a sex maniac," I told him steadily, ignoring his question. "I am—or was—a happily married and reasonably well adjusted man, employed in a position of some responsibility and enjoying what I think I am entitled to describe as a merited reputation for probity, sobriety and morality."

Moving with what I now recognized to be his normal abruptness, Dr. Chernowith stood up and began walking to and fro, keeping the table between us.

"Consider me as your friend," he urged, his voice soothing and wistful. "Remember that our communications are privileged—that whatever you choose to tell me will remain our little secret. Perhaps we might even trade a secret or two, just to prove that I'm in earnest about this thing. For example, as a young man in college, I found myself verging on something closely akin to fetishism. To look at me now, you would hardly believe that there was a time when the sight of a girl in galoshes could send me quite faint, would you?"

"Without wishing to seem offensive, Doctor, I feel I must tell you that I am absolutely indifferent to these sordid disclosures, and I have no wish to intrude myself into your personal problems."

"There was this one little sophomore," Chernowith went on, his eyes hazy with memory, "a blonde—magnificent figure, just maturing into its fullest bloom, so to speak—I used to watch for her on rainy days. Her galoshes were enormous, and she wore them unbuckled. . . ." He paused in his pacing, and his voice lost its musing quality. Now it became stern. "But I got hold of myself,

Lazenby; saw the handwriting on the wall and got hold of myself. And that's what you've got to do.

"I suppose, in your case, it started as far back as junior high school, eh? Crude, smudgy photographs passed from hand to grubby hand after school hours, over illicit cigarettes, no doubt. Hidden away in dark corners, where your mother wouldn't find them. The discovery that more could be obtained if you spoke softly to the unpleasant little man who ran the confectionery shop across the street from school. Makes a pretty sickening picture, doesn't it, Lazenby?

"And down through the years, the habit grew," Chernowith continued, gathering momentum. "Oh, you were normal enough when you weren't gloating over your horrid treasure. Normal enough to marry a fine, healthy young woman; normal enough to make yourself a fairly successful career. On the surface. But deep down, Lazenby, deep down, we know better, don't we?"

It was obvious that there was no point in arguing with this man. He had formed his opinion, and no matter what I said or did he would twist my remarks and actions to suit his concept. Of course, there was always the possibility that I had, in fact, become unbalanced to a certain extent by the incredible misfortune which had, with appalling suddenness, wrecked my life, destroyed my hopes and put me here behind bars. Had my mind, unbeknownst to myself, been playing tricks on me? Had I, all unwitting, undergone some subtle change, unobserved by my wife and associates, and like Dr. Jekyll assumed another personality in some dim, unspeakable semiworld?

Of course not. The idea was absurd. I knew, and was prepared, in the unlikely event that I should actually come to trial before the charges against me were dropped, to prove that I knew exactly how the circumstances in which I found myself had arisen, and that I was completely innocent of any wrongdoing. I must hold on to that conviction or perish, I told myself as Chernowith rambled on, continuing to daub high lights and shadows onto the portrait he was limning of Dorian Lazenby. He had got me into college and was speculating on the opportunities for vice available to a small-town boy in the more cosmopolitan atmosphere of the campus.

"Now you were in too deep to quit," he was saying, still pacing. "Now your miserable aberration was controlling you; now the risk of discovery was more dangerous than ever. You found yourself mingling with a strange crowd—possibly some sort of late adolescent sex cult, innocent enough to all outward appearances but committed to the vilest sort of debaucheries in secret."

"We were a pretty madcap bunch at S.A.E.," I said. "Some of the gang drank beer and said 'damn.'"

Chernowith scowled and sat down.

"Wasn't it like I said?" he asked, almost plaintively. "I mean, about college orgies and that kind of thing?"

"Absolutely not," I declared. Nor had it been. During my entire four years at college, I had been hopelessly in love with Sarah Ellen de Voe, a fine, deep-bosomed girl with the healthiest of instincts who had finally become so exasperated with the knightly purity of my devotion that she had thrown me over for a dashing young Ensign of the Naval Reserve, by whom she has now had, at last news, a passel of brats. Yet were I to admit that I had never laid an improper hand on Sarah Ellen's virginal flesh —would, in truth, have been horrified at the thought of defiling that temple of maidenly virtue, as I then thought of Sarah Ellen —Chernowith would immediately leap to the conclusion that I suffered from a latent homosexuality, and this misconception had at all costs to be avoided.

"Of course, we did some fairly heavy necking," I conceded, and this was, in a sense, true. It was, as a matter of fact, this heavy necking, with never an attempt at thigh or bosom fondling, which had been my undoing. As I was later to come to understand, a girl can take just so much of that sort of thing. "But nothing in the way of what you've suggested," I concluded lamely.

"You know, you're in mighty deep waters, Lazenby," Dr. Chernowith said, and his soft eyes grew even sadder behind his glasses. "I'd like to help you because I think you're worth saving; I think you've a lot left in you to contribute. But I can't help you if you

6

won't help yourself. Try to remember that in these matters I'm absolutely impartial. Whatever I say on the witness stand will be neither for you nor against you; it will be the simple, psychiatric truth as I see it."

"I understand that perfectly. After all, I've written a number of articles about psychiatry, and we've—that is, the magazine has carried several pieces written by psychiatrists themselves. I appreciate what you're trying to do, Doctor."

"Well, then, why won't you try to be more cooperative?"

"Because my case is nothing like what you think it is, and no matter what I say, you'll think I'm either trying to cover up some weird personality flaw or just plain lying. This whole business is nothing more than a dreadful misunderstanding."

"They all say that, you know," Chernowith replied impatiently.

"In my situation it's true, dammit."

Chernowith gazed at me in silence for several seconds, as if he were trying to make a decision. His stubby pink fingers laced themselves together, and he began rapidly to make and unmake a church and a steeple and all the people. "You ever read Frank Harris?" he asked suddenly.

"As a matter of fact, I haven't," I told him. "Henry Miller, yes; Frank Harris, no."

"Might be the answer to your problem. Purge yourself, as it were; mental catharsis, get it out of your system, the whole, ugly mess. You're a writer—"

"Let's say I was a writer."

"A writer," Chernowith went on imperturbably, "and so it ought to come easily. Write it down, Lazenby, write it all down, omitting nothing. Try to think back to whatever it was that started you out on this obsession of yours—perhaps a forbidden book high on the bookshelf of the living room of your boyhood home; perhaps a *Police Gazette* in your favorite barbershop."

"It won't be anything like that."

"Doesn't matter. You won't even have to show me what you've written if you don't want to."

"If I did write it out, as you put it, I wouldn't have anything to hide," I said, as manly a little chap as ever came down the road with his older brothers, Dick and Tom. Or was it fun-loving Tom who was the youngest Rover? Knock it off, Lazenby.

"I can arrange to have you furnished with a typewriter and paper," Chernowith urged, leaning eagerly across the table, or as eagerly as his round little tummy-tum-tums would permit.

I could see the reason for his zeal. If I didn't get the charges against me dropped, if I weren't acquitted, my manuscript would be a valuable addition to the paper he was hoping to write for the edification of his professional colleagues. And if I were to be tried and convicted, what difference would it make what I wrote? Joby could go back to using her maiden name, and I'd go thundering down the corridors of medical history as the prime example of what might even come to be called the Lazenby Syndrome. What the hell? And besides, it would give me something to do.

"All right," I said. "I'll do it."

"Omitting nothing?" Chernowith insisted.

"Nothing."

Chernowith stood up, beaming. "You won't regret this decision, Lazenby. Try to think of yourself as a man who has just attended his first meeting with Alcoholics Anonymous; you're on the right road now, and all you've got to do is stick it out."

"Keep the old shoulder to the wheel, eh?"

"That's the spirit!" He held out his plump, pink pandy. "We're going to lick this thing, Lazenby. I know that now."

"Right," I said, in the manner of the late Richard Dix vowing to avenge his kid brother's loss on the hated von Richthofen Circus as he shook hands with his loyal mechanic, Sergeant Chernowith. We both knew it was sheer murder to send the kids up in these crates, but there was a war to be won.

"You won't forget plenty of paper?" I remarked as the good doctor started toward his door.

"No indeedy," he called back, and gave me a cheery smile. Even now he was probably lost in fantasy, seeing himself at the lectern before the huge, hushed audience of the American Psychiatric Association in convention assembled, waiting for the last coughs to be coughed, brushing a thoughtful finger through his beard as he stares down at the notes before him, perhaps rearranging a page or two and then taking a final sip of water before he begins to speak . . . and a few hours later, rising, blushing, from his seat to walk through the standing, wildly applauding throng of his peers to the dais to receive, in all humility, the coveted Shädelquetscher Medal for the year's most important new contribution to the literature of the science. . . .

"Okay, Lazenby," Guard Hogarth interrupted this pleasant reverie. "Let's go back to the salt mine."

"Fine man, Doctor Chernowith," I ventured as we began the return journey to my little home away from home. Guard Hogarth turned his pale blue, Anglo-Saxon fanatic's eyes on me, and his thin lip curled slightly.

"Question of who's nuttier, him or you guys," he sneered.

"Oh, I don't know about—" I started to say.

"I see a lot of punks come and go around this place," Hogarth continued rudely, his harsh voice distinctly unfriendly. "Dips, pushers, muggers, all sorts of bums, and most of them I can figure how come, but you sex nuts make me sick to my stummick. I got a nice teen-age girl in high school right now; got a nice future ahead, she goes to nurse school like she wants. It's bums like you could wreck a nice kid like that's life. You know what they oughta do with all you kind of bums? They oughta take a knife and caponize you once and for all, you ask me. You're lower than dirt, bud, and I hope they give it to you good."

It was obvious that Guard Hogarth—if, indeed, he had ever heard of it—had little respect for the ancient principle of common law, conceived by his ancestors before they withdrew to the mountains of Virginia and the Carolinas to inbreed, which holds that the accused is innocent until proved guilty. In view of this, it was probable that he would have equally small respect for the regulations which forbid a guard to strike a prisoner, and from the sullen flush in his lean and pock-marked cheeks, I gathered that a smart slap to my chops was not the most distant of Guard Hogarth's thoughts. I therefore maintained a dignified silence. Sidney Carton's situation was no more nightmarish than Frederick William Lazenby's, but at least he had something far, far better to do than get slapped silly by a prison guard. By now we had reached the end of the long, echoing corridor which had given Guard Hogarth the privacy in which to express his views. Opening another heavy, steel door he led me into the cell block.

"And another thing," Hogarth whispered as we reached my cell. "Don't let me hear about you trying to make any passes at any of the other men, see? We got ways and means of takin' care of them kind, bud. No marks, no nothing, but you won't be able to set down or stand up for a week, if you see what I mean." And Guard Hogarth bared his cavity-ridden teeth in an evil grin.

It is possible that if Hogarth had not made this last, obscene suggestion, I would have faltered in my resolve to go along with Dr. Chernowith's idea. But that did it. Suddenly, it was vital that I get down on paper exactly what had happened and how it had come to happen. I'd gone over my story time and again with By Stephens, my lawyer. Joby, my wife, knew the true facts, but now I wanted to write it all out. It might even help By's understanding of my case if he saw my story as a continuing narrative rather than a series of answers to his hundreds of questions.

That is how this came to be written. I make no apology for the somewhat edgy tone that mars certain passages, or for the uneven pace. Despite all the praise that has been heaped upon prisons as being ideal places in which to write, my experience has not led me to join the general chorus. I have tried, insofar as the circumstances have permitted, to preserve that cheerful spirit indicative of the sure knowledge of innocence. If I have not entirely succeeded, put it down to the equally sure knowledge that, from time to wretched time, justice has erred most grievously and innocent men have been dragged, kicking and screaming, up the thirteen steps to the waiting officials, the usual clergy, and the freshly tested hemp.

I

Spring in Washington, D. C., though brief withal is, God wot, a lovesome thing.

The cherry trees around the Tidal Basin burst into mad pink froth. Government girls shed their sensible winter woolens and blossom forth in all their disturbing mammalian splendor. A livelier iris gleams upon the burnished Bentleys drawn up by the De Sales Street entrance to the Mayflower, and down come the tops of the Jaguars and Morris Minors alike as the natives greet the vernal season. The first busloads of high school seniors, slouch-hatted like Stuart's horse or blue-kepied like Meade's stout legions, depending upon their origins, arrive from the provinces, and the souvenir shops display new and startling depravities of the metal-caster's art. The first stenographers to enjoy a picnic lunch on the greensward in Lafayette Square are immortalized by the photographers of the *Star* and the *Post*, and sales of gin and tonic in the bar of the National Press Club rise in ratio to the decrease in orders for double bourbons. Everywhere there is an unnamable joy. It lasts only a few days, and then summer descends, but while it lasts, spring is indeed a lovesome thing in the seat of the Federal power.

I remember I was playing the Roadmaster Game on Q Street. The Volkswagen's four tiny cylinders were thundering out their song of power, and on the sidewalk a coffee-hued Hindu beauty swept along on her way to work at the Indian Embassy, her sari rippling in silken swirls, her forehead dotted and wrinkled in concentration on God knows what mysteries of the Orient. Just ahead of me, a great, fat-bottomed Roadmaster was flatulating along, its driver's little pinhead just visible over the top of his seat as he sighted under the steering wheel and down the limitless expanse of hood. He was, naturally, observing Lazenby's Law of Roadmasters.

This is a law which I formulated several years ago, before the name went into discard and Buick went over to the classics. It states simply that people who drive Roadmasters are really secret and frustrated Cadillac-lovers. Maybe they can't quite meet the payments on a Cadillac, or maybe they're like the people who don't buy Rolls-Royces because they're diffident, but anyhow, these people drive their Roadmasters the way they think people ought to drive Cadillacs. You still with me? Fine. In any event, it was this observation which led me to establish Lazenby's Second Law of Roadmasters, which holds that people who drive these monsters are fair game, and the man who fails to get one in for the common folk is as bad as the dirty little coward that shot poor Mister Howard.

A cynical smile curving my lips—Basil Rathbone in that great scene from *Dawn Patrol*—I eased the VW up alongside the behemoth at the next traffic light and then, ever so slightly, drew a few inches ahead and gunned the motor. The green light against us turned to amber, and my little masterpiece of German precision craftsmanship quivered like a hound on the leash, engine whining. From the corner of my eye, as I stared straight ahead after the fashion of Stirling Moss estimating a curve at LeMans, I perceived Pinhead's cigar tilt arrogantly as his jaw jutted forward.

The light against us turned from red to green. With a tremendous howl, the Roadmaster was away, leaping forward like a cow that has backed into an electrified fence, tires screeching out lost rubber on the black asphalt. Voom! Eeeekkkk! Then, quietly, I let out my clutch and sedately advanced.

At the next traffic light—all traffic lights in Washington are scientifically timed to create maximum delay and confusion—I again drew up alongside the behemoth, my face a study in serenity. Pinhead gave me a single, filthy glare and looked away. But in his heart of hearts he knew—oh, he knew all right. A real Cadillac man would never have descended to such a petulant display;

never have fallen for my transparent little taunt in the first place.
My morning was off to a splendid start. It was with a quiet glow
of satisfaction that I slipped into my parking space in the lot
behind the enormous old mansion on 15th Street above N which
houses the editorial and business offices of *Youth Outlook*.

In the days of its greatness (which ended abruptly in 1932),
the place was known as Mount McVessiter, after its builder, the
late Senator Odin G. McVessiter, of the oil-bearing Oklahoma
McVessiters. His widow, the famed Washington hostess, had been
unable to face even the first Roosevelt Administration and had
pulled up stakes for her only slightly less magnificent palace in
Venice. Less than a month later, with that keen perception that
has made him fabled in the world of magazine publication, Our
Founder and Editor, Dr. Walter Van Meter Mountain, saw that
Washington real estate prices would probably never sink lower
and that the mansion market was at an all-time glut, and so he
bought the vast structure for a fraction of its original cost. Thereafter, Mount McVessiter became Youth House. It was and is to
the earnest young people of the United States what the headquarters of the National Geographic Society, over on 16th at M,
is to the earnest older people; something between a shrine, a museum, a fountain of information and bastion of truth. It is one of
those places in which visitors automatically talk in whispers, and
are very careful of their manners.

"Good morning, Mr. Lazenby," cried Jowett, the guard at the
rear entrance. "Real weather we're having, huh?"

"Good morning, Mr. Lazenby," chirped Miss Emspach, the
receptionist, who sat at her tidy desk to one side of the absurdly
ornate entrance hall, radiating helpfulness, interest and sympathy.
"Isn't this just the grandest weather ever?"

"Mo'nin', Mistuh Lazenbeh," greeted James, the Negro elevator
operator, his quarter-century service pin gleaming in the lapel of
his alpaca uniform coat just underneath the embroidered gilt
initials, Y.O. "A real day and a half, yessuh, a real one."

"Good morning, good morning, good morning," I called merrily.
"That's real weather out there, isn't it." And at this crackerjack

jest, Miss Emspach and James laughed fit to kill. Yes sir, it was really some weather out there.

In my office on the fourth floor, my secretary, Miss Horvath, had laid out *The New York Times* and the *Washington Post & Times-Herald* on my desk. Beside them stood a cardboard container of coffee, its lid still in place, awaiting my pleasure. There were a couple of interdepartmental transfer envelopes in my "In" basket, and a reference book I'd ordered sent up from the library. On top of the *Times* was a little slip of blue memo paper, upon which Miss Horvath had written in her tiny, precise hand: "Pls. call Mrs. Lazenby. 8:55 A.M." It was initialled E.A.H., for Eleanor Alice Horvath.

"Outside line, please," I told the operator, and dialed when the big buzz of the interoffice lines gave way to the softer purr of the metropolitan system. There was a click and my spouse's voice.

"Good morning," Joby cried happily. "Whee!"

"How'd you know it was me?"

"I didn't."

"You'd have felt pretty silly if it had been the credit department at Garfinckel's," I said. " 'Good morning. Whee!' Pretty madcap kid, that's you all right, all right."

"My God but you're getting stuffy. Just because it's a beautiful, lovely, exquisite morning and I feel like saying 'Whee!' you sit in that stuffy office of yours acting stuffy."

"How'd you like it if we took a couple of hours off with the dictionary and you learned a synonym for 'stuffy'?"

"Are you busy?"

"I don't know yet. I just got here. Why?"

"Who do you know in Charlottesville, Virginia?"

"Just offhand, I can't think of anybody I know in Charlottesville, Virginia. And it's 'whom do you know,' not 'who.' "

"Well, you must know somebody there," Joby said stubbornly. These are occasions for patience, I know, and yet I can never manage it.

"Look, Joby, will you get to the point, please?"

A brief second of injured silence and then: "Well, you had a long-distance call from somebody in Charlottesville right after you left the house. I couldn't catch the name, but I told the operator you could be reached at your office any time after nine. Are you keeping a mistress down in Charlottesville, Eff Lazenby?" Joby giggled.

"Not one, but several," I replied. (I should explain that "Eff" is Joby's special nickname for me, and derives from the inexplicable days when I used to sign myself as F. William Lazenby. Or maybe not so inexplicable—if F. Scott Fitzgerald, why not F. William Lazenby? Those were the days when I was going to limn the aimless folly of the post-war forties. Instead, I married Joby.)

"Call me and tell me which one it is," Joby ordered. "And can you stop by Pearson's and pick up a bottle of red wine on your way home tonight?"

"Done and done. Any particular kind, or the usual dago red?"

"The usual. Beef in wine sauce for dinner tomorrow. Love you."

"Love you, too. Thanks for being there."

"Don't mentch."

I made a note on my memo pad to stop for a jug of red wine, and then applied myself to the *Times* headlines, the *Post* editorial page, and then back to the *Times* crossword puzzle. I don't know whether the *Times* realizes it or not, but nothing starts the brain off on the day's labors in finer fettle than their crossword puzzle. Sort of revs up the gray cells for the work ahead. (I am putting in all these little details simply to indicate that this was starting out to be just another normal working day; no omens, no premonitions, no geese over Dupont Circle.)

A few minutes later, my phone rang. My caller was Mrs. Oradean Nonnenmaker, secretary to Samuel K. Nurney, the Senior Ass. More formally, he is the Senior Editorial Associate, who sitteth on the right hand of Our Founder and Editor. SKN, Mrs. Nonnenmaker said, employing the initial system which has long been a tradition around Youth House, desired to see me at my earliest convenience. That's the way we operate at *Youth Outlook*; no curt, direct orders, but with a grave and stately courtesy we make our wishes known.

Tightening the knot of my necktie and settling my coat neatly into place—for it is an underwritten but inviolable rule that no male member of the editorial staff shall appear outside his office in his shirt sleeves—I whistled downstairs to the second finest set of quarters in Youth House. From her desk in the outer office, Mrs. Nonnenmaker gave me one of her "You Lucky, Lucky Boy" smiles, and waved me on to the inner office. The mild tension which a call to report to SKN always produces in me vanished.

"Ah, Frederick, good morning to you." Samuel K. Nurney looked up from his enormous desk and gave me the only smile he had, the "Today's Young Men Mean Well, But They Need Watching" type. Guarded, you might say.

And now, friends, just a word about Samuel K. Nurney before we return to tonight's thrilling episode. Here is your hostess, Prunella Lazenby, with some fascinating facts about this tried and true product. . . .

There is, as we know from William White, a Samuel K. Nurney in every great organization, and ours at *Youth Outlook* was the very model of his ilk. ("Ilk" is a word SKN despises, by the way. He regards it as an example of "fancy writing." Myself, I like "ilk." Ilk, ilk, ilk.) The Samuel K. Nurneys are necessary to the stability and health of an organization because they provide a focal point for all the pent-up hatreds, repressions, complaints and sullen resentments which the day-to-day operations of the organization engender. To their superiors, they are trustworthy, loyal, brave and honest. To their subordinates, they are shifty, vacillating, jelly-spined sycophants, vessels of dishonesty and sons of bitches.

No one at *Youth Outlook* would dream of calling Our Founder and Editor, Dr. Walter Van Meter Mountain, a son of a bitch, but in connection with SKN, the phrase springs naturally and easily to the lips. That Son of a Bitch Nurney is held responsible for all the ills that befall, whether it be the drastic surgery on an article about Australia's sheep-raising industry ("He cut the goddam guts out of it."), or the new decor of the visitor's waiting room ("He's got it fixed up like a Bulgarian whorehouse.").

To the Samuel K. Nurneys are left all the onerous tasks. ("Take your time looking around, Fencible; don't jump at the first thing that comes along. I'm sure you'll find something more in line with your abilities, and one day, you'll realize that this is all for the best.") That Son of a Bitch Nurney. ("Dear Ted: It's never easy to have to tell a Pulitzer Prize winner that, although all of us here thoroughly enjoyed your piece on the St. Lawrence Seaway, we felt that it just didn't quite hit the *Outlook* note . . .") Or:

MEMO: Garment Industry (Scheduled, Aug.)

FROM: SKN

TO: FWL

You seem to have missed the whole point of our "Industry in Review" series. Too may anecdotes; too little solid meat. Grant women's underclothing major part of big picture, but has no place in YO. Returned to you for further work.

That Son of a Bitch Nurney.

SKN had come to *Youth Outlook* in the spring of 1929, on the strength of a series of articles he had sold to Our Founder, entitled, "Our Pitcher That Never Empties: the American Stock Market." Before that, he had edited the house organ of the Chesapeake & Western Railroad. In those days, he had been a dark, sleek young man with the manner of a newly ordained Baptist minister temporarily reduced to selling Bibles from door to door. He had matured, mentally and physically, with his increasing responsibilities, and today bears a strong resemblance to the steel-gray Vicar General of one of the more militant Roman Catholic orders.

I'll be frank to say that I didn't share the general opinion of Samuel K. Nurney. Mind you, I didn't exactly like him, but I had to admit that, for what he was supposed to be and do, he was the right man in the right job; a brave, loyal, courageous, shifty sycophant, a vessel of dishonesty and a son of a bitch with wheels, and without him, *Youth Outlook* would be a much poorer magazine.

Now back to our story. Freddy Lazenby has just grinned subserviently to the Senior Ass, tugging his forelock and shuffling his feet, his honest face aglow with pleasure.

"I've got what I think is going to prove a very interesting and rewarding assignment for you, Frederick," SKN said. "And Dr. Mountain concurs in my view that you are the man to handle it.

"The fact is that Dr. Mountain has been asked to serve on the President's Advisory Commission on Juvenile Correction—you've read about it, I imagine. Quite a number of outstanding people have been named to the commission, and all in all, it should turn out an important piece of work." He stopped and looked at me expectantly.

"Umm," I said with a gravity appropriate to the occasion.

"Quite. But as you know, Dr. Mountain is about to take off on his regular every-other-year survey of world education trends, which means he'll be out of the country, off and on, for the next six months. In view of this, and because he feels the commission has a vital job to do, he requested and received permission to name an alternate to serve in his stead. You will be that alternate, and your duties with the commission will take priority over your editorial chores here."

"I'm sure I'm very honored, sir," I said. ("Well, you have richly merited it, my boy," Captain Putnam said kindly. "I know of no other lad here at Putnam Hall who could acquit himself one half so well in like circumstances." Blushing, the sturdy little cadet drew himself to attention and saluted the smiling Captain.)

"Mrs. Nonnenmaker will give you the correspondence fill-in," Samuel K. concluded. "Plus any other files you may need. Dr. Mountain will want a full report, in writing, on all meetings and, of course, any material issued by the commission: bulletins, interim findings, that sort of thing. We expect a good job, Frederick."

Having said this, he withdrew his attention from me and directed it to the large sheaf of papers on his desk, indicating my dismissal from the Presence.

In the outer office, Mrs. Oradean Nonnenmaker repeated the Lucky, Lucky Boy smile and shoved an immense fiberboard file at me. "There's this, too," she cooed, "from Dr. Mountain's office," and handed me a crisp white parchment paper envelope.

That is a fair sample of the way things happen around *Youth Outlook*. One minute you are a simple Editorial Associate (j.g.), doing an acceptable, steady, workmanlike job, liked by your colleagues, secure in the knowledge that you are contributing your mite to the national welfare, envying no man really. And the next, you are a member—or, at least, an alternate member—of a Presidential Commission. Heady stuff, by George.

I returned to my office on winged feet, clutching my fat file and my crisp white envelope. In the privacy of my cubbyhole, I opened what I assumed was my commission from His Majesty. But it was better than that:

Mr. Lazenby:

Thank you for assuming a burden which my own busy schedule will not permit me to carry. I know you will do us proud. In view of your appointment and the obligations it may entail, I have instructed the Comptroller that your annual rate of compensation is to be increased to $14,000, effective immediately. This should enable you to meet certain unavoidable expenses in connection with your "extracurricular" work.

Regular expenses will continue, of course, to be reimbursed in line with our established policy.

Good luck to you, and my best wishes.

Walter Van Meter Mountain

A thousand buck raise! Why, bless his old heart. Ah'd march to hayull fuh Gen'ral Mountain, seh, ah would that.

For a couple of minutes I just sat there, seeing nothing except in my mind's eye, and what I saw there was ringed with a rosy pink glow. Now, perhaps, Joby might give her consent to trading in the solid, sensible VW on a Triumph—it would be pearl-gray with gray wire wheels; no chrome for this boy.

Another, less creditable thought struck me.

Ho, ho, ho, Nathaniel Walsingham, ho, ho, ho.

Who he?

Him hated rival, that who he.

Well, not actually hated, you understand.

But of him, more anon.

II

Were I a rude, loutish fellow, given to billiards, beer and hanging around the cigar store, I would describe my secretary, Miss Eleanor Alice Horvath, as being stacked like a brick privy, but you'll never get the true picture from such a starved simile. Say, rather, that Miss Horvath is generously endowed with the physical attributes of femininity; that her face, framed in her raven locks (trimmed in the severe yet provocative French manner), with its dark, brooding eyes and full, nay, voluptuous lips, hints of nameless pleasures and a satanic sensuality. Here, you might well feel justified in declaring, is an authentic sex engine. Such, certainly, was my own initial impression.

Yet a sex engine with the comportment of an abbess and the demeanor of a leader of Girl Scouts. She is good to her widowed mother. She regularly attends the gospel feasts and hymn fests of the Thropplestance Memorial Baptist Church, where she is fondly and favorably known for her work among the children in the primary Sunday school. She is also brave, loyal, trustworthy and true blue, and efficient as all get out.

I would be less than honest were I to deny that when she was first assigned to me, I indulged in some truly awesome fantasies. Most of those involved me finding myself working late, asking the luscious Eleanor to join me in some dimly lighted cocktail pit for a nightcap, and ending up in a luxuriously furnished apartment—and you can, if you're half the Yale man I think you are, Stover, guess the rest. Mind you, no more faithful and loving husband is truer to a fine and noble wife than is Frederick W. Lazenby to his Jobiana, but breathes there a man with soul so dead, etc?

I did manage, as a matter of fact, to take her out to lunch one day at Le Tricorne, a pseudo-French restaurant on Connecticut above Dupont Circle, where the food is dismal but the lights are low. Over the lukewarm Martini (one-to-one, and mine; Miss Eleanor went madcap and consented to just a wee drop of muscatel. *Muscatel*, I say!), she told me, her dark eyes lustrous, of the hilarious time she had had at the annual Blue Ridge Encampment of the Baptist Youth Leaders' Conference—oh, the panel discussions, and ah, the fireside hymn-sings! Over the tepid Lipton's Instant Onion Soup, she waxed ecstatic about her widowed mother's recent triumphs in the Senior Citizens' Bowling League. Over the cold ragout she confessed to the deep satisfaction she derived from her work at *Youth Outlook*, for if hers was not a starring role, it was at least a bit part in the soul-stirring drama of teaching America's boys and girls the principles that made this land of ours great.

I could go on at some length about this appalling tête-à-tête, but you will by now have inferred that it was not a smashing success. We did not linger, exchanging meaningful glances over our Benedictine, our hands, hot and moist, meeting and clutching under the table. Nor did we, flashing our Dentyne smiles, grab a cab and whistle off to that luxurious apartment of my dreams where, a cryptic smile curving those full-fleshed lips, my Eleanor would disappear for a moment to change into something comfy; would reappear seconds later, garbed as for a bacchanalia.

We went back to the office.

I also told Jobiana that I had taken Miss Horvath to lunch. That should put you in the picture.

"Why, you old roué," Jobiana cried archly when I told her. Joby knows Miss Horvath. They *like* each other.

My telephone rang. With a genial smile for the reporters and television cameramen gathered about the portico of the White House office ("Sorry, boys, no comment. I will say I thought the President looked very fit, very fit indeed . . ."), I returned from cloudland to the world of men and affairs.

"I have a Dr. Martin Savoury on the line, long distance." came the cool, suggestive, utterly deceptive voice of Eleanor Alice Horvath.

"Right," I cried smartly, as memory's dam burst, flooding me with a torrent of recollection, foaming, dark brown, burdened with dead animals and empty bottles.

"Eff!" came the well remembered voice. Alone among my friends, Marty Savoury has adopted Joby's nickname for me. My best man, my bosom pal, my ancient comrade-in-arms, gentleman and scholar. My downfall.

"Dumbo!" I hooted, employing the name we lads of the gallant 12th Foot had bestowed upon him the night the Walt Disney motion picture so entitled had made its first showing at Post Theater #2, Camp Gordon, Georgia.

We exchanged the obligatory liturgy of affectionate defamations.

"I've got a favor to ask," Dumbo said, when we had completed the ritual.

"*Mi casa es su casa.*"

"Rather, I've got two favors to ask. One, could you give me dinner this evening? Two—"

"*Mi casa—*" I started to say.

"Two," Dumbo repeated, tactfully ignoring my tendency to kick a dead horse, "could you store some stuff for me. I'll fill you in on the details when I see you."

"You'll recognize the old place by the fatted calf simmering on the charcoal grill."

"Spareribs?" Dumbo asked happily.

"Joby's juciest," I replied. Dumbo is one of the most devout Hebrews outside the rabbinate, but he is a sucker for Joby's spareribs. He is also a sucker for peanut-fed, hickory-smoked Smithfield leg of lamb, sliced thin and served with fried eggs.

"I'll bring you back a bottle of Jordan water, and that's a promise," Dumbo declared. "If I get to the Homeland, that is."

"You sound like a man about to travel."

"I'll tell you all about that, too. Europe, the Middle East, the whole works, boy. Tell Joby to save me a kiss."

"March with God," I commanded.

"Shalom," said Dumbo.

I telephoned Joby and warned her that Dumbo was about to descend on us and would she barbecue some spareribs.

"You sound strangely happy," she said. "Two calls in one morning . . . Are you lusting for my lily-white body?"

"The switchboard girl will blackmail me," I answered. "Until later, then, wife, be of good faith."

I hung up the phone, and realized that I'd forgotten to tell Joby about my new status as a member (all right, all *right*, an alternate member) of a Presidential Commission. It could wait. The news would make dinner an even brighter occasion.

Already I could see just the spot on my office wall for my commission, discreetly mounted in a thin black frame, with perhaps a thin gilt strip. With any sort of luck, there might even be an autographed photograph of the President to go with it. Together they would make a nice start toward one of those office collections without which no man can be said truly to have made his mark in Washington. Davis Carter Powers, for instance, had managed to secure autographed photographs of every President since Warren G. Harding, as well as those of a richly varied assortment of military men, explorers, captains of industry, and the like.

Davis Carter Powers, by way of explanation, was the Vice President of Youth Outlook Publishing Company, and the business office peer of Samuel K. Nurney. A remote and mysterious figure, Davis Carter Powers: tall, gray-haired, with the face of an engrossed moose, he could be seen from time to time about the corridors of Youth House, looking vaguely worried.

But enough of daydreaming and Davis Carter Powers. It was time I began the day's labors, and with this end in view, I withdrew the fattest of the interdepartmental transfer envelopes from my "In" basket and unwound the string which held it shut.

MEMO: Tasmanian Christmas Customs

FROM: SKN

TO: FWL

Pls. read & comment on attached Mss. by Dr. Francis Utterbaugh for poss. inclusion Xmas issue. Dr. Utterbaugh wrote "Shahdom's Splendor, a Look at Modern Iran" for us in 1954.

The next transfer envelope contained the proofs of a piece I'd done on "Our Congressional Committees; What They Are and How They Work." Neat, compact, deftly written, if I do say so myself as I shouldn't.

The third envelope contained another manuscript, to which was attached a sheaf of opinions by various of my colleagues. I looked at the first one, From the Desk of Nathaniel Walsingham. Nate's desk was at the top of its critical form; ironic, merciless, blunt.

I didn't bother to look at the other comments, but instead began to read the manuscript. If Nate and his desk didn't like it, that was reason enough for me to give it a sympathetic run-through. Nate is an editorial snob. He is also a social snob, but that can be suffered.

As a matter of record, it wasn't a badly written article. Except, of course, that a magazine aimed at the young folk of America is hardly the vehicle for "Our Drunken Ancestors—New England's Rum Was Barrelled Gold."

Our drunken ancestors and Dr. Francis Utterbaugh kept me occupied for the rest of the morning.

Harking back to that telephone conversation with Dumbo, I can readily see why I did not realize its fateful nature.

It was not too surprising to learn that he had severed his association with the University of Pennsylvania and affiliated himself with the University of Virginia—these things, I am given to understand, happen all the time in the academic world. Nor was I astonished to learn that he was off to Europe. Sociologists are always trotting off to Europe to find out the answers to such problems as why east Baltimore's predominantly Czech population enjoys a slightly lower average per capita annual income than the Lithuanians of west Baltimore. This sort of problem may never have bothered you, but it bothers sociologists no end.

Certainly, too, it was perfectly natural that Dumbo should feel no hesitation in asking me to do him a favor, for were we not bound by bonds of more than comradeship in arms? Had he not steadied my palsied body as I gazed, numbed, upon my Jobiana's rose-fresh loveliness advancing down the aisle of St. Christopher's

Protestant Episcopal Church in Dexter, Pennsylvania, on June 14, 1951? Had he not been our very first overnight guest in the pint-sized apartment which was all my salary as a reporter for the Dexter *Messenger* ("The Paper for All the People") would support?

Equally certain is the fact that Dumbo himself had no idea of the consequences that were to ensue. Rather than imperil our happy home, he would have cut off his right hand—of that I am positive.

III

All right, so we live in one of those ever-so-quaint examples of ex-slum housing which, painted Williamsburg gray, given a shining black front door, a couple of reproductions of brass coach lamps, a fake antique fire insurance marker and a set of completely unworkable shutters, make Georgetown real estate dealers rich beyond the dreams of Midas. It is, nonetheless, home to us Lazenbys, our noble dog, Rafael, and our few pitiful possessions, including the scourings of the Lazenby family unto the cousins three times removed which came to us masquerading as wedding presents.

Into this snug harbor I sailed that evening, bearing rich dainties and exuding the air of well-being I had inhaled during a brief pause in the cocktail dispensary of the Hotel Jefferson, the nearest watering place to Youth House, to celebrate my new eminence as an alternate but nonetheless bona fide presidential commissioner. No sooner was I inside our gleaming black front door than, roaring his pleasure, Rafael launched his enormous bulk upon me, his great, shaggy face alight with glee.

"Down, sir, down, damn you!" I cried as I endeavored to unburden myself of my purchases. "We are going to have to do something about training this damned beast," I continued loudly, if emptily, for Rafael regards all disciplinary efforts as simply another form of sport, and I find it impossible to spank a laughing dog.

Jobiana came out of the tiny closet the reconstructors had thinly disguised as a kitchen.

"Whee, wee wife!" I caroled merrily. "Come, buss your lord."

Wiping her hands on the picturesque-type Pennsylvania Dutch

apron she wore over her black velvet pedal pushers and white silk blouse, the light of my life advanced winsomely and presented her ripe, cherry lips.

"You've had a Martini," she advised me when I had greeted her. Her green eyes were solemn.

"I have had several Martinis, and it is not beyond the realm of possibility that I shall have several more. *Nunc est bibendum*, as we Roman boys are fond of saying, *juvenes dum sumus*. Do you, good woman, crack loose some ice and I shall mix us a batch of the most potent and tell you tales of captains and kings."

"Frederick," said my Jobiana dangerously, using the formal, cautionary full name, which is expected to snap me back to the fact that life is r., life is e., and the g. is not its g.

So I told her about the President's Commission.

"Oh, Eff, that's wonderful," said she, her face lighting with wifely pride and devotion, all wrath forgotten. "It really does mean that Dr. Mountain and SKN have their eyes on you for bigger things. And to think that two months ago you were ready to look around for something else. Oh, darling, it's wonderful!"

Then I told her about the thousand-buck raise.

"You deserve it," Joby declared, leading me back into the kitchen where, pearl among wives, she had laid out the necessary ingredients—vermouth, lemon, gin and ice. The place was redolent with the fragrance of cooking spareribs and Joby's own barbecue sauce.

"I wonder how Nat Walsingham will react when he hears," Joby murmured a few moments later, after she had sampled the produce of my eerie skill with a stirring rod. She grinned impishly, and showed her dimples.

"Hell and confusion to Walsingham," said I, raising my nicely frosting glass.

"Hell and confusion," Joby responded. "And don't forget dear Susanne."

"Susanne, too. Hell and confusion to the both of them."

Susanne Walsingham is one of those women who could bring out the latent cattiness in a female Christian martyr—"My dear, what a lovely stake to be burned at; didn't they have it in your size?" A few minutes of her could turn my sweet and gentle Jobiana into a snarling she-tiger, claws at the ready, fangs bared.

"I've rearranged the back part of the attic for Dumbo's things," Joby observed when we had dealt with the Walsinghams. "I think you'd better get it unpacked and upstairs before you two do anything else. Otherwise it won't get done, if I know the signs and portents."

At which point we heard the metallic clank of our genuine brass fake Federal Period door knocker.

And Dumbo Savoury was amongst us, beaming all over his round, pink face and sweeping Joby into his bearlike embrace to the accompaniment of gladsome cries on the part of one and all.

"The only woman I've ever loved," Dumbo cried, setting Joby back on her feet.

"This is going to be a very large evening," Joby said sternly. "Now get going, you two, and get whatever it is Dumbo wants stored upstairs. Then we can relax. No nonsense now."

Half an hour later, we had finished, and the back of Dumbo's rented station wagon was emptied of its tightly packed cargo of heavy cardboard cartons. We had stowed it safely up under the rafters, in company with my Aunt Claudie's steel engraving of the churchyard at Stoke Poges, my Cousin Lucy's gentleman's smoking stand (complete with cigar clipper, much dulled by years of usage by my late Uncle Ralph), and my Uncle Herbert's alabaster bust of Hermes which Joby refused, despite my pleas, to permit in our living room, where I thought it would lend tone. I wanted to cross his eyes with a few artful dabs of paint.

Our job accomplished, we were allowed to collapse into the sagging elegance of my Grandmother Henning's sofa. Joby had set out cheese and crackers and a fresh jug of elixir.

"We grow old," Dumbo said, ceasing to puff and sampling his glass. "There was a time when I would have called heaving cartons child's play. But seriously, Joby and Eff, I'm terribly grateful to you two for letting me have the space for my stuff."

"Why not, when we've got the room?" Joby asked. "What is it, anyhow?" For the merest fraction of a second, Dumbo hesitated.

"Books and photographs, mostly," he said then. "Actually, it's part of a project, the one I'm working on right now. Been on it for nearly a year now, ever since I left Penn. This trip abroad— did I tell you on the phone this morning, Eff, that I'm being financed by a Heppinstall Grant?—will just about wrap up the field work. After that, it will be simply a matter of getting it into shape. And after that, or so the Heppinstall Foundation people tell me, it will probably go to the United Nations."

"Golly," Joby said. "I'm impressed, Dr. Savoury."

"So you should be, young woman," Dumbo grinned. "Yes, please."

"How long will you be gone?" Joby asked, refilling his glass.

"Bless you, ma'am." Dumbo accepted his drink. "I don't really know how long. It depends on a lot of different factors, and I'll probably be moving around a lot; Spain, Italy, Germany, Sweden, England, very possibly North Africa. On something like this, it's almost impossible to plan an itinerary in advance. You simply go wherever you can find the facts you need, whenever the people you have to see are available."

"It sounds like heaven!" exclaimed my spouse, twisting the old knife in the wound. We've been hoping to scrape together enough for a good, long trip to Europe for years, but it never seems to work out.

Dumbo then startled us by announcing that his plane connection for his overseas flight left National Airport at ten o'clock that evening, and Joby and I protested vigorously at this too-brief visit.

"And I've got the studio couch in Eff's den all made up," Joby said reproachfully. "You're a beast, Martin Savoury; you don't see us for nearly two years, you whistle in, say hello, tell us you're off to Europe and voom! You're gone."

"You know us absent-minded professors and irresponsible bachelors, Jobe," Dumbo replied, giving her his small boy's grin again. "I should have told Eff this morning, but what with the last-minute details and all—forgive me, lady?"

It developed that I was to drive Dumbo and his baggage out to the airport in the rental station wagon. The Washington office of the car-rental outfit would then pick it up from the house in the morning. Dumbo said he'd sold his rackety old Morgan in preparation for the European junket, and planned to pick up a new one in England.

We finished off the spareribs in a fine glow of bonhommie, much enhanced by our preprandial refreshment, and Joby ordered us into the living room while she stacked the dishwasher. There we fell into one of those boring-to-everybody-else-but-fascinating-to-us-old-soldiers sessions of trading notes on the half-dozen or so souls from the old Twelfth Regiment with whom we still kept in touch. Hal Smith was practicing law in West Virginia. Bill Todd was teaching English at a girl's college in North Carolina. Ken Cramsie was a full, bird Colonel and due for retirement on a fat pension. That sort of thing.

I noted that Dumbo did not again return to the nature of the project upon which he was engaged, and it occurred to me that he might, just possibly, be tied up with the C.I.A. A wandering sociologist would make a fine cover—as all us Geoffrey Household and Eric Ambler friends could appreciate. But with my usual exquisite tact and discretion, I forbore to press him for additional details. ("We won't be able to raise a finger to help you, Major; we'll disown you completely. You understand that?" "Of course, sir. But don't worry, I won't get caught. . . .")

Joby rejoined us, bearing our supreme gesture of hospitality to our dearest chums, the Benedictine jug and three pony glasses.

Then, much too soon, it was 9:15, and time to leave for the airport in order to leave Dumbo plenty of leeway in getting his plane, even if we had a flat. I operate on the theory that planes and trains deliberately leave early when they know I'm planning to be aboard. Let's louse up Lazenby, they chortle; let's leave right this very instant, while he's still out there trying to buy a ticket and fumbling for his wallet. For me, the Pennsylvania Railroad runs *ahead* of schedule.

It was not until we had swung out onto Key Bridge to get across the Potomac and onto the parkway that leads down the Virginia shore to the airport that Dumbo told me what it was he was up to.

IV

"Did you know," Dumbo asked, "that juvenile delinquency has increased about 800 per cent in the last ten years?"

"Not amongst our subscribers," I replied smugly, swinging out to pass a Virginia country gentleman steering his battered pickup back to the ancestral acres.

"Eight hundred per cent," Dumbo went on, paying no attention to my chauvinism, "which is one hell of a lot too much. And one of the biggest factors is sex."

"Wasn't it ever thus?"

"Shut up, dammit. Now like I was saying, the big question is how these kids get themselves all steamed up on the sex bit, and one part of the answer is dirty books, by which I mean feelthy litrachoore. Not the pin-up stuff you see on the newstands, and not what the booksellers call erotica, but the real McCoy."

"Like in Paris?"

"Like in Paris, or Havana, or Nogales. The point is that there's a hell of a lot more of the stuff in circulation today than ever before. You hear lots and lots about dope smuggling, or getting diamonds through customs, but you never hear much about the dirty book racket, mainly because the people who buy the stuff aren't very proud of themselves to begin with, and they sure as hell don't want to advertise the fact that they get their kicks out of a book. As long as it was mostly adults, nobody gave much of a damn, but now there's so much of the stuff floating around that a lot of it gets into the hands of kids."

I aimed the station wagon deftly into the Arlington traffic circle, barely missing another F.F.V. After the Volkswagen, it was like navigating a galleon.

"The point is," Dumbo continued, "that you'll probably never be able to stop people from printing this crap, any more than you'll be able to stop other people from buying it, human nature being human nature. What you can do, though, is find out how the thing operates: who prints the stuff, who ships it to whom, how it gets into circulation and who make the profits. Then you can start to work out some sort of coherent plan for controlling it."

"And that's your project?" I guessed as we swung onto the parkway to the south.

"That's it. The Heppinstall Foundation puts up the funds, but I'll be operating under the auspices of UNESCO."

A fearful suspicion was beginning to form—a cloud no larger than a man's hand, as it were. It grew with frightening rapidity.

"That stuff in my attic?" I said feebly.

"Probably the most comprehensive collection of pornography in the country today, outside the Kinsey material, of course," Dumbo replied proudly. "And I've got a few items Kinsey never heard of. Uh, that's why I didn't want to go into a lot of detail in front of Joby. I hope you don't mind, Eff."

"Mind? Me?" I cackled hysterically. "Not me, Dumbo; never in a million years." We crossed beneath the Memorial Bridge overpass.

"You can see how I couldn't risk letting it stay behind in my apartment. I'm renting the place to a nice young couple in the English Department. And I sure as hell didn't want to store it in the library; too many people, and besides, it's tricky stuff. Might produce a real stink if people got the wrong idea about it."

"That it might," I agreed. "But wouldn't it be much simpler to ship the whole works back to this Heppinstall Foundation and let them take care of it for you?"

Dumbo looked bleak. "Two reasons," he said. "One, they're right in the middle of moving their quarters from down on Park Avenue to somewhere up around Morningside Heights. When I was in New York last week to talk over this trip, the executive director couldn't even locate his personal files, the confusion was so thick. Two—" Dumbo paused and sighed. "Two, they'd just as soon not be reminded that this collection exists. So far as they're concerned, it's a messy but necessary detail, and they'd rather not have their name associated with it.

"Mind you, they'll be happy to take their share of the credit when the final report is published, all nice and scholarly and full of statistics on heavy rag paper. But right now—well, they'd hate to have people thinking that the mighty Heppinstall Foundation is buying up dirty books." Dumbo snorted.

"Sort of like 'Give us a report on prostitution but leave out the sex'?" I suggested. Dumbo nodded.

"You've got the general idea. It's a pretty stupid attitude, but there it is. So now you understand why I can't unload this stuff on the Heppinstall people."

"Oh, sure," I said.

"There is one other thing you can do for me, Eff," Dumbo added, having, apparently, failed to catch the note of insane gaiety in my tone. "I've got a couple of things pending—a big collection in Virginia and some new stuff which is supposed to have come in from Mexico. The Virginia collection will probably go for a thousand or fifteen hundred; the Mexican stuff, it's hard to say. If I leave you my check for twenty-five hundred, would you handle the deal for me?"

"Me!" And this time I really did squeak.

"My contacts have your phone number," Dumbo resumed patiently, as one who instructs a backward child. "They don't know your real name, but they'll call you Peter Rabbit, and they'll be in touch with you when they're ready to sell. I wouldn't dream of asking you, Eff, if there were anybody else I could depend on to do it.

"You know how it is around a college campus, where faculty gossip is the only thing that keeps us savants from brooding over our lousy salaries. The head of my department knows what this project is, but when I asked him to help out, he pursed his tiny mouth, looked scared witless and then pious and said he simply couldn't bring himself to dirty his hands with the business, no matter how well intentioned it was. And dammit, Eff, it is well intentioned.

"A kid who gets herself knocked up after she's first got herself all steamed up over one of those damned dirty little books—and a hell of a lot of the stuff *does* circulate among your polite little subscribers, pal—is in just as big trouble as if she'd been introduced to marijuana. And what about the poor kids who pose for this stuff, the ones who think it's the only way to get to be a model, or the ones trying to get themselves enough loot to buy themselves a fix? You talk about battening on misery, chum!"

I hadn't heard Dumbo so angry since the night the Krauts blew up M Company's field kitchen at Mortain. Angry, he can be a most convincing citizen, and he was undoubtedly right, although it was a problem to which I'd never previously given much thought. Much thought, hell; I'd never given it *any* thought. Perhaps, I told myself, I owed it to youth to lend a hand in Dumbo's lonely battle against evil. After all, youth was helping to pay me thirteen thousand bucks a year for my services.

Besides, nobody—not even Joby—need ever know what was in those big cartons in the attic.

"Okay, pal," I said, as we drew smartly up to the brightly lighted entrance to the airport. "You can count on ol' Eff."

"Thanks, Eff," Dumbo said simply, and then grinned. "I knew you would, you old bastard."

"Peter Rabbit yet."

"I sort of thought you'd appreciate that touch."

"If we play our cards right, you're going to have just time enough to buy me a drink before your plane leaves."

"Be my guest, pal."

It was not until I was driving the station wagon back to Georgetown that the immensity of my folly dawned upon me—that I really began to realize the hideous possibilities in my position.

Here was I, Frederick William Lazenby, holding a responsible editorial position on the staff of one of the most respectable magazines in the United States, expected to provide a sterling example of rectitude for the emulation of the nation's youth, and about to begin a tour of duty as a member of a commission appointed by the President of the United States to investigate youth's problems.

And in my tiny garret reposed one of the biggest collections of feelthy litrachoore ever assembled on the North American continent.

Even more appalling, I was about to become, freely and voluntarily, a wheeler and dealer in the pornography trade.

Lascivious Lazenby, Lazenby the lecher. Filthy Freddy.

High above me as I parked the station wagon—illegally—in the alley behind our residence, a mighty airliner climbed with thundering engines toward the stars, winking its red lights in brave defiance of the night. Perhaps it carried Dumbo on his way to— and then I went numb.

To where? To where, for God's sake?

To Europe, yes, but *where* in Europe?

Of all the bloody fools that ever drew breath! In the mental turmoil into which I had been tossed by Dumbo's revelations, I had completely forgotten to ask him how I could get in touch with him, just in case. Nor was there any point in trying to reach him through UNESCO or the Heppinstall people; hadn't Dumbo himself declared that on such a project it was impossible to plan an itinerary in advance? Supposing an emergency were to arise, I had absolutely no means of letting him know. Not that there was any reason to expect anything to go wrong, of course, but just the same. . . .

I was all alone. I mean, *all* alone.

In that grisly realization, I also knew that I had enjoyed my last moments of mental peace until Dumbo Savoury should return. For me, tranquillity would be only a word.

And that's how it all began.

Brother!

V

If only Joby hadn't decided to turn in before I got back from the airport, matters might have arranged themselves very differrently, I keep telling myself. Because if she had been up, I would undoubtedly have discussed the situation with her, freely and fully, as we've always talked over everything that has affected our lives. We don't wallow in the sweet syrup of togetherness, but I like to think that we're both reasonably sensible people, in love with each other, and that a marriage worth the powder to blow it to hell should be based on complete mutual confidence. If that makes me Dr. Norman Vincent Lazenby, I'm sorry, but that's the way I feel. Look at it this way: if we goof, we're in it together. Like the year we decided to try free-lancing. We went broke, but nobody went around blaming anybody.

Mind you, this is not an attempt to shift the blame onto Joby. But she had gone to beddy-bye, and I decided that, since she'd had a pretty full day, what with one thing and the spareribs, she deserved her rest. After all, it was my problem. So I mixed myself a nightcap and sat down to analyze the situation. There's no point in denying that I've grown so accustomed to discussing things with Joby that, left to my own devices, I am not a hundred per cent sure thing. On this occasion, I outdid myself. I decided not to say a word to Joby about the true nature of Dumbo's collection and the deals I had agreed to negotiate for him.

In Heaven's sweet name, sire, why? you ask. And well you may.

As best I can remember my scrambled reasoning, the major factor in this decision was my fear that she would worry herself silly over the possible consequences to my career should something untoward occur. Not too long before, an eminently respectable citizen had been in grave trouble with our highly moral District cops for his possession of a collection of pornography gathered, as was Dumbo's, for purely scientific purposes. The courts ruled that the collection would have to be turned over to a court-approved board of trustees which would then make it available to qualified scholars. The whole thing worked out fairly well for all concerned, but before it was settled, the local press had a fine, sniggering time and the citizen's good name was temporarily much besmirched.

In my case, the damage was potentially much more disastrous. A dope fiend unmasked among the student body of the Union Theological Seminary would enjoy no shorter shrift than I, accused of hoarding a trove of pornography, at the hands of Walter Van Meter Mountain. With the job would go the house, and. . . .

I had a shawl-wrapped Joby selling matches on a wind-swept corner before I'd taken my second swallow of nightcap. Wisps of gray hair kept blowing across the ravaged beauty of her face, and a terrible abiding sadness clouded her lovely eyes.

"Ah, there, my good woman, I'll have a box of—Great Scot! Why, it's—but it can't be—Jobiana Lazenby!"

"God bless and keep you, kind sir." The tremulous smile, the wrinkled blue hands fumbling with the snaps of a frayed purse. "Matches, matches, who'll buy my matches?"

I took a good stiff snort and tried to think straight.

"And you persist in telling this court—you expect the jury to believe, Mrs. Lazenby, that you were not aware of the presence under your own roof of this incredible mass of sheer filth?"

"As God is my witness." The firm little chin forward, the green eyes clear, the voice steady and sure—Jobiana wrapped in the snowy mantle of truth. My lawyer leaping to his feet, shouting; the judge, infinitely wise.

"Objection sustained. The District Attorney is aware that it is not Mrs. Lazenby who is on trial here. The Court is prepared to accept her statements as true. The jury will disregard that last question, and it will be stricken from the record."

But why go on? The fact is that I arrived firmly and resolutely at the wrongest decision I've ever made in my life, and I speak as a man who has made some beauts. For her own protection, Joby must not know about Dumbo's collection; protection from need-less worry, and legal protection, just in case the balloon went up.

Oh, I should have known better; should have recognized and heeded the signs. That feeling of smug satisfaction which accompanies the completed deed: Yessir, I've given this thing some pretty deep thought and here's my decision. Bang! No nonsense. That's the Lazenby way, lads; up, Guards, and at 'em.

Ha!

I finished my nightcap and ascended to our bedroom. Joby had left the lamp on my bedside table alight, and I gazed down at her, smiling fatuously. Her auburn hair lay gracefully adrift on the soft whiteness of her pillow, and a gentle smile curved her lips, and altogether she was so downright wonderful my eyes watered.

No harm shall befall this sweet child, I vowed, unbuckling my scabbard and leaning my massy shield, brave with its many quarterings, 'gainst the chaise lounge Joby's Uncle Urban had given us on our third anniversary. Nay, though hell shall vomit flame, Sir Cedric of Lazenby will ne'er cry Hold! Enough!

And then it occurred to me that I had not yet examined the problem of how to explain those telephone callers who would be wanting to talk to Peter Rabbit.

Very quietly, in stockinged feet, I went back downstairs and poured myself another nightcap. But this time it was easy. I let the old imagination roam at large, and one cigarette was sufficient to the task in hand. The mind, relaxed after the strain of reaching a major decision, purred smoothly, and within minutes had produced a perfectly suitable cover story.

Then I returned upstairs, and this time went to bed. Now that I had calmly thought this business through, I marvelled at the baselessness of my fears earlier in the evening. Just a matter of applying mature intelligence to a reasoned analysis. Nothing to it, really.

Slept like a babe.

VI

In euphoric mood, I descended to my breakfast that next A.M.

Joby, ever dutiful, was long up and about, and a most marvelous fragrance filled the air. She was seated at our miniscule breakfast table, inhaling her wifely mug of coffee and reading the *Post* editorial page when I entered, showered, shaved, lotioned and sprightly.

"Canadian bacon," cried I ecstatically, bending to give her the morning kiss on the top of the head.

"You smell lovely," Joby said. "I wish you'd use that stuff all the time. I take it you got Dumbo on his plane and off to Europe all right."

"I did that," I replied as she fetched me my plate.

"Drink your tomato juice first. Or would you sooner have orange? Or there's a half grapefruit."

I braced the tomato juice with a jolt of Lea & Perrins and quaffed same. Then I set to work with a will.

"I wish it had been us on that plane last night," Joby murmured. "Just think, we'd be in London now." Her eyes were shining.

"One of these days," I said.

"What about Dumbo's station wagon?" Joby changed the subject.

"I'll call the rental people from the office. Then they send somebody around to pick it up. Dumbo left me a check to cover whatever the bill comes to."

"I'm sorry I pooped out on you last night. After you left, I tried to read for a while, but I simply couldn't keep my eyes open. I think I'll make an appointment with Dr. Loveland and have my eyes examined. Maybe I need bifocals. Would you still love me if I wore bifocals?"

"This bacon is simply magnificent," I mumbled, munching.

"God, but you're romantic in the morning."

"Well, dammit, it *is* good, and I love you for buying it."

"We can't really afford it, but there was a special on. Did you and Dumbo," my wife went zooming into one of her spectacular non sequiturs, "have a good yak session on the way out to the airport?"

Here was my opening.

"It was pretty much how I had it figured," I said knowingly. "Of course, he couldn't say too much, but I got the general idea. I imagine you had it pegged, too."

"Had what pegged?"

"Oh, come on Jobe. You know what I'm talking about; this junket he's on."

"What about it?"

"Now just think back for a second. You'll remember he never did say, really, what it was all about."

"Well, sociology, I guess. What else would it be?"

"Ah."

"Eff Lazenby, you are *the* most maddening person in this world when you put on that sickening smile. You know something, and you're teasing me."

"Keep a secret?" I asked.

Joby crossed her arms over her handsome bosom, pouted her lower lip and gazed at me with distaste, plainly indicating that she, personally, simply couldn't care less one way or the other, if *that* was the way I was going to act. All a pose, of course; she was hanging on my lips, if the truth be told.

"The fact of the matter is that Dumbo's really tied in with the C.I.A.," I said quietly and, I think, impressively. "This so-called project of his is what they call a cover. Hell's bells, Jobe, you've read Eric Ambler; you know what I'm talking about."

"Eff." Joby's voice was infinitely tolerant, infinitely infuriating.

"So all right. Forget the whole thing. Forget I mentioned it. The hell with it." Now it was I who was doing the pouting. There followed several seconds of uneasy silence.

"I don't care what you say, I think he's pulling your leg," Joby said, her curiosity getting the better of her.

"If you would be good enough to hear me out, and whether or not you believe what I've been telling you or not," I declared with a fine flourish of negatives (cunningly designed to provide that extra soupçon of nervous emphasis), "we're a little mixed up in whatever it is Dumbo's doing." The effect was as desired. Joby's expression turned mildly anxious.

"Now Eff . . ." she said uneasily.

"Just take it easy, Jobe. There's nothing cloak-and-daggerish about it. What happened was that Dumbo asked us—or that is, me—to act as sort of a check point for him. If it turns out he has to communicate direct with C.I.A., he'll send me a cable in one of their codes. We won't know what it means; all we do is forward it to the C.I.A. And a cable sent to us won't mean anything to anybody because we're not connected in any way with the C.I.A."

Joby was beginning to look intrigued. So far, my story line was going over just fine.

"The chances are, of course," I pressed on, "that Dumbo won't have any occasion to cable direct, so, actually, we're not really involved at all, except in case. But because we're acting as sort of a relay station, Dumbo had to give the C.I.A. my name, and every so often they'll be phoning me, just to make sure I'm still paying the phone bill, so to speak, or haven't moved to Upper Oatmeal, North Dakota. Kind of a security check."

"Suppose a cable arrives or they phone and you're at the office, do I phone it on or answer or what?" Joby asked. The bonny lass was swallowing my absurd story lock, stock and barrel.

"It won't and they won't," I reassured her. "That is, you, yourself, won't have to be mixed up in it at all. If a cable should come, I'll phone it in when I get home. If they call, they'll ask to speak to Peter Rabbit. That's my code name. They ask for Peter Rabbit, and then you ask them for a number where I can reach them. You see? It's simple."

"It sounds silly."

"It does, at that," I conceded handsomely. "But you know the government, Jobe, and especially the C.I.A. They like doing it the hard way. Plus the romance and mystery angle and everybody wearing trench coats; all the old cornball routine."

Joby's slender shoulders started to quiver as she began to giggle. "Peter Rabbit," she gargled. "Really, Eff . . ."

I shrugged.

"Peter Rabbit!" she shrieked, tears streaming from her eyes as mirth took over and she began to whoop.

I finished my coffee in my best we-are-not-amused manner, and Joby gradually subsided into a series of muffled, spasmodic giggles.

"You might keep in mind," I advised her, "that, funny or not, this is one of those things about which we do not gabble over the bridge tables."

"Yes, Major North." Joby gave me a brisk salute. "Sir."

"I mean that."

"Oh, Eff, you're priceless. Don't you give me any credit at all? Of course I won't say anything to anybody. Now you'd better run along or you'll be later than usual."

"I'll call you later."

"Could you remember to bring home some dog biscuits? Rafe finished the last box yesterday."

"Remind me when I call."

As I stepped through the back door into the midget's play pen of our garden patio—the phrase is not mine, but good, Georgetown realtor's jargon, signifying nothing—I heard behind me a mocking cry: "Have a good day, Major North."

It was not without a certain amount of quiet satisfaction that I proceeded into the converted piano crate which houses the Volkswagen: What a practiced web some of us can weave when we wangle to deceive. Joby had accepted my fabrication entire, and another problem had been disposed of with little or no difficulty.

My normal route was blocked that morning by a fire in a small house on P Street, and as I swung off onto the route indicated by the policeman guarding the approaches to the disaster scene, I could see smoke billowing from the windows of the stricken structure and helmeted and raincoated firemen dashing in and out, bearing hoses and axes.

My complacency of a few seconds previous quivered, split down the center and collapsed. Suppose the wiring in our house were even now smoldering, waiting only for some breath of air to burst into a small flame . . . Suppose Joby had left a cigarette lying unbalanced in an ash tray while she hurried about some household chore. . . . "You, O'Brien! Heave them cartons out of the window! Or chop a hole in the roof, but get 'em out of here." "Yessir, Chief!" "Sa-a-a-y, Chief! C'mere a minute. . . ."

I arrived at Youth House in a frame of mind which can only be described as troubled.

VII

What amazes me is that any hanky-panky ever succeeds. Take even the simplest caper, one that isn't so much dishonest as involving merely a certain blurring of the truth, and consider all the angles that have to be covered. Mind you, I do not admire these morally unstable bankers who make off with a few hundred thousand dollars over the course of the years, but I have to take my hat off to their mental discipline and agility.

What galls and maddens me, on the other hand, is that my situation wasn't dishonest and it need not have involved any blurring of the truth. To be more accurate, there was no situation to begin with. I created it, all by my very own self out of my own tiny head, and thereafter, like some monstrous plant, it simply grew and grew. What stimulated and nourished its horrid growth was my continuing effort to cover all the angles.

I did not take my morning mental constitutional through the *Times'* crossword puzzle, but devoted myself instead to an analysis of the storage problem. Stashed in the attic, the Savoury Papers represented a clear and present danger, and it seemed perfectly obvious that the solution was the removal of the collection to some safer location. Indeed, it occurred to me, in this wise I could also disassociate myself from the stuff. Would it not be a simple thing to telephone some storage outfit and, under an assumed name, order Dumbo's cartons to be hauled away to the fireproof inviolability of a warehouse?

It would, and that was the trouble, I perceived. Doubtless Dumbo had long since thought of the same solution and rejected it for the same reasons which came to mind as soon as I had taken thought of all the angles. Suppose a careless workman were to drop one of the cartons as he struggled down the narrow stairs from the attic. Suppose the storage van were to become involved in an accident on its way from Georgetown to the warehouse. And in any event, such a plan would establish a definite connection between Dumbo's cartons and my home and hearth, and this must be avoided at all costs. No, the idea was unsound, although it had one feature of merit—the assumed name.

If not a storage warehouse, then where? Rent some farmer's unused barn over in Virginia, rent a truck and haul the stuff over by myself? No good. Barns have mice and sometimes they leak and sometimes they catch fire. I had, after all, promised Dumbo to keep his unseemly treasure intact.

A brisk review of the qualifications requisite to adequate storage indicated that what was needed was an area reasonably safe from fire and available only to me. The transfer of the collection would have to be made by myself, who would also have to remain unknown to the owners of the premises. With my thoughts in a row, the problem solved itself. Under another name, I would rent an office in one of the older but fireproof business buildings far downtown. Here, a carton at a time, I would bring the collection.

But what about the cleaning women? Would they not be tempted to peek? Would not the building superintendent feel some curiosity concerning a tenant who filled his office space with cardboard cartons? But filing cabinets were something else again. Very well, then, I would rent enough steel filing cabinets to house the contents of the cartons. No one would find anything strange in the fact that my office was filled with locked files.

So far, so good. But it was only when I turned the great brain loose on the question of what name I should assume that the true beauty of this scheme revealed itself to me. My new office would be much more than mere storage space. It would give protection to the collection, to be sure, but it would also be equally a protection for myself. It would be Peter Rabbit's warren. In it, I could conduct whatever negotiations might be necessary to the acquisition of the additional material Dumbo had arranged to purchase. Beyond it, I could never be traced.

Now, as to the name. For my purposes, it would have to be a

simple name; one that would evoke no comment. Not John Smith, of course, but not T. Sylvester Plantagenet, either; just a plain, unmemorable American name. Why I finally selected the name "George Burnley," I'll never know. It just came to me, possibly from some dim association in my past, but it seemed to have the right ring to it. George Burnley. Good old George, the hardest worker in the whole shop. In sales.

Ah, but wait! George Burnley's contacts with the owners of his office building and their superintendent must be held to a minimum. The rent will be paid by check, sent through the mails. And how explain Frederick W. Lazenby's name on George's rent checks? There must be absolutely no connection whatever between George Burnley and Frederick W. Lazenby. George must sign his own checks, which meant that George would have to open a checking account. Which meant problems. The trouble was that the banking institutions in Washington—so far as I knew—would not accept a new account without some sort of identification, even if the initial deposit were in hard cash. And how did I know this? Because I had edited the manuscript of "How Bankers Guard Against the Swindler," and I knew the writer had gathered his material in our fair capital. That's how I knew this, and a good thing, too. If George Burnley had walked into a bank and tried to open an account and hadn't been able to produce some identification, somebody would have remembered him, and if I could help it, nobody was going to remember anything unusual about old George.

So it was necessary to create an identity. Without a bank account, who would give Burnley a credit card? Nobody. But suppose George could produce a driver's license. Ah-ha! Who questions a driver's license? And come to think of it, why don't they?

Once more, the problem resolved itself. What could be simpler than driving out to Rockville and renting a post office box? Thus George would have an address, and in Maryland. As a Marylander, he would have every right to apply and be tested for a driver's license. Armed with this evidence that the State of Maryland believed he existed, he could walk into any bank, plunk down his cash and open an account. And as for the knucklehead who wrote "How Bankers Guard Against the Swindler," he reckoned without the brilliant mental processes of Frederick W. Lazenby, the spiritual heir of Fu Manchu.

In sum, dear hearts and gentle people, I honestly believed that I had covered all the angles.

Actually, it struck me, my mental processes had not been too very different from those involved in the construction of a novel. It was largely a matter of logical development and leaving no loose ends dangling.

There was just one hitch. I have never constructed a novel.

Nevertheless, with my whole program now clear before me, I could apply my skills and labors to the interests of *Youth Outlook* in good heart. I turned to my "In" basket with a will, and so do-ing happened to glance at my wrist watch. The hands stood straight up at noon. My ratiocinations had blown an entire morn-ing to hell.

On top of the papers in the basket was a long, official looking envelope bearing in its upper left-hand corner the imprint of The President's Adivsory Commission on Juvenile Correction. Inside was a letter on top-quality government stationery, advising me how happy was the commission's chairman, Dr. H. Broadus Whatcoate, to know that his group would have the benefit of my extensive background and thinking in the great tasks that lay ahead, tasks demanding of each of us every resource of heart and mind in the service of our glorious nation. It also noted that the commission would conduct its organizational meeting at 10:30 A.M. on Wednesday of the following week in Conference Room D in the Health, Education and Welfare Department Building on Inde-pendence Avenue. Dr. Whatcoate concluded with the hope that I would be able to join him and the other members of our stout company at an informal lunch afterwards.

Even now my life was being lived on two planes, one high and honorable of purpose, the other low and furtive but, in the final analysis, equally high of purpose.

VIII

There's not much point in going into all the details, but the fact is that by the time the organizational meeting of the President's Commission on Juvenile Correction rolled around, my program had been pretty well worked out. The Maryland cops had seemed perfectly happy to accept my Rockville post office box address, and the driving test was no trouble. Equipped with my new driver's license in the name of George Burnley, I went to my own bank and withdrew, in my own name and in cash, the twenty-five hundred dollars which, in the form of Dumbo's check, I'd deposited earlier. This sum I took to another bank, where a junior assistant vice president accepted my license as all the identification necessary, and George Burnley had a bank account and was ready to do business. Then, after a simple check of the *Star's* classified section and a couple of telephone calls, I found a one-room office in an elderly building well down E Street, and by Wednesday all that remained to be accomplished was the actual transfer of Dumbo's collection from my attic to my seedy hide-out. The office rental and the charge for the rental of the steel filing cabinets could, I felt, legitimately be charged off as necessary expenses and taken from the fund Dumbo had left with me.

All tickerty-boo, in other words. No sweat, as the military men put it.

Then I went to that damned meeting.

Our Nation's Leader had certainly picked himself a jim-dandy little commission. The members came in all shapes, sizes and voice ranges, but they shared two qualities in common so far as I was concerned: all of them were older and appeared to be considerably more prosperous than I. Dr. H. Broadus Whatcoate, our gifted and able chairman, looked like the late British actor, Mr. H. B. Warner, in the role of Jesus, and he wasted no time in getting the show on the road. First off, he gave the twenty of us gathered solemnly around the vast, coffin-shaped conference table an expanded version of his welcoming letter, and then without further ado divided us into four five-man committees. There was a committee on career guidance, another on youth problems in urban areas, and still another on aspects of rural delinquency. I was beginning to feel left out as he finished announcing the membership of the third committee, but then he got around to appointing the fourth committee and I felt the roof sag.

"And finally, but certainly not least importantly, I come to the committee which will have a vital role to play if the mission of this group is to be achieved in a manner which will reflect credit upon it," declared the good doctor gravely. "I refer to the Committee on Salacious Literature." There was a murmur of agreement from my fellow committee members and several spinsterish types smiled thinly to demonstrate that no matter how horrid things got, they were dead game to the end.

Dr. Whatcoate's mild features grew stern, as if he were about to rebuke a band of moneychangers. "We are all aware of the proportions of this problem, of the obscenity which floods the newsstands in an ever-swelling torrent of corruption, as cheaply and readily available to young people as a candy bar. Yet any attempt to control this turgid flow is invariably greeted with countercharges of censorship and interference with the freedom of the press.

"What, then, is the solution?" All of us looked uneasily down at the yellow scratch pads on the conference table before us, searching heart and mind for the answer. None forthcame to break that rhetorical silence.

"That is the question to which I hope our Committee on Salacious Literature can provide, in part at least, a measure of reply. From their studies will emerge, I trust, recommendations which the President has assured me will be incorporated into legislation by the Congress. Thus a grave responsibility rests upon the members of this committee, whom I will now name. I have selected these members on the basis of their qualifications, but in the event that any one named does not feel morally willing to subject himself to what must be, I am afraid, a frequently distasteful chore, I will naturally attempt to relieve him or her and arrange an exchange of committee assignments.

"Those who will compose the Committee on Salacious Literature are: Chairman, the Honorable Martin Luther Brackett, formerly chief justice of the Supreme Court of North Dakota and an authority on the laws governing the press and the use of the mails; Mrs. B. Eugene Dailey, past president of the South Atlantic Region of the National Congress of Parents and Teachers; the Reverend Doctor Theodore R. MacIlvaine, director of the Presbyterian Youth Conference of California; Rabbi Milton W. Whitestone, of Temple Beth Israel in Baltimore and formerly editor of young peoples' publications for the Rabbinical Council of the Greater New York Area, and—standing in for Dr. Walter Van Meter Mountain, whose many duties will keep him out of the country during the initial phases of our work—Mr. Frederick W. Lazenby, of the editorial staff of *Youth Outlook*, certainly the most reputable publication of its sort in the world today."

As each of our names was called, we half arose from our chairs to acknowledge the introduction, smiling modestly and nodding amiably to our fellow members. When my turn came at last, I managed reasonably well and was rewarded by a kindly inclination of the noble Roman head of Judge Brackett. It was the sort of nod he probably used to put brand new attorneys at their ease, and from it I gathered that in the future deliberations of the Committee on Salacious Literature, Master Freddy Lazenby would be expected to be seen and not heard; there's a good boy. Which was just fine in my book, and I was grateful to Dr. Whatcoate for having defined my status as a stand-in.

"Now that we all know who we are and what we have to do," Whatcoate picked up the ball again, "I want to take the occasion to introduce you to the chief of our full-time, professional working staff, but before I do, I want to tell you just a little bit about this gentleman's background. This is a fact-finding body, and the man I will introduce to you is one of our government's most experienced investigators. He is a former Special Agent of the Federal Bureau of Investigation. He served as a staff investigator for the late Senatory McCarthy, and most recently, he has been chief investigator for the Senate Committee on Corrupt Practices. I think you will all agree with me that we are fortunate, indeed, in having secured the services of this gentlemen.

"Will you come forward, please, Mr. Julian? Thank you."

All of us at the conference table turned in our chairs and followed with our eyes the progress of this very paragon among investigators, who had appeared at the door of the room precisely on schedule and was now moving briskly to join Dr. Whatcoate. Mr. Julian sure as hell didn't look like my idea of a hot-rock investigator. He was short and tubby and had that shade of sandy hair which, against his ruddy complexion, made his eyebrows almost invisible. His face was that of a tiny Herbert Hoover wearing rimless glasses and, so help me, a pencil-line mustache which he probably darkened with his wife's mascara. He wore a tan suit, a silk necktie of Maxfield Parrish blue, and (I observed later) white socks with high black shoes of the sort that Sears, Roebuck used to and may still sell to retired postmen, with elastic gores set into the sides. In his left lapel gleamed the insignia of the American Legion. I'd say he was probably in his middle forties, but with that hair and in that get-up it was hard to tell; he might have been ten years younger or older. In all fairness, maybe he wanted to look the way he did for business reasons: who expects to be investigated by a man who looks like a small-town mortician?

"Ladies and gentlemen, Mr. Don Julian," Dr. Whatcoate introduced. Mr. Julian beamed upon us all through his glistening spectacles and shook hands heartily with Dr. Whatcoate, as if they were meeting for the first time. "I will ask Mr. Julian—or Don, as you all, too, will soon be calling him—to give you a brief summary of his organization and the work they are equipped to do for this commission. So Don, the floor is all yours."

Don! It figured; the clown had to compensate somehow for his absolute normalcy (and I use "normalcy" intentionally; this boy looked like what Warren G. Harding must have been talking about). He'd probably grown that absurd mustache when he left the F.B.I. and dropped the "ald" from his name. Rakehell, madcap Don Julian, the demon sleuth, and I'll bet his wife called him "Donnie."

"I promise to be brief, folks," Donnie began ("folks"!), flashing his pearly teeth and crinking up the edges of his baby-blue eyes for an instant and then becoming strictly business, yessir. "Our professional staff exists for just one single purpose and that one single purpose is to serve you, the members of the commission. You tell us what you want to know. Our job is to find out the answers; it's as simple as that. We're prepared to go into the farm areas and find out what forces of corruption are at work there among the young people, and we are prepared to go into the cities and do the same job." Donnie paused to let the significance of these brave words sink in. Was there no place to which these daring devils would not venture?

"Now as Washington staffs go, ours is pretty small," he resumed with a we're-all-insiders-here chuckle. "But I can assure you that each and every staff member is an expert in his or her field. I won't take up your valuable time to introduce each of them (and thus, I thought unkindly, take the spotlight off yourself), but you'll be meeting all or most of them as the work of the commission goes forward.

"Now as to organization: With Dr. Whatcoate's approval, I've broken the staff down into specific groups, each of which will be assigned to work hand in glove with one of your committees. Together, you will make up what I like to think of as task forces, each capable of carrying out your own mission independently but, of course, coordinating and exchanging programs and information. Each committee chairman will have his opposite number on the professional staff, and—because our group is, as I say, on the small side—I will, in addition to exercising over-all control of the professional group, also serve as operating head of one of the subgroups.

"I think that pretty well wraps up our organizational chart, and I want to say right now that this is one of the most challenging assignments I've ever worked on, and I look forward to the opportunity of working closely with each and every one of you.

"As Doctor Whatcoate told me when I reported aboard for duty, he said, 'Don, I want this to be an action outfit.' Well, folks, if you want action, all I can say here and now is that we of our professional staff will do our level best to give you plenty of it. I thank you all very much." And Donnie sat down in the chair Dr. Whatcoate had brought forward from the side of the room during this stirring call to arms while we all gave a great big hand to this great little trouper as he stared modestly down at his white socks.

"And now, ladies and gentlemen," Dr. Whatcoate said, standing up, "after that perfectly splendid briefing, I believe we can safely say that we are well and truly launched upon our work. Before I adjourn this first—and if I may say so, very successful—meeting, I want to repeat my invitation to lunch and to hope that your very busy schedules will permit you all to stay. I believe we are scheduled for Private Dining Room B . . . ?" He looked questioningly down at Julian, who nodded efficiently. "That is correct, then; Private Dining Room B it is. Each committee will have its own table, and in that way we can all get to know the people we'll be working with on a more informal basis. In addition, the professional staff member assigned to each committee will also be lunching with his or her group.

"If there are no further questions, I declare this meeting of the President's Commission on Juvenile Correction closed until the next call of the chairman. You will receive at least two weeks' notice of each meeting of the full commission, and I leave it to committee chairmen to arrange for convenient meeting times for their groups. Thank you all very, very much."

And off we all traipsed to Private Dining Room B.

IX

That Don Julian! Well, sir, now don't you just know he never misses a bet? Thinks of every little detail, that boy does. Including, of course, place cards for one and all. The place cards were in the form of little clear plastic envelopes, with a pin arrangement on the back, containing white cards bearing our names and affiliations. Once we had found our places, each at his very own committee table, we were supposed to pin these things on our bosoms, and I'll bet it took every ounce of Old Don Boy's self-restraint to omit nicknames.

Once we all got sorted out and were standing behind our chairs, Dr. Whatcoate asked Rabbi Whitestone to offer grace, and when I bent my head I saw why the chair next to mine on the right was still unclaimed. There on the service plate was Julian's place card. I imagined the demon investigator was somewhere out in the service pantry making sure the soup was just right. It was going to be a jolly lunch, sitting on the left hand of Old Don Boy.

The good Rabbi finally finished getting us right with the Lord God Jehovah, and there was the customary uproar as we all sat down. Everybody at Salacious Literature's table seemed to know and, at one time or another, to have worked with everybody else on some worthy project and before the soup arrived the air was filled with the merry laughter and gay badinage of these cheerful crusaders. Judge Brackett was asked how the fishing was these days out in North Dakota; the Rabbi was asked how he saw this whole integration situation as it shaped up in Baltimore's public schools; and Mrs. Dailey came out 100 per cent for uniform bastardy laws. The Reverend Doctor MacIlvaine, about as muscular a Christian as you might wish to find in ten day's hard marching, said yes, it was a damned shame and that he'd run across this one really pathetic case out in San Bernadino: it seems this girl had moved there from Nebraska and really wanted to keep her baby but, well . . . that was the hell of it.

"Well, my feeling is that if more parents got their children to reading the magazine Mr. Lazenby here represents, we'd have a lot fewer problems on our hands," Judge Brackett said, hauling me bodily into the general conversation.

"Very kind of you to say so, sir," I replied, ever urbane.

"I guess I've known Walter Mountain for the past thirty or so years," the Judge announced to the table, having given me my line, "and I'd be hard put to it to think of any other single individual who has done as much for this country's young people." There was a murmur of unanimous assent to this generous estimate (typically, my mind had zoomed away happily to play with the problem of His Honor's redundancy. Did he know of any double individuals? Schizos? And Julian had kept pounding away at his "one single purpose" . . .) At which point my meditations were interrupted by Don Boy himself. His duties in the pantry presumably accomplished, Julian slipped into his chair and immediately stood up again as Judge Brackett introduced him around. Close up, he had the complexion of a baby, but his blue eyes gleamed with the cold, cold light of the man on the make. His firm, manly handshake lasted a little longer with the others than with me, and his first remarks before he took over the conversation entirely were addressed mainly to Rabbi Whitestone and the Judge. No point in wasting time on a mere alternate. And then, as I say, Donnie took over.

"Of course, this is hardly the place to discuss it, but I'm sure you'll understand that in a job like this we all have to get used to living with some pretty harsh facts, and I'm just wondering if any of you here at this table realize that you can now join a sex club by mail?" Julian asked, jabbing his fork into a slice of tomato on his salad plate. Now there was a real opener, and it got the results it merited—silence and total attention. "You can rent obscene films by mail," he went on, "and you can order obscene phonograph records by mail." He popped a bit of tomato into his round little mouth and chewed briskly for a second or two. "All, mind you, advertised in publications sold right here in Washington, Dee Cee."

"How awful," breathed Mrs. Dailey from the depths of her monumental mezzanine.

"But not," quoth Julian, "as terrible as it might be. Now I agree, these mail-order filth dealers are one aspect of the problem, but after all, in a properly run home, where there is a real family life—"

"Where Jesus shares the hearth," murmured Dr. MacIlvaine, smiling winsomely.

"—er, yes, where there is a truly religious atmosphere," Julian said, neatly dodging the sensibilities of Rabbi Whitestone, "why, there the parents can exercise a certain amount of control over incoming mail. But what control can even the strictest parent have over the retailer of obscenity?"

"Retailer?" asked Mrs. Dailey, bewildered.

"Let me put it like this, ma'am. Your average retailer of pornography operates in many ways like a regular salesman or peddler. Drop the word in certain quarters and a representative will call with the goods. We know for a fact that some of these people also operate out of established quarters, like a confectionery store near a school, say, or a used-book shop, and so on, during certain hours of certain days. Now it's certainly not for me to tell you here at this table how you should run your committee, but I will say this; I will say that in my humble opinion, a study of this traffic and devising methods of controlling it is vital."

"No, no," protested old Brackett. "We want your thinking on this, Mr. Julian, and we deeply appreciate your views. It's quite obvious that you've given this problem a lot of advance thought."

"Yes indeed," put in Mrs. Dailey, and Rabbi Whitestone nodded solemnly.

"Just how would you proceed along this line?" asked the Reverend Doctor MacIlvaine.

Julian lowered his voice and narrowed his eyes and we all leaned forward tensely as the master sleuth prepared to divulge a few of the secrets of his arcane trade. "Infiltration," he said slowly, tapping an index finger significantly on the table. "Infiltration's the answer. Assuming the committee decides to attack this angle, here's the way I'd play it. Our people would move in as buyers. They would establish their sources of supply and then, like dope addicts on the hook, they would, ostensibly, become sellers. Thus we would be in a position to study the retailing aspects of the pornography racket from the inside." Even as Julian described his proposed scheme, I began to feel a certain unease.

"Sounds like that might take a good deal of time," Judge Brackett observed. Julian's smile was purest self-satisfaction.

"That, sir, is why you have a full-time professional investigating staff. One of the first missions I assigned, when Dr. Whatcoate asked me to assemble a staff about six weeks ago, was this very problem. I felt reasonably sure at the time that it would have a top priority in this particular committee's studies. As a result, I think I can safely say that we've got a pretty good head start. Two of my people are working undercover on that assignment at this very moment."

Oh, no!

"We're going to find out who markets this stuff, and who buys it," Julian declared. "Mind you, it's not only the kids, —er, young people who are customers for this filth. We're going to find out who the big buyers are; who makes the trade profitable. After all, a high school kid can spend only his allowance, say, but an adult now, now there's a different color of horse entirely. Take Mr. Lazenby here—" Merciful God! "—and say, just by way of illustration, that he spent what he might normally spend on the game of golf for pornography. You can see how it would mount up."

"I'm afraid it wouldn't mount up to much in my case," I babbled, restraining the impulse to throttle this clot for scaring the wits out of me—suppose I'd just been taking a drink of water! "I don't play golf." What was intended as a genial chuckle came out dry and rasping.

"Nevertheless, you see my point," Julian said, giving me a thin smile.

"You've certainly gone right to work on this thing," Judge Brackett handsomely allowed. "I'm sure the rest of the committee will agree with me that you ought to go right ahead. When can we expect to see the first results?"

"It's a little early to say yet, sir, but I can tell you that our people are making wonderful progress. We already know, for example, that a very large shipment of pornography of Mexican origin is due to arrive right here in Washington any day now." Lordy, Lordy!

"And you are going to try to intercept this shipment?" Rabbi Whitestone inquired.

"No, indeed, sir. We're not going to risk compromising our people just yet. We don't know just who this Mexican importer will be—he may not even be a Mexican national—or who he plans to sell to, but you can bet your bottom dollar we're going to try to find out. Remember, sir, we're not a law enforcement organization; we're purely investigative. But I can say that naturally we're prepared to cooperate very closely with the police when we have information they can use."

My shirt collar now bade fair to strangle me, and the air in Private Dining Room B was abruptly stifling. I can recall little or nothing of the remainder of that grisly luncheon, but somehow I must have retained control of myself and fought down the urge to precipitate flight.

One fact was dreadfully clear: I was now in the absurd position of a man chasing himself. Frederick W. Lazenby, the upright honorable member of the President's Commission on Juvenile Correction, was, through the agency of Don Julian and his furtive liegemen, hard on the heels of Freddy Lazenby, the pornography king. And if Julian's past record were any indication, Beastly Burnley didn't stand a chance.

Dutifully, I returned to my office in Youth House and wrote out a full report of the organization meeting for Dr. Mountain but my heart wasn't in it. I couldn't have dictated it if my life had depended upon it; my voice would have cracked and squeaked like a thirteen-year-old boy's. Shaken, that's what I was.

"Golly, Mr. Lazenby, it sounds positively fascinating," rippled Miss Eleanor Alice Horvath when she finished reading my report preparatory to typing it. "Why I had no idea . . ." And she blushed prettily.

"Neither did I," said I firmly. "It's not a very nice subject, once you start digging into it."

"I suppose you'll have to look at all the evidence that this Mr. Julian collects?"

"It's part of the job, I guess."

"What sort of things do you think he'll find?"

Now what was all this about? "Oh, books and pictures mostly, I would imagine." I chuckled tolerantly. "But don't worry, Miss Horvath, I won't be allowed to remove any of it from the commission's offices, so you won't be shocked by finding anything lying around on my desk here."

"Oh, now really, Mr. Lazenby, you know I didn't mean anything like that. You want me to make the usual three copies of this?"

"If you please. Better start a file on it, while you're at it." I suddenly remembered something. "Here," I said, extracting a small packet from my pocket and heaving it toward Eleanor Alice. "Add this one to your bracelet." In the packet was a little sterling silver replica of the White House.

Eleanor Alice's charm bracelet was a kind of running gag that had begun when I'd asked Joby to pick out a Christmas present for my secretary the first year Eleanor Alice had been assigned to me. Since then we'd added charms to the bracelet to commemorate various absurd or notable occasions: a miniature silver lobster the year Joby and I had toured the New England coast, for instance, and now the tiny White House, in honor of my vicarious association with the President.

"Cute as a button," Eleanor Alice announced when she'd unwrapped and inspected this latest addition. "I'll put it on tonight, between the Washington Monument and the Lincoln Memorial." (Respectively, my last promotion and the day we signed the settlement papers for the house in Georgetown.)

"Do that," said I heartily.

X

God bless the C.I.A. and all who work therein. Tell you why in a minute.

By the end of the afternoon, reason had once more restored calm to the fevered brow. Life was, after all, still proceeding along its normal channels. I'd remembered to stop in at Garfinckel's to buy the silver charm for Miss Horvath; I was still holding down a responsible job in a respectable organization; the mind was still functioning. Besides, maybe there were two shipments of Mexican pornography due into Washington. Plus which, Julian still didn't know the identity of his Mexican, and perhaps never would. But suppose he did. Suppose Julian's agents traced the unknown Mexican to George Burnley—would they be able to establish a connection between George Burnley and F. W. Lazenby? Not if George watched his every step, guarded his every move. All that was requisite were the skill, infinite cunning and bold daring of a Bulldog Drummond. In any event, by the time the end of the working day came around, my spirits had so far risen that I decided to take Joby out to dinner.

"But I've got a roast in the oven," wailed spouse when I announced this generous intention over the home-coming Martini. "You could have called earlier."

"We'll have it cold; tastes better cold than hot sometimes. And I would have called except that I didn't get the idea until just before I left the office and it would have been too late then, anyhow. Go slip into something glamorous."

"First tell me about your meeting."

"Later."

"Well, who else was there? Did you meet any celebrities? What sort of people were they? I mean, were they all terribly old and stuffy, or what?"

"Later. Now go get dressed."

"Eff, there are times when I could murder you." And so saying, the lady of the house flounced out of the living room toward the kitchen to deal with the roast. There came a purposeful clanking of kitchen gear as she hauled it forth from the fiery furnace, and then she flounced on upstairs. I permitted myself another Martini. A man must be masterful in his own home, by God.

The phone rang in my teensy-weensy study next to the living room, and I strolled in and answered its summons. "Yes?"

"Federal seven, two-five, two-five?" I didn't recognize the voice at the other end of the line, but it sounded fat and comfortable.

"That's right, the Laz—" I started to say and stopped short, warned by that subtle instinct that serves us Drummonds so well in moments of crisis. "You've got the right number," I finished instead. The voice at the other end of the line grew soft.

"Peter Rabbit?" it asked.

And thump-a-thump-a-thump went my heart.

"Speaking," I replied, lowering my voice to my caller's conspiratorial level.

"I believe you were expecting some Mexican shipments?"

"Go on."

"I'm prepared to make delivery. Would this evening be satisfactory?"

"No!" I practically shouted before I got the vocal cords in hand. "Sorry, but this is not a good evening for me. How about tomorrow afternoon, late?"

"You're the buyer, my friend."

"Say five o'clock. Room four-oh-nine in the Gerlacher Building. That's on E Street between Eighth and Ninth. Think you'll be able to find it?"

"Oh, I'll find it, friend, never you worry. Five P.M., room four-oh-nine, Gerlacher Building. Got it."

"Right." I heard Joby's footsteps at the head of the stairs. "See you then." And hung up.

"Who was that on the phone?" Joby asked, descending.

"As a matter of fact, it was a 'Peter Rabbit' call."

"Oh!" Joby was instantly all wifely concern.

"Relax. It wasn't anything serious, but it's going to be sort of a nuisance."

"What do you mean, nuisance?"

"Well, it seems they want to check over some of Dumbo's records, and they want me to bring them all downtown."

"Well now, isn't that big of them. *They* want *you* to haul all that stuff downtown. If they want it so badly, why don't they send some of their own people out here to pick it up?"

"You know how these cloak-and-dagger outfits are, Jobe. Maybe they figure there's some sort of risk that somebody might recognize one of their people coming into our house. You know how people are; they ask all sorts of questions."

"Well, you surely can't get all those cartons into the V.W."

"Probably have to rent a station wagon, like Dumbo."

"And who exactly pays for this station wagon?"

"Now don't worry. I'll be reimbursed. We won't be out a nickel, believe me."

"I still say it's one hell of an imposition," said my wife vigorously. "Eff, you're just too easy."

"Profanity proves nothing," said I piously.

"Oh, come on then, if you're going to take me out to dinner."

"You're beautiful when you're mad, wife."

So, as I said, God bless the C.I.A., and all who work therein. I mean, who argues with those magic initials? Having bought the C.I.A. story in the first place, Joby now had no option but to accept this latest mysterious dictate from that fabled, inscrutable agency. Man proposes, the C.I.A. disposes.

We decided that we probably wouldn't be able to park the car conveniently near Armand's, so we strolled through the spring evening toward Wisconsin Avenue. Armand's is one of the capital's fairest approximations of a good New York imitation French restaurant, and if you narrow your eyes and get a few belts of Chateau Neuf du Pape into you, you can almost imagine that you are in one of the capital's fairest approximations of a good New York imitation French restaurant. Joby and I reserve it for gay, madcap evenings of lighthearted fun and frolic.

We had just turned the corner onto Wisconsin and were headed for M Street when a thought struck me. "By the way, Jobe, when you answer the telephone do you always say whose house it is?"

Jobiana looked momentarily thoughtful. "Why, I guess I do, although I've never thought about it. And most people seem to know who they're calling. On second thought, maybe I don't, unless somebody asks. Why?"

"Well, it's just that while this Peter Rabbit thing is going on, it might be a good idea if you found out who was calling and what they wanted before you told them our name, that's all."

"Halloh, zizh is der Rawshyan hembazzy spikking. Ish thish ze razzidance of Major North, plizz?"

"Dammit, Jobe, I'm serious. Now knock it off."

"I am sorree," she persisted, "but ze Mazhurr he ees chassing ze spy. I am ze oopstairs maid, Marie. Can I halp you, M'sieur?"

"Very funny-ha-ha."

"Well, *honestly*, Eff. Good Heavens, this is Georgetown, D. C., and you're acting as if we were in the middle of Warsaw or someplace. Knock three times and give the password."

"Will you for God's sakes please not step off the curb when the light's red!"

"You're my escort. You're supposed to be looking after me. You're supposed to be a gentleman and take my arm at street corners, remember?"

Conversing in this spritely fashion, we proceeded down Wisconsin Avenue past the various small specialty shops which line that thoroughfare thereabouts. As always, Joby made frequent stops to inspect and criticize the contents of the show windows, and at length we came to my own very favorite shop, a splendidly cluttered, one-room, antique emporium. Calvin Coolidge was still there, peering stonily down from the top of an early George V china cabinet filled with tarnished silver and glass Lazy Susans, matched sets of Sheffield fruit knives, yellowed meerschaum pipes carved in the shape of Turks' heads, and dusty china saucers filled with Indian-head pennies. The Prop. and his wife were seated in wicker rocking chairs just inside the open door, perusing *The Evening Star.*

"Promise you'll buy him for me some day," I begged Joby.

Hearing my voice, the Prop. glanced up from the freshest advices domestic and foreign, recognized me and gave me a dirty look. Right after we'd moved to Georgetown, I'd spotted that portrait of Silent Cal, done in oils by an earnest but ungifted hand. The Prop. had set the price at seventy-five dollars, and I had been so struck by the absurdity of anyone's paying seventy-five dollars for even a *good* portrait of Calvin Coolidge that I had laughed most heartily, at which he had taken umbrage (every time I write that phrase I have to master a terrible urge to add "and smiling, the boy fell dead"). Apparently everybody else had thought that seventy-five dollars was too high a price to pay—or perhaps nobody since me had wanted a portrait of Calvin Coolidge. At any rate, it was still there.

"Why are you so crazy to have that thing?" Joby asked as I bowed courteously to the Prop., who snorted and disappeared behind his newspaper.

"I want it to hang in my office, on the wall behind my desk. It would lend an air of mystery and enchantment to the place." And I meant it. I mean, think of it. You never explain why he's there. People come in and people go out, and there is Calvin Coolidge looking like a prune in pain. Bear in mind that this will be the only decoration in the whole office—no European travel posters, no English sporting prints, no old maps of Colonial Virginia, no autographed photographs, no reproductions of Joan Miró, Chagall or Braque. Just Calvin Coolidge, badly done in oils. People ask you: How come him? and you simply shrug and change the subject. As I say, it would lend an air of mystery. Was he a relative? Did your maiden Aunt Edith paint it in therapy? Is it, maybe, just somebody who just *looks* a lot like Calvin Coolidge? Oh, no, you'd say quickly; that's Calvin Coolidge all right all right. But that's all you'd say.

"Someday I'll buy him for you, Eff," said Joby affectionately, hugging my arm. "And I promise I won't give our name to any strange people on the telephone, either."

Peace was restored and harmony did reign as we crossed M Street and made our way into Armand's.

Over dinner I told Joby about the meeting of the President's Commission on Juvenile Correction, and of my assignment to the Committee on Salacious Literature. She was, bless her heart, unimpressed.

"It sounds to me just like another one of those book-burning operations," she declared righteously. "Let's all go out and lynch Vladimir Nabokov, and all that kind of idiocy." So I explained that such was far from the high-minded purpose of our grand little group.

"You wouldn't know the sort of thing we're trying to get at," I said, my manner patient, tolerant, and insufferable. "Or at least, I hope you wouldn't." There followed on my part a concise but, I like to think, remarkably clear discourse on pornography and its potential for evil among our nation's youth, at the conclusion of which Joby appeared to have a much clearer idea of the nature of the work in hand.

"Don't you go getting any wild ideas now," she cautioned when I conceded that we committee members would probably be called upon to examine the evidence amassed by Don Julian and his under-coverlings.

"Why Mrs. Lazenby, the very idea! Fie, for shame!"

"I'm not at all sure I like the idea of you staring at a lot of nekkid women."

"You've seen one, you've seen 'em all, I always say."

"Eff Lazenby!"

"Excepting, of course, Chinese girls."

"They say when a man gets middle-aged, he turns into an old goat, and I must say you're no exception."

"Do you know what I've always wanted to do?"

"If you speak just a trifle louder the people across the dining room can stop straining."

"It's got nothing to do with sex. I'd like to have a supply of little round pieces of paper with cryptic messages on them to slip under people's water glasses. They'd take a deep swallow of water, see, and there through the bottom of the glass they'd read something like 'You are warned,' say, or 'Everything is known. Flee.' " Joby gave me one of her looks.

"Sometimes I wonder," she murmured. Our waiter, garbed in the undress uniform of a subaltern of Hungarian hussars, sidled up with a wine card.

"A cognac, pootettruh?"

"Double brandies for both of us," I cried. Life was good here at Armand's, life was sweet and we were lovers in the spring, my Jobiana and I.

Fool's paradise enow.

XI

That next day, Thursday, saw the start of yet another series of events which were to contribute to my ruin. Eleanor Alice, attired in a sensible gray flannel skirt and gray sweater brought me the morning's mail and there on the top of the pile was a bulky envelope richly adorned with West German postage stamps and purple *mit Luftpost* legends. The name in the upper left-hand corner, Horst von Eggar, and the street address in Munich, meant nothing to me.

"Unsolicited manuscript," observed Miss Horvath with her customary acuity. As she placed the stack of mail on my desk, I noted that she had, indeed, added the White House to her charm bracelet.

I opened Horst von Eggar's envelope first. Inside was a Manila folder containing a letter and some twenty pages of typescript, all in English. The letter promptly cleared up the question of von Eggar's identity:

"You will not have remembered me, I think, but since about one year I have the great pleasure to meet you at lunch in your wonderful National Press Club in Washington. I was a member of the group of young German journalists visiting in your country under the auspices of your State Department. You were a member of the club committee which arranged a lunch for us, and I had the honor to sit beside you."

Now I remembered, except that I hadn't been a member of the committee but had been hauled out of the bar and pressed into service when one of the committeemen got tied up at a Senate hearing down on The Hill. If the old memory was still functioning, Horst von Eggar had been a dark, eager young man, full of beans and earnestness, whose ambition it was to become the United States correspondent for his newspaper.

"I send you this manuscript," von Eggar's letter continued, "because there is probably in my country no one who would publish it.

"You will by now have read in your press of what has been happening here; of the desecration of synagogues and of other incidents of equal shame. Perhaps you have said to yourself that this is the work of only a few rowdies, or perhaps you have said that the Germans will never change.

"I am a journalist and I am a German. In my work, I am talking at all times with young people throughout West Germany, hearing their innermost thinking, and what I have heard frightens me. I think there is still a sickness here like a cancer, and until it is cured or somehow removed, Germany will in truth never change. What I have written here is what I have with my own eyes seen, and what I know about this cancer. If there is no place for it in your splendid magazine, would you do me the favor of sending it to some other publication. I am not worried about payment, only to have this published."

Normally, that last sentence would have put me off, and I'll tell you why. The fact is that a great many of the unsolicited manuscripts that come in to *Youth Outlook* are accompanied by a letter explaining why its absolutely vital that the author's work be published, and that payment is a matter of indifference. What's loot, when the safety of the world is at stake? Most of these world-savers turn out to be fairly dismal writers, and in some cases maniacs out to prove that the Pope of Rome is a tool of International Jewry, or vice versa. But if Horst von Eggar had been considered by his superiors to be good enough to be sent along on a tour of the States, his writing could be expected to be reasonably accomplished, and thus deserving of attention.

It was. In fact, when I finished reading the manuscript I felt fairly certain that we had something on our hands. Without getting hysterical about it, von Eggar had produced a disturbing analysis of German neo-fascism and the forces that nurtured it. He named names in those instances where former Nazi civil and military officials had been returned to positions of power and influence, and cited specific examples of their efforts to subvert the democratic processes of the Bonn government and to foment the spread of fascist doctrine among German youth.

I called Eleanor Alice and asked her to come in. When she did, I dictated a memo to Samuel K. Nurney, urging his serious consideration of the von Eggar piece and noting the circumstances through which the manuscript had reached me. This could be, I argued, one of those think pieces which set *Youth Outlook* ahead of and apart from the average magazine directed at a teen-age audience.

"You want this this morning?" Eleanor Alice asked, snapping shut her notebook and straightening up in her chair, the gray sweater straining against its magnificent contents.

"Please." I succeeded in tearing my gaze, which tends to become a bit glassy in these situations, away from the gray sweater. When she had gone—those superbly rounded buttocks swaying tantalizingly beneath the sensible gray flannel—I reread von Eggar's manuscript. This was definitely a bread-cast-upon-the-water deal. I hadn't particularly knocked myself out at the Press Club luncheon; in fact, I'd let von Eggar know that I'd visited the Fatherland the hard way, via the Huertgen Forest. But apparently he'd remembered me kindly, and this manuscript was the result.

You may wonder why I'm making so much of what was, on the surface, a routine incident. Well, you see, if Samuel K. Nurney agreed with me that von Eggar's article was a good one, another skill point would be added to my column when he and Dr. Mountain finally got together to decide who would succeed to the chieftaincy of *Youth Outlook's* Foreign Department, which had been vacant at that time for six months following the retirement of Willis H. Voorhis. The job carried senior staff status with salary to match.

My principal rival for this most coveted position was, as you will have gathered from my earlier remarks, Nathaniel Walsingham, the Missouri School of Journalism's triumph and the State Department's loss.

That's not being entirely fair. Nate Walsingham was all too damned competent. He and I had joined *Youth Outlook* the same month, and like all novices in that imposing organization, we gave each other a certain amount of moral support. Joby hadn't yet moved down from New York and Susanne Walsingham was still in Chicago. Sensible chaps that we were, Nate and I were assaying the climate around Youth House before we risked moving our wives. Strangers in a far country, we found ourselves thrown together fairly often as we discovered the best places to have lunch and the cheapest package stores. Nate was, and is, tall, dark-haired and what the ladies' magazine writers would describe as craggily handsome. He affected a crew cut, which he could get away with, and conservatively tailored suits, cordovan shoes and neckties of well-nigh incredible discretion, and he would have been caught dead before folding his breast pocket handkerchief square, with the initial showing. His manner was urbane and courteous, and all in all he was a credit to his mother's upbringing, his college and his country. In those early days, I looked forward to a long and mutually enjoyable association as we twain grew gray together in the service of *Youth Outlook*, eventually exchanging graceful speeches at the banquet marking our quarter-century on the staff. But this was not to be.

Mind you, we were never overtly inimical. Our courtesies each to the other were charming to behold, and in the commission of our official duties only an observer trained in the niceties of inter-office intrigue might have detected certain tensions that existed between us. For the fact was that we had both realized at about the same time that one of the main reasons we had been hired had to do with the imminent retirement of Willis H. Voorhis.

The difference between us was that Nate began actively to buck for the job. The army has a scatological phrase to describe the manner in which he accomplished this. In nonmilitary circles, it's called apple polishing. But we Lazenbys are fatalists. Assuming you are doing your work to the best of your ability, you'll either get the job or you won't. If you do, fine and dandy. If you don't, it's just one more proof that the world is run by whim, which you'd suspected all along anyway. Either way, you don't end up with a nervous breakdown or stomach ulcers.

Chances are, Nate's apple polishing could have been tolerated if he hadn't graduated to the next logical step, as he saw it: get right with Walter Mountain and Samuel Nurney. Next, sabotage the opposition, but so subtly that neither Walter nor Sam are aware of the operation.

To date, Nate's efforts at sabotage hadn't been too effective. In the main, they consisted of disagreeing ever so tactfully with me in the critical memoranda we wrote concerning incoming manuscripts and story suggestions. If I wrote that a manuscript had promise and might, with a little rewriting and editing, work into a suitable story, Nate would wonder, in his memorandum, whether we weren't dropping our standards. If, on the other hand, I thought an idea or a manuscript stank, Nate would offer a gentle caution against what he described as "editorial Shintoism" which denied fresh approaches and stifled potential bright new additions to our contributor's list.

There was one other angle to our uneasy relationship. Nate and I might have fought it out in the good old-fashioned American way, kicking, gouging, rabbit-punching and groin-kneeing, and still remained, superficially at least, the jolliest of pals, but when our wives had met for the first time, they had taken an instant and irrevocable dislike to each other. Where Joby's nature was as warm as the color of her auburn hair, Susanne Walsingham was as icily remote as the glitter of her pale blond locks. We had tried on a couple of occasions to get together for dinner, but the end of the evening invariably saw the two girls smiling and chatting to each other with such steely gentility that only the absence of firearms prevented the outbreak of open hostilities.

So now you know why the arrival of Horst von Eggar's manuscript was something more than a routine incident. To be perfectly honest about it, I wanted the Foreign Department and wanted it badly, but not so much for myself as for Joby. If Nate got the job, Susanne would be intolerable, and I was not going to see her patronizing my spouse.

Eleanor Alice returned, bearing my typed memorandum. I initialed it, attached it to von Eggar's manuscript and bade her dispatch it to the office of the Senior Ass. The day was off in fine style.

Then I remembered my five o'clock appointment. The hell with it; there was work to be done, a career to be won. I would worry about five o'clock later.

Scarlett O'Lazenby.

XII

At 4:30 Post Meridian, I laid aside my editorial chores. It was time to proceed to my first assignation with the forces of evil. Out on Fifteenth Street, I hailed a cab and ordered the driver to take me to the corner of Ninth and E Streets, where I intended to dismount and thence make my way casually toward the Gerlacher Building, keeping the eyes well peeled to ensure that no one I knew was present to observe my entrance to my lair. I had seen James Mason manage the business in a number of spy movies and foresaw no difficulties.

My driver—a Mr. Howard Murtagh, by the name on the hack license affixed to the sun visor—proceeded with that slow gravity of pace so typical of the capital's older operators of public vehicles. There was a small plastic statue of the Virgin Mary stuck on top of the dashboard and a St. Christopher's medal clipped to the top of the hack license. From Mr. Murtagh there emanated a low, monotonous murmur, barely audible over the cab's badly tuned engine. He was telling his beads. If nothing else, his piety precluded the dismal possibility of our whiling away the journey in one of those inconclusive surveys of the Senators' chances of staying out of the cellar or the deep-dyed villainy of the city's traffic policemen. In due time, we arrived at my destination coincidental with Mr. Murtagh's concluding prayers.

"This son-a-bitching five-spot the smallest you got?" he snarled when I presented my fare. "Christ Almighty, goddam tourists!" I said I was sorry. Muttering further imprecations, Mr. Murtagh dug into his coat pocket and produced a grubby roll of bills and a handful of change. I handed him back fifteen cents as a tip, not because I felt he deserved it but because he had given me such a beautiful exit line. As I got out, I paused and said softly, "*Ora pro nobis*, you bastard." If this seems unduly harsh, it will seem so because you have not had too many occasions to ride in Washington taxicabs. Many of the younger men in the field are fellows of wit, intellect and dashing courage, like Hemingway bullfighters, passing their fenders very true and well and close in, but the older men seem to have adopted hacking as a final, tight-lipped gesture of contempt for the whole human race, a revenge, as it were, for unsuccess.

The Gerlacher Building may at some period after its construction in 1907 have been an address of some pretention, but it has long since fallen into that category of structure which awaits only a reasonably fair offer to be torn down to make way for a parking lot. Of Roman brick with red sandstone trim, it raises its ornately-façaded bulk a full seven stories above E Street. In the basement and reached by a curving cast-iron staircase from street level, is the McWhortle Sanitary Barber Shop. The main lobby is large and shabby. Above a six-foot-wide paneling of cracked and yellowed marble, the walls are painted in a shade of pea soup green, the grisly effect of which is much enhanced by a couple of very dusty fluorescent lighting fixtures suspended from the embossed tin ceiling. In addition to a wire-grilled elevator enclosure, painted long ago with gilt and now far gone in grime, the lobby contains a newsstand, operated by an ancient man and heavily stocked with pin-up magazines, turf bulletins and pamphlets devoted to the numerical interpretation of dreams.

From the lobby extends a dark and sinister corridor leading to the rear of the building, its drabness relieved by small signs hung vertical to the entrances to the various business firms having their quarters there: Sydney J. London, for example, Tax Returns Prepared & Notary Public; the Federal Direct Mail & Business Service Co.; the Fair Deal Vacuum Cleaner Exchange, and so on. The building directory on the wall beside the elevator enclosure listed the occupants alphabetically, floor by floor, and in dealing with this potentially compromising listing, I had managed to kill two birds with one stone, and rather neatly, too, I think you will agree. I called myself the Old Dominion Genealogical Researchers, which name at once explained the large number of files I'd rented as well as my prolonged absences from the office. We genealogists have to spend a lot of time in the field, rubbing tombstones and checking out family Bibles. And besides, it seemed exactly the sort of dim and hopeless business which would fit right in with the whole atmosphere of failure the Gerlacher Building was steeped in.

"Four," I said to the elevator operator, who may have been the aged son of the newsstand proprietor. With some reluctance he laid aside his copy of *The Wolf Girl on Venus* and set about the task of putting his antique mechanism into operation. No push buttons for this boy. Slamming the folding gate shut with a fine crash, he twirled a large brass wheel and stomped a pedal set into the floor of our aerial car and by George! up we started at the pace of a bubble of swamp gas rising in a marsh, accompanied by an exhausted whine from far overhead.

"Hotcherstep," warned my conductor aloft, skillfully bringing the cage to a halt four inches below the level of the egress.

Hardly had I time enough to install myself behind the scarred yellow oak desk which, with my bank of filing cabinets, formed the principal furnishings of Room 409, when there was a furtive knock on the glazed glass panel of my door. "Come in," I cried, and if there was a slight edge to the voice it must be ascribed to that natural tension which is the inevitable concomitant to any deviation from one's normal mode of living. I had never in my life met a pornography merchant, but I had formed a dim concept which varied in appearance between Peter Lorre and the late Bela Lugosi.

The office door opened to reveal a tall, stooped, starved-looking man clad in an ill-fitted suit of a shade of light blue best left undescribed. Atop his skull he wore one of those yellow plastic artifacts which are cast, like molten iron, into the semblance of straw hats. The expression on his face was that of an embarrassed elk, but it would be inaccurate to say that his manner was furtive. He shambled in, closing the door behind him carefully.

"Mah name is Snaveley," he announced in a reedy voice.

"Um." I nodded, giving nothing away.

"Snaveley. Loudon County, Vuhgenya. That mean enehthin to you?"

"Should it?" I asked, playing it close to the chest. The query appeared to unnerve him momentarily. Then he gathered himself together.

"Ah'm pretty sure theayah was a Snaveley killed at Cowpens," he said tentatively. "Trouble is, Ah can't prove it. Went to a fellow uptown but he wanted too much money and said he couldn't gahrntee results. Same thin with an old lady in Leesbug."

Then, of course, it dawned on me that I was hoist on my own petard. The Old Dominion Genealogical Researchers had a client which the firm needed like a hole in the head.

"Come in here to see a fellow on business," Mr. Snaveley went on. "Seen your sign and figured Ah might's well drop in." A slow flush crept over his gaunt cheeks. "Mah wife's a Daughtuh," he explained wistfully. "She was a Dowdie from Fauquier. She's been afteh me to be a Son." A great grin split his face. "Guess Ah'm too old to be a Chile!" He yelped happily at this sally, then cut it short and looked at me anxiously. "Thenk you can hep?"

I glanced at my watch. It was 5:10, and it was essential that I get rid of this hayseed before my Mexican importer turned up. And yet I couldn't bring myself to be nasty to poor old Snaveley; it must be hell to be married to a Daughter and not be a Son. In the mind's eye I could see Snaveley cringing under his wife's taunts, unable to face his sneering family and contemptuous relations. Here was a man who genuinely needed help, but help I was in no position to give. Only encouragement.

"I don't think you're going to have any trouble, Mr. Snaveley," I said heartily. "That name certainly rings a bell with me, especially when you mentioned Cowpens. But unfortunately, my case load right now just won't permit me to take on any new work. I've got this one woman wanting to be a Daughter of the Barons of Runnymede and I'll tell you, it's kept me hopping twenty-four hours a day. Now there's an outfit that's really tough. In your case, I don't think you'll have anything to worry about."

"You think there won't be too much trouble, huh?"

"I'm sure of it. Try the South Carolina Historical Society to start with. May take a little time, but it'll work out."

"Well, at least that's somethin'." The Snaveley shoulders made a brave if pathetic effort to square. "Ah'll have to tell the wife that, by God. Ah owe you anythin' for your advice?"

"Not a blessed cent, sir."

"Well, anyhow, thanks a lot. Ah'll write them South Carolina people first thin tomorra."

Snaveley withdrew, followed by my beaming smile of hope, and I like to think he returned to his broad acres in Loudon County that evening and gave his wife a bad time of it. Nevertheless, his visit had taken a lot out of me, and the old hands were not as steady as they might have been when I lit a cigarette to calm the nerves.

XIII

At 5:20 there was another rap on the door of the Old Dominion Genealogical Researchers and my call to enter was answered by not one but two men. The first and by far the more prepossessing of them gave the impression of being taller and heavier than he actually was: florid of face, with a frank, open expression, honest as the day is long; a fine head of hair, iron gray and curly, worn just a trifle long over the ears, and a deep, smooth voice. His dress was conservative, and his mien that of a public relations man for some vaguely dubious project, like an international beauty contest. The second man looked much more like the type to be engaged in the pornography trade: short, pudgy, blue-bearded, with tiny pig's eyes tucked in deep beneath black eyebrows that met above the broken nose. This second man carried a large black fiberboard sample case on which was stenciled in white the legend, "Nifty Novelty Leather Co., Bergen, N. J."

"Mr.—er—Rabbit?" inquired the big man amiably, with a wink that told me that both us men of the world knew this was all pretty ridiculous, but one did have to take precautions. I nodded. Pig eyes stared at me fixedly and malignantly. "I imagine we can be private in here?" The big man nodded toward the office door.

"I'll lock it," I said, and did so. Pig Eyes moved to the only window and peered through the dust of generations. The window faced onto the blank wall of the building across the narrow service alley that ran alongside the Gerlacher Building. He turned and nodded shortly to the big man. "Okay this side."

"That's just fine, just finé. Well now, if we're going to be doing a little business together, maybe I ought to introduce myself. Any friend of Dr. Savoury's is a friend of mine. Fine fellow,

Savoury; very interesting tastes. One of my best customers." I hadn't realized that Dumbo had used his own name in acquiring his collection. Well, that was his worry.

"Yes, indeed," I said. "An old friend. Yes. I'm, er, taking over for him while he's abroad. He doesn't want to miss anything new while he's out of the country."

"Well, I can understand that. And, of course, a man in his position doesn't want to take any chances bringing anything back through customs. Very smart of him. Oh—I was going to introduce myself. Tombes is the name, B. J. Tombes, Los Angeles, California." He stuck out a large, pink, well manicured hand and I had no choice but to shake it. "This is my assistant, Mr. Johnny Salvi." Happily, Pig Eyes simply nodded.

"Burnley," I said. "George Burnley. We can forget the Peter Rabbit thing."

"Glad to know you, Mr. Burnley. Look forward to doing business together." He chuckled archly. "But I guess you're pretty anxious to have a look at what we've brought along, eh?"

Here it came.

"As good a time as any," I said hoarsely. My tone was the result of nervousness, but probably it sounded like the lustful panting of the veteran voyeur eager to sample new debaucheries.

"Let's unpack the bag, Johnny," Mr. Tombes commanded.

Mr. Salvi plumped the sample case down on the corner of my desk and proceeded to unlock and open it. "Glossies first, then the color slides," Mr. Tombes directed. "I'd like you to note the quality of these glossies, Mr. Burnley—the detail especially."

Then, with the manner of a securities salesman displaying prospectuses to a new client, Tombes spread out upon my desk a batch of some of the most fantastic photographs these old eyes have ever beheld.

"Would you believe that little blonde is just fourteen?" Tombes asked proudly, stabbing a plump finger at one of the more extraordinary group shots. "But wait until you see her in one of the films we've brought along. Name's Dolores; that's her older sister with the boy on the other bed." Mr. Tombes giggled and pointed at yet another photograph. "And there's Johnny. What was that broad's name, Johnny?" There, indeed, was Mr. Salvi, strenuously, if unexpectedly, engaged with a large, naked brunette of grotesque proportions.

"Rosie," Mr. Salvi grunted, a slight gleam of pleasure lighting his beady little eyes. I stared at him, fascinated not so much by the fact that here was a character who actually posed for obscene photographs as by the conjecture as to what wild stroke of harsh fate had reduced Rosie to surrendering her enormous charms to his antic variations on a theme.

In something under three minutes I'd seen all the stomach would tolerate, and then some. "If the rest are all as good as these, I'll buy," I said, as Mr. Salvi began to gather up the first batch of pictures.

"Oh, they are, and better, believe me," Mr. Tombes declared stoutly. "Shall we go on to the color slides? Or would you prefer to run through the films? We've brought a hand viewer along."

"Frankly, Mr. Tombes, I'm going to take you at your word on the whole lot. You understand I'm simply acting as Dr. Savoury's agent in this matter, and I guess that if the goods aren't up to your usual standard, he'll let you know soon enough."

"By George, Mr. Burnley, I like your thinking, yessir, I like your thinking. And you're perfectly right—why, I'd be a plain damned fool to sell Dr. Savoury anything that wasn't right up to top quality; it'd be like killing the goose, you might say, that laid the golden egg, although I don't mean that personally in any way, of course. But I'm first and foremost a businessman, and I like to deal with another businessman. Now tell me, sir, did Dr. Savoury give you any idea what sort of a price he was expecting to pay?"

"He pretty much left that open for discussion."

"Sensible, Mr. Burnley, very, *very* sensible. Now let's just see what this material comes to: approximately two hundred glossies and about the same number of color slides. You know, I *am* sorry you don't want to take the time to look at those color slides, Mr. Burnley; we've got one series featuring these two real honest-to-God American college girls and brother! what those two girls would have thought up next I just don't know; ten movie prints and forty-five readers."

"Readers?" I asked before I could remember that I was supposed to be an old hand at this game.

"Sure. Books."

"Of course."

"Like *The Clinic of Dr. X*, all about how this mad doctor runs this sanatorium and experiments on these beautiful Egyptian girls. You a bondage man, Mr. Burnley?"

"A little bondage goes a long way with me," I said. What the hell was a bondage man?

"My own reaction entirely," Mr. Tombes agreed heavily. "There's something about seeing a woman tied up I just don't care for. Whips I don't mind; bondage makes me sick to my stummick."

There being absolutely no reply to be made to this, I remained sympathetically silent.

"You're sure you don't want to run one of the films through the hand viewer, Mr. Burnley? Wouldn't take long." B. J. Tombes turned to his aide-de-camp. "Johnny, unpack the hand viewer for Mr. Burnley and get out that reel we made where the girls meet that tramp in the woods."

"No, really," I said hastily. "I'd love to see it, mind you, but I'm a little pressed for time. Got to take the wife out to dinner with some friends this evening. You understand how it is." I was rapidly getting sick of this whole transaction and the sight of B. J. Tombes and his associate, but despite my better instincts, my curiosity got the upper hand. "You made these pictures and films yourself, Mr. Tombes?"

He laughed merrily at my naïveté. "Not personally, no indeedy. I couldn't even work a box Brownie. No, sir, all this work is done by high-class professional photographers and printed on high-quality stock. Best in the trade, sir, absolutely the tops. And our sound equipment is the finest manufactured."

"These are *sound* films?" I croaked.

"Yes-sirree-bob! Makes it seem like you're right there in the same room."

My God! Blue movies with full, stereophonic sound!

"I take it all the girls in these films are professional tarts?" I asked, still curious. Mr. Tombes looked arch.

"You'd be surprised, Mr. Burnley. Some of our best performers are strictly amateurs: bored housewives, secretaries out to make some extra cash and have a thrill, bona fide models out of a job. That's in the Los Angeles area, you understand. Now in Mexico, on the other hand, you find more professionals working. Don't know just why that should be, but that's been our experience."

Again, I found no suitable comment.

"Same thing in Cuba, or used to be," B. J. said musingly, and then seemed to haul himself bodily away from his philosophical speculations and back to the world of men and affairs. "What would you say to six-fifty for the whole lot, Mr. Burnley? That strike you as a fair price?"

As if I knew what constituted a fair price for this unholy mess! It was like asking me what I thought would be a reasonable rate for an assassination. Plus which Dumbo had said he had no idea what the cost of this Mexican pornography might be. On the other hand, I supposed that there was always a certain amount of give and take in these dealings.

"Seems a little on the high side," I suggested.

"You've never seen anything like these films before, Mr. Burnley. I can personally guarantee that Dr. Savoury will go nuts when he sees them, especially the one with that little Dolores . . ."

"Still and all, six-hundred-fifty . . ."

"She's taking a swim in the nude, see, and along come these other boys and girls on a picnic, like, and the first thing you know the other girls are swimming around naked, and . . ."

"It's a deal."

"Mr. Burnley, I'll tell you what I'm going to do, because you're a good sport and a good businessman. I'm going to throw in another film about this girls' school where the head teacher has this bull whip—"

"There's just one thing," I interrupted hastily. "I've got to give you my personal check in payment." B. J. Tombes, stopped in mid-explanation, gave me a long hard look, his eyes no longer frank and honest but steely and appraising. "It's just that Dr. Savoury left me some funds to buy this with, and I want to give him a correct accounting of everything I've spent. Of course, I could get you cash tomorrow when the banks open, but it seems to me in a deal like this you'd sooner have a check than write out a receipt."

"I usually deal in cash only, Mr. Burnley," B. J. Tombes said evenly and, it seemed to me, ominously. "And I never give receipts. I expected you to have your cash on hand."

"I wasn't even sure you'd show up. Or how much your price would be. You don't think I'm going to walk around town all day with that kind of money on me, do you?"

The pornography merchant's manner became genial again.

"Well, maybe you've got a point there, Mr. Burnley. Normally, I'd have to say Absolutely No to a check, but in your case I'll make an exception because you're a friend of Dr. Savoury's and because I like the way you do business. And besides, Johnny and I have a very busy schedule tomorrow and I wouldn't want to have to make a return call if I could help it. So a check will be okay. Make it out to me, B. J. Tombes, Treasurer, the Nifty Novelty Leather Company."

"That's very kind of you, Mr. Tombes. I was sure you'd understand about my wanting to give Dr. Savoury an accounting."

"Why of course, Mr. Burnley, of course I do. There's just one thing, Mr. Burnley . . ." I paused in the act of making out the check.

"What's that?"

"In a confidential business like this, we can't afford to take any unnecessary chances, you understand." I nodded. "Now if you were, say, to try to stop payment on this check first thing tomorrow morning, why that would look pretty bad, wouldn't it?" B. J. Tombes' Rotarian smile did not extend to his eyes.

"But I have no idea of trying anything funny like that," I protested righteously.

"Well now, that's fine, Mr. Burnley, and mind you, I never would of suspected you would. But like I say, just in case somebody in your situation did try to stop payment, why it wouldn't be a good idea at all." He turned to Pig Eyes. "Would it, Johnny?" Mr. Salvi's reply consisted of a more than ordinarily evil leer in my direction. "Johnny is in charge of Collections and Delinquent Accounts," B. J. added smoothly. "I must say he does a fine job of it, too. I'm sure you understand what I'm getting at, Mr. Burnley?"

"Yes," I said faintly.

"Then we all understand each other," B. J. declared in tones ringing with Kiwanian good fellowship as he accepted the check from my palsied fingers. "Unpack the bag, Johnny, and then we must be on our way. Got to remember that Mr. Burnley's going to take his little lady out to dinner tonight."

In a trice my desk was covered with the remainder of the contents of the black sample case: round tin cans of motion picture film, stacks of glossy photographs and color slides, and a pile of books, some appearing to have been professionally printed and bound, others looking like the product of some revolutionary printing press. "Don't forget to leave the hand viewer for Mr. Burnley, Johnny," B. J. commanded. "He may change his mind and want to have a peek at some of the films after we've gone." He gave me another unspeakably knowing wink. "Always more fun when you're alone, eh, Mr. Burnley?"

Then, finally, Messers Tombes and Salvi were on their way.

"I may be making another swing around the East before Dr. Savoury gets back," Tombes said cheerfully at the door. "I'll look forward to seeing you again."

"Hey!" cried Mr. Salvi suddenly, staring at the simple black lettering on the open office door. "If you're a woman doctor, how come you go in for this stuff?" He held up the sample case and shook it significantly.

"Come along, Johnny," said B. J. Tombes, smiling tolerantly. "I'll explain it to you later."

Thus they departed. I locked the door behind them and sat down behind my desk, feeling queezy and, somehow, contaminated. And what the hell was that "woman doctor" bit about? Then I understood and felt better. And now that I was alone, I decided that maybe—in all fairness to Dumbo—I ought to inspect my purchase.

XIV

All right, all right—so one minute I'm saying that filthy pictures make me want to throw up, and the next I'm poring over them, eyes a-bulge, a trickle of saliva drooling from the sensual lips curved in a depraved grin. But I'm trying to keep this account honest, and in all honesty I was curious. I was damned if I was going to display my curiosity before B. J. Tombes and Pig Eyes, on the other hand. And after all, aren't most red-blooded American lads of my age curious? (What do you mean, "curious," Lazenby? Stop rationalizing.) And you may believe it or not, as you choose, but this was the first—so help me—sizable mass of pornography I'd ever laid eyes on. As Dr. Chernowith had surmised, I'd seen the grubby, crumpled, badly-lighted and worse-printed snapshots that sometimes get handed around after the meetings of the high school debating society, and I'd seen and disliked what are euphemistically described as cartoon booklets, "The Kind Men Like!" But never anything like the collection on the desk before me that Thursday evening.

A more detailed inspection disclosed, to my astonishment, that the female subjects of the photographs were not the horrid creatures who had peopled the cracked snapshots of my youth. In fact, many of them were downright good-looking, and most of them appeared to be enjoying themselves hugely as they conducted experiments which might have fetched a puzzled frown from even the most detached and calloused member of Dr. Kinsey's staff. I found myself wondering what manner of person might earn her living in this fashion, and then I found myself wondering what it might be like to live thus wildly for the moment, heedless of repute or the morrow. What Freud would doubtless have described as a sexual fantasy took possession of the Lazenby wits, and I let the imagination roam to some improbable time and place. I should have left my job (Jobiana's status never really cleared itself up—perhaps she would have left me to marry some terribly decent chap, having discovered me for the beast I really was) and—again, just how is not quite clear—convinced Eleanor Alice Horvath that we two should offer our services to some maker of lewd photographs. Together, as the cameraman gasped, we would disport ourselves in mad, naked orgies of the flesh. In each new depravity, Eleanor Alice would take the lead, inventing strange new caresses, lending her voluptuous body to unheard-of usages, insatiate with passion, ever eager for more novel embraces, more unusual perversions. Our films, in full, stereophonic sound, of course, would quickly become collectors' items; our fame would spread in certain circles until no especially private debauch could be considered a success until, before a hushed, lascivious audience, Eleanor Alice and I had performed personally a few of the intricate exercises for which we had become noted. Our prices—for we would, naturally, charge for these services—would be astronomical. We would be flown to the Riviera for a single evening's employment. . . .

"We've an invitation to a thing at the de Sangremont's place outside Antibes," I heard myself remarking casually to Eleanor Alice as we shared a continental breakfast in our Parisian hotel suite. "Sound fun?"

"Such dreadful parties, really," Eleanor Alice would reply, her tone bored. "Such a dreadful little man, de Sangremont, always wanting to paw one. Still, some of the others aren't too fearfully dull. And I've a new costume—all sheer black and too wonderfully intriguing . . . I'd like to try it out. . . ."

I was building up nicely to the de Sangremont's orgy when a knock on the door of the Old Dominion Genealogical Researchers brought me crashing back to the world of morals, convention, and Jobiana Lazenby, the finest wife a man ever had, simmering at home as a perfectly good dinner went to pot whilst her husband dreamed unthinkable dreams.

"Cleaning woman," came a hoarse cry from beyond my door.

"Later," I yelped frantically, snatching together my bawdy trove. "I'll be about ten minutes and then the place is yours."

"Okay, but don't make it too long," returned the minatory voice. "I ain't got all night."

"Nothing under it, of course," whispered the departing shade of Eleanor Alice Horvath, softly and brazenly, her eyes hazy with lust. . . .

Without further ado, I set about stuffing the latest addition to the Savoury Papers into one of the tall steel filing cabinets. The little white card in the holder affixed to the top drawers still bore the legend, "Personal Data Sheets." That was as good a name as any by which to label the contents of the cabinet, and I let it stay in place.

Then I locked the cabinet and the office door and prepared to wend my way Georgetownwards.

XV

Descending sedately in the Gerlacher Building's antique elevator, I chided myself mercilessly for giving way so easily to my baser instincts. I, with the finest, loveliest, sweetest wife any man might hope to wed, dreaming lascivious dreams of Eleanor Alice Horvath! Was this, then, the base goatishness alleged to be the lot of the male in his advancing years? Would not the next phase inevitably be some unmentionably sordid episode, the outcome of which would find me charged with one of those offenses which the newspapers periphrastically describe as a "morals count"? Indecent exposure? In that he did willfully lay his hands upon a minor female with intent to. . . . Alleged to have had carnal knowledge of. . . . No!

In any event, I determined to avoid inspecting any further purchases I might make on Dumbo's behalf; I had experienced its pernicious effects and would have no more of it.

Ah, virtuous, upright and honorable Lazenby, stepping briskly out onto E Street and breathing deeply of the carbon monoxided dusk—and remembering suddenly that he was, for the nonce, George Burnley, buyer of pornography, traveler in the murk. Fool, fool, Bulldog Burnley! . . . who should have left the building by the tradesmen's entrance in the rear instead of tripping thus blithely into the public view from the main entrance. Oh, inept, dullard, Bulldog Burnley . . . to have emerged from the offices of the Old Dominion Genealogical Researchers without so much as a glance up and down the dim hallway! What had the dusty shadows hidden?

Too late to worry about that now.

Steady, Burnley. Sweep the street with slow, searching gaze, eyes narrowed, steely. . . .

Juvenile delinquent, gleaming in black leather motor-siccle jacket, jaw slack, face vacant, pausing across the street to pick its nose before a display window full of war-surplus trench knives and machetes. Beside it, its consort, nubile, empurpled lips moving sensuously to the subtle rhythms of chewing gum, brazen breasts upthrust against taut, luminous-pink jersey sweater, bulging buttocks all but bursting out of black toreador pants. . . .

Knock it off, Eff!

Yonder a tourist agape. At what? Cheap reflex camera bouncing against the thin, sport-shirted bosom, red, bony hand clutching the small, grubby paw of his issue. A few steps behind, the little woman enrapt before a windowful of red plastic furniture.

But of Pig Eyes Salvi there was not a sign. I could relax.

To tell the truth, it *had* occurred to me briefly before I left the office that I might find Mr. Salvi loitering around, waiting to shadow me home so that knowledge of my whereabouts would be readily available to Mr. Tombes in the event that I attempted to cancel payment of my check. Indeed, I'd prepared a merry chase for him: In the 17th Street entrance to the Statler Hilton, out the K Street taxi corridor, double back into the hotel through the airline office, reexit on 17th Street and away! Eric Ambler could not have improved upon it, but I now saw that such evasive action would not be required.

Stepping to the curb, I hailed a cab and bade the driver, a Mr. Ernst Voelker, deliver me to Thomas Circle, a destination within easy walking distance of Youth House.

"Fayhre on Dhomus Zircle?" Mr. Voelker wanted to know, giving me a bloodshot glare over his shoulder. He wore a rakish black-vizored cap and, given a white turtle-neck sweater to go with his blue jaw, might have stepped straight from the conning tower of the dreaded U-48, Scourge of the North Atlantic.

"Just Thomas Circle," I replied, a trifle impatiently. I desired to be away from the vicinity of the Gerlacher Building.

"Oh-gay, puddy." Leutnant zur Zee von Voelker threw his gears into mesh and we surged forward. We had gone less than a block when I ventured a hasty glance through the rear window. Nobody appeared to be following us, but I had committed an error for which, had it become known back in Whitehall, I might have received the very devil of a dressing down from the Chief. Voelker had, by means of his rear-view mirror, observed my backward glance.

"You vorriet avout somesing, puddy?" he asked significantly.

"Who, me? No. No, no. Nothing at all."

"I mean, sumpuddy tailin' you, mebbeh?"

"No indeed." I laughed gaily at this absurd suggestion, possibly too gaily, for by way of reply von Voelker crash-dived. Jamming his foot down upon his accelerator, he gave us full right rudder and swerved into a swooping turn that sent us hurtling at flank speed down a narrow alley, out the other end into another, tighter turn that put us out on F Street. He laughed harshly.

"Anypuddy tailin' us iss gonna haf a pisspotful of drubble vit det alleh," he snarled, and of a sudden we were no longer the dreaded U-48; now the great, gaunt Mercedes was thundering out of Munich just minutes ahead of Roehm's thugs and it was good to be together in a fight again with Ernst, Willi, Hans and all the rest of us who went through hell with Erich Maria Remarque.

"Fare's gonna be seffenteh," this gay, gallant *Freiheitskampfer* said tautly over his shoulder as we neared Thomas Circle. "Getcher monneh readeh and I'll let you out on a green light. That weh, the other guy has to keep moofing. You duck into the druckstore; it's got two vays out."

Ah, that Ernst Voelker! Timing it perfectly, he zoomed up to the curb at the 14th Street entrance to the circle, nodded grimly at my cry of "Keep the change" as I thrust a dollar bill at him, and was away even before I had reached the door of the drugstore on the corner. God help him make the Swiss border . . . *Wiedersehen, Kamerad.*

Once inside the glaringly bright interior of the drugstore I stepped into a phone booth and called Joby to tell her that I'd been detained downtown and would be right home. She was, rightfully, a bit miffed.

"I'll hurry," I promised.

"Take your time," she said coolly.

Then I walked to Youth House, picked up the Volkswagen

and drove home. Home! To sanctuary, to peace and the well loved, familiar hearth, haven from the evil world, cozy womb, alma mater dear.

And Rafael, noble dog! Come here, boy! Good boy, good Rafe! Rumple the old ears and pound the mighty rib cage and dodge the great, pink, joyfully flickering tongue. . . . Oh, good and noble dog!

And wife! Sweet, gentle, lovely, my Jobiana, paragon of virtue, helpmeet, mistress and mother; come, oh come, buss your lord!

"What on earth's got into you, Eff Lazenby?" Joby asked as I released her from a massive hug and kiss. Her distant expression had collapsed into a quizzical smile.

"Happy to be home, Jobe, that's all, just happy to be home."

"Want a drink?"

Ah, sweet Heaven, was ever such bliss, ever such a wife, ever such a safe harbor? The cheery glow of the tiny parlor, the gentle clink of ice cubes into the gleaming crystal beaker, the soul's comfort of liquid chortlings—three chuckling gins, one lightly laughing vermouth, the merriment of the mixing spoon. . . .

"Czar Nicholas," I said, raising on high the frosting glass. "His early return."

"His early return," Joby echoed solemnly as we took our inaugural sips.

"Holy Mother Russia," I said, proceeding.

"Mother Russia," murmured Joby. "Not so fast."

"His Imperial Highness, the Czarevich."

"Eff." There was that note in Joby's voice which, experience had informed me, meant that enough was enough and that now we would get to the bottom of all this.

"Yes, love?"

"You haven't done anything foolish at the office, have you?"

"You mean did I walk into Samuel K. Nurney's office and belt him one?"

"Eff! You know very well what I mean. You can't fool me. You come home nearly two hours late, sweep me off my feet, give me your best imitation of Cary Grant and finish your first Martini before I've even made a dent in mine. Or did you spend those two hours in the Jefferson, living it up with some strange blonde?"

"Now you know very well—" I started to say and realized that we twain were beginning to sound alike—they say that's the sign of an ideal marriage and that, in life's golden dusk, the truly happy couple even come to resemble each other. "Look, Jobe, the fact is that I've been put on this odd-ball committee at the Press Club and today just happened to be the day when we were supposed to have a meeting and so that's where I was. At the Press Club."

"That's the most convenient club in Washington, D. C."

"Well, it happens to be the truth. There was Roy Hoopes and Stu Jones and Charlie Rayner and a couple of other guys I didn't know, from *Time-Life*, I think."

"You could have left word at your switchboard where you could be reached," Joby replied, only slightly chastened by the patent honesty of my explanation.

"My God, Jobe, what am I, a child at its mother's apron-strings? Can't I even go downtown to a committee meeting without letting somebody know where I am? My God, that'll be the day. God damn!"

"Do you know that you're getting so that you can't get through a simple sentence without shouting 'God damn'? You never used to swear the way you have these past few weeks. Goddam this and goddam that; honestly, you're beginning to sound like a broken record."

"I'm beginning to wish I'd stayed at the club. One minute I'm home and all's right with the world and everything's wonderful, and the next minute, Blam! All right, I agree; I have been forgetting myself about the swearing, and I'm sorry. Now let's knock it off and have another Martini."

"Well—" Joby permitted herself a forgiving smile and nodded. "Just a small one this time. And I'm sorry too. I didn't mean to make a fuss, but it's just that I didn't know what to do."

"What do you mean, 'what to do'?"

"This afternoon. You had a call from the C.I.A."

Now wait a minute. The C.I. . . . what the hell was the C.I. . . . Oh, goddam! Of course, the *C.I.A.* "For Peter Rabbit?" I asked, a trifle hoarsely. Joby nodded.

"I guess it was one of their operators," she said. "At least it was a woman's voice. Very efficient; she sounded British or something: 'Is Peetah Rebbid theh?' So I said No and she said, 'Thenx veddy mutch, I'll cull laytah,' and before I could say another word, she hung up. If I'd known where to reach you I could have told her. Maybe they don't want you to move those cartons after all."

"Oh, I doubt that, I doubt that," I said hurriedly. "They probably had some change in the instructions about where to take the stuff."

"Just when *are* you going to move it?"

"Saturday morning, bright and early. Frankly, I'm sort of glad to be getting it off our hands. Not that I think there's anything dangerous about having it around, mind you; it's not that, but just the same, I'll be glad to turn it over to them."

"All I can say is I wish Dumbo had thought it through before dumping it all on us. I had plans all made for us to do some work out in the patio Saturday morning. I want to do something about that big rose bush."

"Maybe Saturday afternoon," I suggested without enthusiasm. Gardening, even on the microscopic scale suitable to our patio, fails to arouse anything but apathy in me. "Or maybe the rose bush will just die, and then we can get one in plastic or cast-iron."

"In case you've forgotten," Joby replied, ignoring my blasphemous suggestion, "we are supposed to be going to the Lampreys' for cocktails Saturday afternoon."

"Hell."

"Double hell," Joby agreed. "I turn green every time I set foot inside that house; absolutely sickening green all over."

"The girl with the chartreuse bazoom," I murmured evilly. "Not to mention . . ."

"Finish your drink," my wife commanded firmly. "It's time for dinner."

"Grass and vines and young Rhenish wines,

"That's what little girls are made of," I caroled as we set forth for the groaning board.

XVI

You will have noted in the preceding paragraphs the steadiness of manner, the coolness of mind with which I received intelligence of the second Peter Rabbit message; the ease with which I dismissed it from my thoughts to devote myself to the pleasures of my wife's company and cuisine. Here, I like to think of you as muttering to yourself, is a calm customer, a man well used to dealing with danger. You will have sensed, in brief, the swift development of this new facet of my character.

It would be nice if this analysis squared with the facts, but the unfortunate reality was that I took the coward's way out: I simply refused to think about it until later.

But when later came, with Joby beside me lost in gentle sleep, the body went rigid, the brain churned and the bright, mad eyes stared straight upward at the Rorschach blotch of light on the ceiling, created by a street light beaming through a gap in the interior shutters that ensured our privacy.

Actually, it wasn't really very late; say about eleven.

The second caller had not called later, as she had said she would. What, if anything, did this portend?

But this was not the main burden of my anxiety. What worried me was the fact that this second caller had been a female. Surely it was not possible that there were female pornography merchants? Yet, come to think of it, why not? After all, females constitute the major subject of most pornography; why should they not share in the profits derived therefrom? And was it not true that in the area of bordello management, women predominated? Granted, then, that a girl might select pornography sales as a career field, where did that leave me? Surely I could not be expected to engage in negotiations looking to the purchase of filthy literature from a woman. The mind might not, perhaps, have boggled so badly if she were to be some toothless old harridan, a kind of petticoated Fagin—but a female with a crisp British accent?

Dju tek tee, Majeh Lazenbeh?
Whiskyn splesh, few don't mind.
Dottatall.
Thenx. Veddy kind.
Such a loveleh deh, don'tju think?
Rathuh!
Well, now. . . .
Er, yes, quayte. One would rathuh like to . . .
Of cawce. Do come sit by muh.
I say, these are smeshing! Leica?
Contaflex, but not bed, ektualleh. . . .

This and similar scenes flashed across the eyeballs like one of those montages the television people put together to depict the rise and fall of the Third Reich. Major the Hon. Freddy Lazenby, late the Grenadier Guards and known as Rakehell Freddy to the demimonde of two continents, might bring it off, but George Burnley . . . ? Moot, that's what it was, moot.

Suddenly the telephone rang, shattering the stilly night like the alarm bells of hell. I sat bolt upright. The damned telephone was still downstairs. We had paid handsomely for the installation of a jack in our bedroom so that when the shades of evening fell and we retired to restore the day-wearied tissues, we could haul the telephone upstairs with us, thus obviating the necessity of navigating the steeps of our narrow and potentially lethal staircase whilst still half-encapsuled by sleep. This had been Joby's idea of economy; instead of a couple of extension phones, install jacks. Except that we could never remember to transport the phone. I fought my way through the dark and out of the bedroom to the imperious clangor of the bells, not turning on the bedside light for fear of waking Joby, and consequently ramming the door frame rather heavily.

"I wish you'd turn on the light instead of bumbling around in the dark," spouse observed crisply as I started to ease the bedroom door shut.

With a muttered oath I descended to the first floor and answered the phone. It was exactly who I was afraid it was going to be.

"Peetah Rebbid?" Lady Constance inquired.

"Yes."

"I s'ppose you know why I'm calling?"

"Yes." The accent wasn't pure British, I felt, but as near as no matter. International set?

"Good-oh. When can you get out to Middleburg?"

"What! Now see here . . ."

"Surely you don't expect me to bring this—ah—material into Washington?"

"Well, it seems to me . . ."

"Shall we say Sunday, then?"

"Sunday?" I mumbled weakly.

"Sunday evening," Lady Constance replied firmly. "After eight, dju undehstend?"

"Yes, but how do I . . . ?"

"When you get to Middleburg, ask for Peace and Plenty."

This was getting silly. "Directions would be more help," I said with a trace of crispness in the voice. We Lazenbys can be bullied just so far, and to be made a figure of fun by a lady pornography merchant was, it seemed to me, intolerable.

"That," replied my fair caller, her own tone distant, "is the name of the farm. Any filling station will be able to tell you how to find the road in. I shall expect you Sunday evening." With which she hung up.

Well, now. Well now, indeed. This would require thoughtful appraisal.

Sunday evening. Why had I permitted this unknown female to dictate to me, to dominate me? What were Joby and I supposed to have on for Sunday evening? Suppose we were tied up for dinner? I searched the memory. So far as I knew, Joby had announced no plans for us. On the other hand, why accede thus meekly to this strange female's command? I knew now where to find her; why not go when I, Frederick W. Lazenby, should elect to go? Ah yes, but—she had specified a day and hour, which probably meant that she wished to conduct her nefarious trans-actions with me at a time when she could be assured of privacy. Which, in turn, indicated the existence of some other person, someone whom she desired to keep in ignorance of her wicked business. Obviously her husband. Her husband!

Shaken by this line of reasoning, I made my way into the kitchen, found a pack of cigarettes and lit one. It tasted ghastly. I had lighted the filter. I lit another and decided I needed a drink.

Of all the complications I had anticipated, the possibility of involvement with an irate husband was the last I had envisaged, and certainly one I wanted absolutely no part of. The ramifications staggered the imagination. Clearly, the only sane thing to do was get out from under the whole sticky business right now. I would simply not keep the Sunday evening appointment, and there would be an end to it, and Dumbo would have to make the best of it.

But stay! The chatelaine of Peace and Plenty had my telephone number. Come to think of it, what reason had I to think that she was the lady of the manor? Perhaps she was some sex-starved British governess who, when I failed to keep our tryst in her em-ployers' absence, would call Joby and blurt out some antic tale too lurid to bear thinking on, and then what? Middleburg, Virginia, and its fox-huntin' environs are crawling with any number of splendid establishments, and he must needs be a fool who would overlook the possible presence of a sex-starved British governess in one or another of them.

It was a risk I dared not hazard; the lesser danger must perforce be accepted. We military men understand these things. I would keep the appointment Sunday evening at Peace and Plenty, but it would require some really brilliant staff work to prepare for the operation. Somehow I must absent myself from home without arousing Joby's suspicions. Not that my Jobiana has a jealous nature, you understand, but a Sunday evening separation was un-usual in our lives.

The Press Club was out. No right-thinking Press Club committee would dream of conducting its meeting on a Sunday evening
when, under the District of Columbia's eerie sumptuary laws, the
bar is forbidden to serve aught save beer, and Joby was aware of
this. Besides, I'd just used the Press Club excuse.

Aha! Judge Brackett! What more logical than that the chairman of the Committee on Salacious Literature should call together the members of his group for an informal evening of conversation and togetherness before we really got our teeth into
our work? As artists are said to recognize the brush stroke that
completes a painting, so I knew that the Judge Brackett bit was
perfect for my purposes. Indeed, I would be able to pretend that
I did not want to give up my Sunday evening, and then Joby
would insist that I go.

Subtle, subtle.

This small triumph of the mind nearly succeeded in obliterating
the more disturbing aspects of my appointment at Peace and
Plenty, and it was with a distinct air of well-being that I finished
my neat bourbon and repaired once more to my bed. That's the
way we get things done, boys, crossing each bridge as we come
to it. And with any luck at all, burning it behind us.

XVII

If I do say so myself, the transfer of the Savoury Papers from the attic of the Lazenby residence to the office of the Old Dominion Genealogical Researchers was logistically beyond cavil and tactically impeccable. The rented station wagon proved entirely adequate to the bulk of its cargo, and the Gerlacher Building was, except for a janitor who operated the service elevator, seemingly deserted. The moving job was finished by noon of Saturday, and I spent another hour transferring the contents of the cartons to my filing cabinets. Happily for my peace of mind, much of the material was contained in sealed heavy cardboard envelopes bearing such unsettling labels as "Fetishism, Scandinavian," and "Incest, 1700–1812, decline of." The motion picture film was, of course, encased in the usual round tin cans, and the books I forbore to open. My arrival at and departure from the Gerlacher Building were superbly screened, since the delivery door is located well down the service alley alongside. By two o'clock Saturday afternoon I was, as I saw it, out of the woods.

The day had begun well with Joby's total acceptance of my Judge Brackett gambit, and her insistence that I owed it to Dr. Mountain to put in an appearance, no matter how badly it fouled up what was to have been a quiet Sunday evening. Grudgingly, I conceded that she might be right and it would probably be best to go, at that.

"Although," Joby concluded, "between the C.I.A. and that Presidential Commission, it seems to me you might just as well go to work for the government."

"Just doing my citizen's duty, love," I answered happily. If I could manage to keep my various stories straight, I was in like Flynn.

Late Saturday afternoon, as scheduled, we trundled the Volkswagen through streets wide and narrow across Georgetown to the Lampreys', where we maneuvered into a wee parking space between an enormous Cadillac convertible and a Facel-Vega which made it look absurd. The Lampreys occupy what *Town and Country* would describe as a showplace, when they are not occupying their showplace near Warrenton or their town house in London.

Brad Lamprey was the youngest member of the board of directors of Youth House. He'd inherited his seat, together with one of the big, family-size American fortunes from his daddy, who owned New Jersey or something, and for a brief spell during the period just after I went to work for *Youth Outlook*, Brad had held down a staff writing job, on the theory that he ought to know how the thing worked if he was going to help run its affairs. He'd done a pretty fair job, too, and when he ascended into Heaven and sat on the right hand of Walter Van Meter Mountain he did not forget his former associates. In consequence of which, Joby and I found ourselves from time to time in receipt of invitations to the Lamprey establishment. There was, besides the natural, gnawing envy Joby and I felt for the Lamprey accumulation of worldly possessions, only one drawback to these splendidly hospitable occasions: we could be reasonably sure that we would find the Walsinghams in attendance as well.

We found the atmosphere to be, as usual, one of restrained merriment. Two white-jacketed blackamoors bearing trays moved silently and efficiently among the clusters of people standing or seated about the vast, high-ceilinged rooms, offering drinks and canapés, and the scene was altogether one to delight the soul of one more accustomed to the jam-packed, howling, elbowing, steerage-deck condition which is the average Washington cocktail fight. I recognized a couple of senators, Her Britannic Majesty's Ambassador to the United States, and a clutch of political pundits trading punditry. Sound party.

Joby and I made our manners to Brad and his wife, Natalia, and proceeded to mingle. Joby, having caught sight of Susanne Walsingham in a group by the tall, black marble fireplace which dominated the drawing room, steered us firmly toward the library and thus straight into another group containing in its number no less than Samuel K. Nurney.

"My dear Joby," said Samuel K. Nurney, bowing gracefully, "you're looking lovelier than ever." And didn't my Jobiana simper, didn't she just? Damn the man, he could exude charm at will, like Bishop Sheen (to whom, at that moment, he seemed to bear an uncanny resemblance), and no female, least of all my wife, appeared able to withstand it. How often had I heard Joby ask me why on earth people thought so harshly of such a sweet person as our Senior Ass.

We were introduced around and were chatting inanely when SKN took my arm and led me tactfully a few steps away. "I hope you won't mind my talking shop, Frederick," he said easily, knowing damned well I couldn't, "but I did want to tell you how impressed I was with that German piece you sent in. Of course, it will need some touching up here and there—I'd like to see a new lead, something a little less dramatic, perhaps—but basically it's just the sort of piece, as you pointed out in your very well presented memorandum, that *Youth Outlook* ought to run. I sent it along to Nat Walsingham for an additional opinion, but unless he comes up with something I missed completely, I think we can pretty well count on buying it."

"I'm very glad you liked it, sir, very glad."

"Well, it's always been my feeling that when a man does a good job of work he ought to be told about it. And now I see your lovely young wife looking in our direction, so maybe you'd better be getting on back to her or I'll be in serious trouble."

Well sir! The Knight's Cross with Oak Leaves, Swords and Diamonds, from the hands of the Field Marshal himself! Rise, Sir Frederick Lazenby. SKN had liked not only the story but the memo as well—jackpot. I started toward Joby to draw her aside and impart the happy news when my progress was interrupted by the abruptly materialized form of Nat Walsingham. Beside him was a trim, beautifully tailored character I'd never before seen.

"Doctor Walsingham," I said, keeping up the empty banter which passed as cameraderie between us.

"Doctor Lazenby," Nat returned cheerfully. "Like to have you meet a friend of mine, Heinz Hohenlohe-Furtha." I shook hands with the impeccably tailored citizen, who gave me a friendly smile and a good, firm grip. Nice guy, apparently.

"How marches that one, the Senior Ass?" Nat asked, nodding towards SKN, who was just strolling from the library.

"He defends himself."

"He say anything about that piece by whatzisname, the German chap?" Nat asked, too casually. The guard went up.

I shrugged. "Seemed to feel it might work into something. He said he'd whistled it along to you for an opinion."

"I haven't really had a chance to give it a thorough reading yet. Thought I might ask Heinz here to have a gander at it before I send it back to our Samuel."

I suppose I must have looked appropriately quizzical.

"Sorry," Nat said hastily. "Should have finished my introduction. Heinz here is the cultural attaché at the German Embassy."

Poor Hohenlohe-Furtha couldn't help himself. He gave me the old Kraut bow-from-the-hips, heels together, hands extended, thumbs along the trouser seams, and back to *Achtung*.

"I thought," Nat continued, gazing vaguely past my left shoulder with that appearance of unconcern the late Manolete was said to have displayed as he prepared to kill his bulls, "that Heinz might be able to help out on this guy—von Eggar, that's it— on his background, and maybe even have a few comments on the material itself."

"We're always happy to help out any way we can," Hohenlohe-Furtha said amiably in almost unaccented English. He gave me another one of his likable grins. "I wish we got more calls for help on things like this. Sometimes I feel as if I ought to back up to the pay table." Which gave me to suspect that Happy Heinz might have spent some time in an American P.O.W. camp. Not that that was anything against him, Heaven knows. As a matter of fact, at that moment I would have put a lot more trust in Hohenlohe-Furtha than in Nat Walsingham, and, as it turned out, I would have been dead right, too.

"I'll be interested in your reactions," I said, and then I got the hell out of there after the formal "Glad to have met you." Walsingham was out to torpedo the von Eggar story, and the laurels of a few minutes earlier were rapidly doing a fade. Maybe I *had* reacted too fast in sending it along with a favorable memo; maybe I *should* have checked the State Department first to find out if von Eggar was still in good repute. Maybe, in my mad questing for the bitch goddess, I'd pushed too hard.

"Eff, take that terrible frown off your face. You look as if you're planning to commit mayhem," Joby muttered as I eased alongside. "Is anything the matter?"

"Hmm? Oh! No, nothing's the matter. Everything's just fine and dandy. I'm going to have another drink."

"Me too, please. Who was that nice-looking man with Nat Walsingham just now?"

"The German cultural attaché," I said. "Guy named Hohenlohe-Furtha; probably a baron at the very least." I secured two fresh Scotch and sodas from a tray floating past.

"Joby! Freddy! How simply wonderful to see you both!"

It was Susanne Walsingham, flashing insincerity and looking ultra Harper's Bizarre in a cocktail dress that must have set Nat back a month's salary, and the sort of eye make-up a blonde Egyptian might fancy.

She was all I needed to make this party a thundering success.

Crossing Wisconsin Avenue, Joby broke a silence which can only be termed strained and which had obtained since we had taken our leave of the Lampreys.

"You didn't need that third highball, you know."

"I know."

"And you barely spoke to Brad and Natalia Lamprey."

"I know." I rammed the VW into second as we spurted across in front of an oncoming bus.

"Why do you let Nat Walsingham irritate you so, Eff?"

"Now dammit, Joby!"

"You let him spoil a perfectly lovely afternoon."

"I did not."

"The way you stood around looking like a storm cloud, I'll be very much surprised if we're ever asked back."

"I'm sorry."

"That Susanne Walsingham," hissed my Jobiana.

And then we were home.

XVIII

To say that Sunday passed without anxiety would be to tamper with the truth, for although I essayed to soothe the soul with great draughts of the Sunday *Times* I found it impossible to quench the increasing qualms which were a-building concerning the evening's rendezvous. Thus far my tactics had been, I felt, reasonably sound, but now, like the Federal fleet upon the approach of the Confederate iron-clad steam ram, *Virginia*, I was face to face with something for which there was no precedent. Nor, as the day drew on, did any satisfactory method of dealing with a female dealer in obscene literature suggest itself. I would have to play it by ear. Constantly, too, I reproached myself for having been drawn from my lair into the open. It would still be possible to be George Burnley, but a George Burnley deprived of his natural cover. Worse, it would be a George Burnley driving a Frederick Lazenby's Volkswagen. I made a mental note to park the car well out of sight so that curious eyes might not espy its license number and thus trace its ownership.

Despite these and multitudinous other worries, I managed to preserve an air of outward calm, responding civilly to Joby's comments about a spectacular sale at Lord & Taylor, and even affecting a display of interest in a Giant Green Thumb Garden Special advertised in the *Post*. The morning was so fine that for the first time since winter's snows had melted we took our coffee out into our little roofless cell and enjoyed what the realtors grandly call "patio living." Rafael, the beast, was beside himself with glee and after upsetting only one cup and saucer, suddenly disposed himself to that utterly contented coma dogs seem to go into when their human kinfolk are nigh. Fortunate Rafael.

Just before noon there was a thunderous pounding on the wooden walls that separated our terrace from that of our neighbors, and the commanding voice of Bayard Stephens: "Thirsty time, people!"

Our occasional Sunday morning thirsty times with the Stephenses alternated between our two houses, and this was almost the only contact we had with them, which was just the way we all liked it. Both Anne Stephens and Joby have a profound distaste for neighborhood gossip and weekday kaffee klatches, and By Stephens and I have just enough in common to make our brief every-other-week-or-so get-togethers fairly enjoyable. This Sunday I was especially glad to get my mind off my own affairs, and it was with some alacrity that I advised By that we would be over as soon as we got decent.

Anne and Joby, equipped with tall glasses of milk punch, disappeared into the house to inspect the new wallpaper in the Stephenses' dining room, leaving By and me to encompass our Martinis in the peace and quiet of the great outdoors. By Stephens is a rising young barrister with Kempt, Traught, Couth & Ruly, one of the ancient, expensive law firms down on Fifteenth below Eye Street, and of a sudden it occurred to me that he might very well be able to provide the answer to a question which had haunted me from the moment Dumbo Savoury had divulged the nature of his collection. But it would require delicacy and the tact of a Talleyrand to fetch the conversation around to the subject upon which I desired enlightenment.

Then By himself managed the chore for me with the comment that he'd seen the newspaper stories announcing the first meeting of the President's Commission on Juvenile Correction. "What have they got you doing, Fred?" he inquired, refilling my glass. I described my status as a member of the subgroup studying salacious literature.

"Just what does the law say about this sort of thing?" I asked in elaborately casual passing. "I mean, suppose we go ahead with our studies, does the law have any teeth in it to back us up? Or are we just another bunch of do-gooders?" By studied his glass solemnly, making like Justice Learned Hand about to deliver an opinion. (Do they have courses in Judicial Frowning & Preliminary Throat Clearing: 1 hr. lecture, 3 hrs. practicum at Law School, or do people with flexible foreheads and plenty of phlegm just naturally turn to the law?)

"Of course, it's pretty much out of my line," By said gravely, "and to be perfectly frank, I don't know just what the law does say with reference to pornography. You understand we're in a Federal District here, and that can complicate matters. What I mean to say is that what the United States Attorney might call one thing, the District Corporation Counsel might call something else again, if you follow me . . ."

Oh, Lord! *The United States* versus *Lazenby!*

"Go on," I urged weakly.

But By needed no encouragement; he was off on the lawyer's favorite pastime of leading the innocent layman down the little-known byways of tort and writ, felony and misdemeanor, infang and outfang, soccage in fief and barratry on the high seas.

"Then, too, we must consider that the nature of the offense, susceptible as it is to various interpretations, may itself vary. If memory serves, the Federal law doesn't prohibit mere possession, so long as there is no intent to display for profit or sell the material. And I believe the Federal statutes are pretty definite concerning interstate transportation of obscene materials, although this is probably, if I'm not in error, applicable in the main to improper use of the mails. As to the District laws, I just can't say offhand. I could look it up for you." I was sorry I'd brought the whole thing up.

"Let's not worry our pretty little heads over it on this beautiful morning," I said, with a heartiness I by no means felt. Interstate transportation . . . ?

"Now as I say," By droned implacably on, "my line is corporation law, but we have, in the past, represented a number of publishing firms and I'm aware that there is some difference of opinion, legally speaking, as to what constitutes pornography. There was this English book just recently they had all the fuss over—*Lady Chatterton's Lover*, I think it was . . ."

"Chatterley," I put in automatically. *"Lady Chatterley's Lover. D. H. Lawrence."*

"Oh? Okay, well now there was one example, but then that's not the same thing, say, as some of these French books people bring back from Paris."

"That's for sure," I murmured, and we fell silent. The conversation thus far had profited me nothing. Somehow, without arousing prurient minds to base suspicion, I must ascertain what, if any, crimes I was committing. A discreet call to the Corporation Counsel, perhaps? No. There would be too much explaining involved there. No, it would probably be much better to put a hypothetical question to Don Julian. That was the answer.

Suppose I were absolutely in the clear! Suppose it were no crime to secrete a trove of pornography in my attic so long as I had no intent to display it for profit or sell or otherwise dispose of it or whatever the hell the law forbade. It was, I perceived, essential to my sanity to establish my true legal position.

All very well, but what about the moral position? I knew I was working in a good cause, a noble cause, by assisting Dumbo, but would anybody else believe it? Would Joby understand?

Of course she would.

Would Dr. Walter Van Meter Mountain? And Samuel K. Nurney, and Judge Brackett?

An appalling thought smote me like a mallet. Suppose Dumbo's story were a tissue of lies, of falsehood all compound! Suppose that, unbalanced by too arduous an application to his scholarly researches, he had turned inward upon himself and now found his sole pleasure in the evil delights to be derived from the contemplation of obscenity—a Krafft-Ebing case loose in Charlottesville! Then, obliged to pursue his studies abroad, he had simply unloaded his libertine's library on me for safekeeping. . . .

"Hoy!" By Stephens' jovial cry roused me from this waking nightmare. "Your glass is empty." He waved the shaker at me.

Now no one should indulge in three Martinis before lunch.

"I don't mind if I do," I said, extending my empty glass in a hand as steady as a rock only because its owner was numb. This way lay madness.

I took a swallow of this third injection and the imported botanicals started to take hold and do the job of calomel without the danger of calomel, giving four-way relief without upsetting my stomach and easing the pangs of neuritis, muscular ache and head worms. The main thing, indeed the only thing, was to remain calm and collected. Just play it cool and take it easy.

There was a low, peculiar, bubbling sound, and it was borne in upon me that By Stephens was chuckling as he slumped deep in his tubular aluminum chaise lounge and gazed with favor upon his glass. "Y'know, 'sfunny," he observed. "I mean your asking me about pornography. Because I really ought to check the law out on tha' stuff myshel—myself."

"How do you figure? You're a corporation law man."

By gave me a leer and giggled. "So? Man's corporation law man don' mean he's a goddam fairy. So happens I get to Paris myself every s'offen, 'fyou follow me. Got some stuff upstairs would curl your hair, Daddy-oh, jus' cur-rell yoh hayah." He laughed aloud and I stared. By Stephens! "Started picking up a few items for ol' Kempt, th' senior partner. Smart ol' bastard, ol' Kempt." I realized that during my revery of a minute before, By had seized the occasion to have his third Martini and was now on his fourth. "Y'see," he continued, narrowing one eye and closing the other to reduce me to one from two, "ol' Kempt sees it as ninves'ment, *as an investment*, goddamit Martinis always foul me up. Well, anyhow, the stuff is jus' like diamonds, 'if we ever have 'nother depression. Y'can always get your money out of it, pro'lly more'n you put in."

"But what about Anne?" I asked in a daze. By Stephens! "Does Anne know about it?"

"She thinks it's the funnies' thing sh' ever laid eyes on," replied my neighbor with a hearty laugh, and knocked back the remnants of his fourth Martini.

What was happening to my world? Who was in charge here?

"That's probably as healthy an attitude as any," I said idiotically.

"Poss'bly, poss'bly," By conceded, his face growing somber, "jus' poss'bly. But it made me think when she laughed the way she did, and it sh—, it still bothers me a li'l."

Now what, for God's sake?

"Look at it from this point of view," By said, his tone troubled. "Could it be, and mind you it couldn't be, and I know that, but could it be, I asked m'self, could it jus' be that she laughed like hell because she's got some kind of latent Lesh—Lesbian tendencies? 'Sworried me. . . ." He lapsed into another silence, and I wondered just what kind of reply you made to that kind of remark and I had just decided that a peal of manly laughter was the very thing when Anne and Joby emerged again into the Stephenses' garden and I saw their expressions and shut up. They both looked flushed and furious.

Thirsty time was over.

XIX

"Will you for God's sake kindly tell me what happened between you two women?" I pleaded when we were back inside the Lazenby residence after one of the curtest leave-takings we had ever achieved. By and I had been able only to stare bewilderedly at each other and then Joby and I were off the property, and sobriety descended upon me like a bucket of cold water.

"Disgusting," snapped Jobiana, still ablaze of cheek and eye. "Sickening. Nauseating."

"Now look . . ."

"And I always thought Bayard Stephens was such a gentleman! Ha! Oooh, such men make me positively want to throw up. Do you know what that man has upstairs in his den?"

I knew all right. But . . .

"Dirty, filthy, horrible pictures, and that Anne Stephens, actually pulling them out of a desk drawer and *showing* them to me. Can you imagine two people living together with that kind of thing under the same roof? And her actually taking some kind of *pride* in them! Do you know what she said, actually *said*? She actually said they were the funniest things she had ever seen in her life. She *laughed*."

"Is that all?" I asked, a trifle tensely.

"What do you mean, is that *all*?" Joby returned, steaming. "Wasn't that *enough*? Oooh, that Bayard Stephens, dragging a nice girl like Anne down to his level—I could kill him, Eff."

If nothing else, my worst fears had not been realized; Anne hadn't tried to make a pass at Joby. That would really have made for a difficult neighborhood situation.

"Now, Joby," I remonstrated soothingly, "you've got to be

broadminded about these things. Some people have different views, that's all; different sets of values."

"Well! I sincerely hope, Eff Lazenby, that it never comes to the point where you'll expect me to approve of those different values, as you call them."

"Chances are Anne meant it all in fun. You know Anne well enough to know she wouldn't deliberately try to offend you, Jobe. And after all, you're both married women and well, hell." But I could see that this approach to reconciliation was making not the slightest impression. It would, in all likelihood, blow over, but in the meantime the girls would have to work it out for themselves as best they could.

I could also see, with icy clarity, that no matter what my legal position might be, Joby must never learn of the Savoury Papers, my custody of them, or my efforts on Dumbo's behalf to enlarge their scope.

Joby disappeared upstairs to restore her emotional equilibrium with a hot bath. I took a cup of coffee into my study and pondered. Why, of all times, had Anne Stephens chosen this particular Sunday to disclose the existence of her husband's foible-cum-retirement-program to my Jobiana? Would not a prudent man discern in this seeming happenstance an omen of ill to come? Was not some malignant force obviously at work, patiently weaving a hideous web which must eventually and inevitably entrap him?

Don't be ridiculous. Anne's indiscretion had been, in fact, a boon, for there was no longer any doubt as to the course to be pursued with regard to Joby's sensibilities. That she would in time come to understand and indeed approve of my actions I felt certain, but the interim period would be too horrible to contemplate.

In sum, the events of that Sunday morning had been nothing more nor less than pure and fortunate coincidence. Twice fortunate, for, if worse came to the worst, I knew where to lay my hands on a lawyer who would conduct my defense with a zeal based not only upon his professional duty but upon enlightened self-interest as well.

It was roughly half an hour after our return from the Stephenses' residence when, seated as I was in my armchair and appearing to peruse the theatrical section of the *Times* as I sorted out my thoughts, the subconscious became aware that I was being observed. I let the theatrical section crumple into my lap and glanced up to behold Joby standing in the doorway.

"I'll bet I'm as attractive as any of those girls in By Stephen's pictures," she stated, gazing modestly down at the tips of her green silk mules. Which comprised her complete attire.

"Promise you won't ever have any of those things around the house," she said softly and sleepily some time later as I reached for a cigarette from the pack on the bedside table.

"Promise," I replied, nuzzling the small, warm, pink ear. Thank God for the Gerlacher Building; honor was preserved.

"Lover," came the small voice of my love as sweet slumber o'ercame her. And for once, the small voice of conscience was still.

XX

Given a well tuned Ferrari, say, or an Aston Martin, nerves of steel and a casual contempt for the speed limits, it is probably possible to drive from the District of Columbia to Middleburg, Virginia, in something less than an hour. Given a Volkswagen and a spring shower of a Sunday evening, on the other hand, the journey takes on some of the grimmer aspects of the west-ward march of empire, with overtones of hell. U.S. 50 runs in an almost straight line from Fairfax to Aldie, but for the six miles from Aldie to Middleburg the highway builders let their fancies roam free, and it was this last six miles, of course, which provided all the sport: a pick-up truck with no taillights; a horse van in dreadful need of a ring job; a Rolls-Royce limousine whose owner had obviously told his chauffeur to rev it up to twenty miles an hour and keep it there, no matter what; a station wagon jammed full of children and driven by a young matron with visions of tiny skulls pulping against the dashboard. To mention only a few. But, if nothing else, the problems presented by our erratic progress as we accordioned along served to take my mind off what lay ahead.

"God blast Virginia, dat little ol' Virginia," I sang in a loud, harsh voice as we slowed and speeded, speeded and slowed, and by the time we started oozing into the environs of Middleburg my morale was in a measure restored. Just past a black and silver Virginia State Historical Marker commemorating some aspect of the Late War for Southron Independence, I pulled into a service station and stopped the car. Then I walked into the office, where a group of lantern-jawed youths held conclave beneath a riotously colored calendar depicting a bare-bosomed young maiden archly untying the strings of her bikini, fore and aft.

"Excuse me," I ventured, interrupting a spirited discussion as to the relative merits of the Olzmobeel Nahnny-ate and a Merk, "but I'm looking for a place around here that goes by the name of Peace and Plenty Farm or something. Could anybody help me out with directions?"

"Ain' thet the ol' Crozier place?" one youth inquired of his nearest companion as the others present stared at me, their honest faces wearing baffled frowns as they searched their memories.

"Ol' Crozier place bun down fahve yea 'go," the companion answered. "Peace and Plenteh?" he asked.

"That's the name," I said.

"Who owns it?" another youth put in.

"All I've got is the name of the place," I said, feeling foolish but restraining the impulse to entangle msyelf in any explanations.

"Hayell, ah know thet place," spoke up one who had heretofore been silent. "Khrass, yes! Go awn raht through Middlebug, baht a mal, mal enna half, y'come to Zulla Rud, tuhn layuff, anuthuh two, mebbe three mal, big gates on yuh layuff."

"Hayell, ah know wheh 'tis now," said the first youth, and there was a general murmur of agreement. I observed, too, that their gaze had become more interested, and from this deduced that the establishment I sought was held in some regard by the natives, but what sort of regard was difficult to ascertain.

"Thanks very much," I said.

"Happy to hep," chorused the Motor Boys cheerily.

Only after I had eased the VW back onto the highway and was well into Middleburg proper did it occur to me that I had completely overlooked the opportunity of discovering the name of the owner of Peace and Plenty. On second thought I decided that it was probably just as well that I hadn't pressed the matter; one of those alert youths might have become suspicious of a visitor to a neighboring farm who didn't know the name of his hosts, and so alerted the local constabulary. Indeed, his suspicions might already have been aroused; even now a police car might be roaring into position to intercept me.

What story could I tell to account for my visit to Peace and Plenty? I broke into a light sweat. The police would want to see my identification. If I showed them George Burnley's license, they would want to know what I was doing without my registration card. I could stall them on that, perhaps. Left it at home on the dresser, officer. Damn' fool thing to do. Why am I looking for Peace and Plenty, officer? Oh, just dropping by for a few drinks; little party, you know the sort of thing. . . . And one telephone call would disprove *that* story. All right, Burnley, let's have it.

But soft! These are the merest phantom worries, conjured up by a guilt-sick conscience. If the cops stopped me, I was going to Peace and Plenty on business. By all means telephone, officer, and they'll confirm the appointment. That's quite all right; you fellows were only doing your duty.

But, of course, no police car materialized. I was simply succumbing to combat fatigue.

Thus, with nerves twanging melodiously, I arrived at Zulla Road and, turning left, eventually at two imposing brick gateposts into each of which were set marble plaques inscribed with the words "Peace and Plenty." I eased the VW through the gateway and down a blue-stone drive lined with magnificent old trees, and after topping a slight rise I perceived a twinkle of lights ahead betokening the presence of the great house. It was time to turn the VW out of the drive and into the darker darkness behind the trees.

Wrapping myself in my raincoat and pulling my Professor Higgins tweed hat well down over the eyes, I set out on foot. The distance to the house was considerably farther than it had appeared, but the shower had moderated and it was not an unpleasant stroll. No doubt about it, Peace and Plenty was definitely in the gentleman's estate league.

The drive looped grandly into a large circle in front of the house, which loomed up, vast and Georgian, against a background of still more splendid trees. No ostentatious white pillars here, by

George; just a formal, pedimented doorway beneath a fine Palladian window. On either side of the door glowed two elegant brass lanterns burning honest-to-John kerosene in their glasschimnied lamps and casting such a hospitable yellow glow that I was enabled to avoid tripping over a large marble mounting block set to one side of the drive.

Gathering my courage together, I raised the heavy brass doorknocker several inches, held it there until the gathering process was completed, and let it drop—Clank!

From the house, silence. Doubtless old Cato was shrugging into his tailcoat and straightening his green-striped vest before hastening to respond to the knocker's summons. How wonderful it would be to see his dear old face again! "Marse Ashley, is it really you? But we all thought you wuz daid, Marse Ashley!" I huddled a little deeper into my threadbare greatcoat with its tarnished galons and saber-ripped collar, shabby remnant of the once elegant uniform I first put on in '61. And how old Cato's eyes would moisten when I leaned heavily upon his ancient shoulders and allowed him to support me to the nearest horsehair sofa. . . . "But youse *wounded*, Marse Ashley!"

The massive, polished mahogany door swung suddenly and silently open to disclose a softly lighted hallway of great depth and width and a willowy blonde clad in one of those knee-length silken hostess coats and whatever the hell they call those slim trousers that go along with the rig. The coat was green-gold and the whatchamacallits were dark green, and the total effect was fairly stunning.

"You're late, Mr. Rebbid," she said crisply. "Now do come in out of the damp." I did so. "Please take off your coat." I divested myself of the raincoat, a genuine Young Raleigh trench model, all straps, buckles and odd flaps and vents, and in the process succeeded in entangling myself momentarily, which put me somewhat off my form, but the incident, trifling as it was, served to bring me back into focus. This was not Ashley Lazenby returning to the ancestral hearth after Appomattox; this was George Burnley, the clandestine buyer of obscenity. "Throw it over there," my hostess bade me, motioning toward a superb antique sofa standing against the wall. I tossed hat and coat as directed.

In the glow of the chandelier I seized the opportunity to observe the woman. She was, I judged, about Joby's age, but taller and more slender, with a certain gauntness of cheek which gave her an expression of wry amusement. There was just the beginnings of those tiny wrinkles at the corners of the eyes which seem to come early to women who laugh easily and spend a major portion of their lives out-of-doors. Handsome is the word I would select to describe her, a deuced handsome woman. And one I found impossible to connect, even remotely, with the merchandising of pornography.

"We'll talk in the library," she said, motioning again, this time through a tall door into precisely the sort of room that should have Hercule Poirot explaining to a circle of fascinated suspects just how Sir Hubert met his untimely death. The sort of room, in short, in which Bulldog Burnley might find himself at ease, albeit on guard for the slightest rustle from behind the heavy draperies at the deep-set windows. It was a really proper library with books, to use the grand old phrase, lining the walls and a small, cheerful fire flickering in the fireplace.

"If you'll sit on that sofa over there," suggested my hostess, waving a casual hand at an enormous and deep leather sofa facing the fire. "Can I mix you a drink?"

Her British accent, which I have not attempted to reproduce here, strongly tempted me to come back with my whisky and splash line but discretion won out, up to a point.

"Thenx," I replied brusquely, and the point was passed, for I had, quite involuntarily, fallen into mimicking her, just as I find myself starting to say "yawl" and "ah reckon" when I am among Southerners. I don't know why it happens, but it happens, and so my "thanks" had come out sounding like Sir Laurence Olivier or Trevor Howard. In a flash, my decision was made: why not carry on with the British bit? It would add still another layer to George Burnley's disguise: Blacksheep Englishman, ticket-of-leave type—rum chap, Burnley, shouldn't be at all surprised if he weren't something of a blackguard, eh? Wants horse-whipping in the High Street, by Gad!

Lady Constance mixed us a couple of whisky-and-sodas at the bottle-laden tray set up to one side of the room, and I was pleased to note that she did not add ice. I accepted my glass from her and when she sat down, I did too. Before us was a large leather-topped coffee table upon which lay about half a dozen leather-bound albums, a large silver cigarette box, several capacious ash trays, and a heavy silver table lighter. I raised my glass silently and took a swallow of the lukewarm contents. Lady Constance simply took a swallow, but I noted a faint flicker of approval in her glance. One doesn't raise one's glass to my sort, of course, but I was up one skill point because I hadn't murmured "cheers." Chap may be down on his luck, but he doesn't forget that sort of thing.

I leaned forward to set my glass down upon the table and as I did so my gaze fell upon the large silver cigarette box and I damn' near fainted dead away.

It was one of those presentation-type gifts and upon its lid was engraved a message which burned itself into my brain with the searing power of molten steel:

THE ORANGE COUNTY HUNT
Davis Carter Powers
M.F.H. 1956, 1957

XXI

FIRST LITTLE GIRL: Oh, Alice, do come quickly and see the curious ancient man sticking straws into his snow-white locks!

SECOND LITTLE GIRL: Nannie, Nannie, whatever can the matter be?

NANNIE (*kindly*): There, there, children, it is not polite to stare so. The poor gentleman is merely unbalanced.

MAD GENTLEMAN: Keeks, keeks! Gurk. Hoo-ha? He-hoo!

(Nannie and her little charges walk on. The gentleman continues to gibber. He is Frederick W. Lazenby, and he is gone quite 'round the bend.)

Do you know, my first reaction was a wild, an almost overwhelming urge to giggle. The very enormity of the situation was absurd. . . . I was doing, or was about to do business of the basest sort with what must be—for surely here was no governess —the wife of the Vice President of the Youth Outlook Publishing Company, Inc.

Earlier in this narrative I have noted that Davis Carter Powers was, to those of us on the editorial staff of *Youth Outlook*, a remote figure, and the foregoing should give you a fairly sound idea of just how remote he was. I knew vaguely, as one does in a relatively small organization, that Powers was wealthy and that he lived somewhere in exurban Virginia, but of his interest in blood sports and that he was married to an Englishwoman considerably younger than himself I had not the faintest knowledge. Yet more staggering than these discoveries was his connection with an assemblage of pornography which Dumbo Savoury felt was important enough to want to supplement his own formidable collection.

Only one factor, at this instant, prevented my sliding into deep shock attended with pallor and shallow breathing, and this was the realization that Mrs. Powers hadn't the foggiest notion who I was.

Somehow, in the split second during which the foregoing thoughts raced through my stunned brain, I managed to set my glass down safely. Since I dared not, for the moment, risk looking at Mrs. Powers until I should have collected my wits, I assumed a frown of concentration and stared at the albums on the coffee table as one who estimates their probable contents and monetary value.

"Now then," said she in a businesslike tone, "I understand that you are acting as the agent for the principal in this matter."

I nodded, unwilling to trust my voice just yet. Best test the nerves first. I picked up my glass again and brought it to my ashen lips. The hand was fairly steady, and I swallowed deeply. The British know what they're doing when they leave the ice out of their drinks; lukewarm, the stuff gets into its splicing-the-mainbrace routine swiftly and efficaciously.

"I may as well say straight off," Mrs. Powers continued, her tone laced with distaste, "that I consider this a filthy business, and the sooner it's done the better, so far as I'm concerned."

"I quite understand," I said, remembering the bogus accent in the nick of time. Now I was able to look at her, and saw that her face was troubled. She had been staring straight ahead as she talked, but suddenly she turned on me furiously.

"No, you don't understand, damn you! You don't understand a bloody thing." I observed that she was close to tears, which was not a reaction I had anticipated, insofar as I had anticipated anything. As abruptly as she had given way to anger, she resumed her previous attitude of cool disdain. "I shall want fifteen hundred dollars for this material."

This was not, I decided, an occasion for bargaining. I, too, desired this business to be accomplished with a minimum of delay; indeed, if I could have managed it, I would have aborted the whole operation then and there. Cool thought processes were absent, and I seemed to have no choice but to go along quietly. Even as I was arriving at this unsatisfactory conclusion, Mrs. Powers finished her drink in one swift swallow, arose, seized my glass and took it, with hers, to the array of decanters on the side table where she poured out two more noggins. This time she left out the soda. It occurred to me that she may have passed the time in waiting for me to turn up by previous applications of the stuff. As she returned to the sofa, I noted with some alarm that the reason she had omitted the soda was because there had been no room for it.

"Fifteen hundred dollars sounds a fair price," I said, accepting my glass. "D'you mind taking a check?"

Mrs. Powers sat down again, her pose less formal than before. She tucked one slim and shapely leg beneath her, and her expression was somewhat less severe.

"I should have thought you'd prefer to deal in cash," she said, giving me a wry smile. "No names, no pack drill." She stared into the depths of her glass. "You know," she went on thoughtfully, "you don't really look the type to be in this ugly sort of business." I shrugged.

"Chap does what he must to keep from starving. Doesn't always have too much of a choice."

"Ah," Mrs. Powers breathed. "One doesn't always have too much of a choice. God, how well I know that."

This conversation could, I realized with a sinking heart, rapidly become sticky. Mrs. Powers contemplated her glass for another long moment and then drank deeply. "What do they call you?" she asked bluntly.

"Burnley. George Burnley." Oh, dear. Dear, oh dear.

"George Burnley," she repeated, and smiled, sadly, wistfully. "Did the war do this to you, George Burnley?"

"The war?" I asked blankly.

"Put you into a world you never made; left you flapping about like a stranded fish? As it did me?"

"The war did so many things to so many people," I said, and there, by God, we were, sounding like the script of *Random*

Harvest, starring Greer Garson and Ronald Colman. But as I say, there was no place to go but along.

"The excitement's done and everything's flat, stale and unprofitable," she said with a mirthless laugh. "Did you fly?"

Oh, what the hell, why not? I shook my head and smiled inscrutably.

"Oh." There was understanding in her voice, and approval, and more—a slight vagueness that should have put me instantly on the alert, but didn't. Let me make it quite clear that I am not attempting to excuse myself, but the fact nevertheless remains that, as a general rule, I am an ice-cube man and I was, at this point in our dialogue, well into my second iceless flagon. Moreover, my nervous equilibrium had received an unsettling jolt. And less than three feet away from me in the depths of that enormous sofa was a deucedly handsome woman. To the combination of these various circumstances may be attributed what, in the cold light of retrospect, must necessarily seem the sheer idiocy of my subsequent behavior.

"Balkans mostly," I murmured. "The usual thing: bag of sovereigns, dealing with the partisans and that." My face hardened into a mask of bitterness as I threw myself into the role. "All gone now, of course—sovereigns, the bright promises—everything." I took a large gulp of my drink and nearly choked, having momentarily forgotten that it was undiluted. My bowels turned to fire, but the external effect, on the other hand, was to make me wince as from an evil memory.

Mrs. Powers's eyes were misty. "Poor George Burnley," she said softly. "Poor Diana Joyner. Poor lost people." Diana?

"Diana Joyner?" I asked.

She raised her glass in a mock toast. "You may call me, Diana, George Burnley." I raised my glass, but forbore to sip until my stomach had ceased to smolder. "I was fourteen when the war ended," she said, her words betraying the beginnings of fraying at the edges. "Everything I'd known was gone—vanished. But there was school to be finished; there was enough money left for that. And then a job in an advertising agency in London, seven years of it, and then I met Davis—my husband, that is—

and wealthy American sweeps poor little English girl off her feet and carries her away, and here I am . . ."

"And here you are." The late Ronald Colman himself could not have put more depth of understanding into that simple sentence.

"Am I so terribly unattractive, George Burnley?" Mrs. Powers asked abruptly, moving toward my end of the sofa, her eyes (and I now perceived that they were blue) hazy with what might have been emotion but was probably Scotch. "So unattractive that my husband would sooner spend his time with his photograph albums than with me?" She leaned toward me in such a manner as to dispose the neckline of her silken coat in a most immodest fashion. "Do you see anything wrong with me, George Burnley?" Her voice was soft, and she moved a centimeter or two closer.

"That's why you're selling them, then?"

"Not all of them; not this time." By now, her arm had slipped casually along the top of the back of the sofa; the soft pressure of her bosom made itself felt against my right bicep, a firm but feminine thigh pressed mine, and the zephyr of her breathing as she spoke fanned my ear. "Half now, half another time. I don't want him to miss it all at once." I felt her fingers ease into the hair at the back of my head. "That's not really true"—her voice was a whisper now—"I don't give a damn whether he notices or not."

I cleared my throat.

"George . . .?"

"Yes?" The pressures of mammary and thigh were increasing, and if I had turned my gaze, inflexibly fixed straight ahead in simulated worldly disenchantment, I would have been nose to nose with her.

"Davis has one of those Polaroid cameras—p'raps, if he were to see me, my picture, that is—like those other women—" Her mouth was touching my ear, and her other hand had rested itself as lightly as a feather upon my knee.

No Freudian fantasy of mine had ever approximated this present reality; no wildest wanderings of the gland-spurred imagination had encountered such perfection of situation—I had but to narrow my glittering eyes and inhale sharply, nostrils quivering, and there would ensue a voluptuary's holiday beyond dreaming. Such an opportunity comes seldom if ever to a man. Who scorns it, scorns it at the peril of a lifetime of bitter self-reproach; who denies it, knuckles under to the moral code of a puritannical world inhibited unto madness by the immolation of its earthy instincts. Benvenuto Cellini recognized no such absurd strictures, nor did, in his different sphere, the Corsican Buonaparte confronting the Countess Walewska. Byron did it, Wagner did it, Antony and Cleopatra did it—

I prepared to quiver my nostrils.

And then I thought of Joby.

"I'll go and fetch Davis's camera," Diana Powers murmured, "and slip into something more suitable." With a throaty farewell, she arose and left the room. That is to say, she started to leave the room, by way of the decanters on the side table, where she paused to refill her glass. Her gait was not what could be called entirely steady. It was at this critical juncture that I did the most sensible thing I had done that evening: I succumbed to blind panic.

Let no one ever, in future, denigrate in my presence the wonder-working powers of blind panic. Fully conscious of my actions, I would never have been capable of extricating myself from what had so swiftly become an untenable situation, for with the thought of Joby my short-lived lustings vanished completely. But in the grip of blackest fear, the mind functioned automatically and with lightning speed. Without being aware of why, I knew what had to be done, and, like a striking cobra, my arm shot out and knocked one of the leather-bound albums from the top of the coffee table onto the floor. At the same instant, the vocal chords produced an explosive "Damn!" and the leg muscles worked to send me onto my knees in the position of one who attempts to retrieve a fallen object. My skull slipped smoothly into just the correct position beneath the edge of the heavy table, and I stared down at a photograph which had slipped from the album for the barest fraction of a second before the back muscles snapped my head smartly up against the bottom of the edge. The effect was precisely that of a well-aimed rabbit punch delivered by a powerful hand.

To the impact of wood on skull was added, in that last instant of consciousness, yet another mind-shattering shock, and if I hadn't knocked myself out quite so thoroughly, I might well have yelped in astonishment. The photograph which had slipped from the album was that of a handsome young woman caught in a moment of wildest abandon as she engaged in an act of which society cannot be said to approve without benefit of clergy. There was not, for me, the slightest possibility of mistaking the identity of the young woman, even in the dim light beneath the coffee table. She was unquestionably Miss Eleanor Alice Horvath, pillar of all things respectable.

But, as I say, I was out cold.

XXII

I couldn't have been unconscious for more than a minute at the most, and if, during that brief period, I went into one of those dream sequences so popular as a cinematic device whereby the protagonist's subconscious desires may be visually realized, I have no recollection of it. No orchestra swept to a crescendo of passionate noise; Ginger Rogers did not whirl into my arms for a fast tango over the furniture, nor did Jobiana and I stroll through the mists of an English spring morning, counting the seconds before I should have to return to my squadron.

Nonetheless, my distress was apparently real enough to halt Diana Powers in her tracks and fetch her swiftly back to the side of my procumbent figure, for when the lights went on again, she was kneeling on the carpet, adjusting a pillow beneath my battered skull. Her expression was a curious commingling of sympathy and contempt, and I knew that, for the moment, the old moral fiber would not be put to the ultimate test.

"I'm most terribly sorry," I announced in a low but clear voice, thus indicating that the brain was relatively undamaged and still capable of commanding lucid speech. (A certain obscure pride urges me to note that even in my delicate condition, I retained the mother wit to continue with my bogus B.B.C. accent. If I had emerged from the Land of Nod speaking pure Washingtonian, the position might have been very awkward indeed. Not that it wasn't odd enough as it stood.) I started to sit up, and the consequent wave of anguish made it abundantly clear that I had given myself much more of a clout than was really necessary.

"What on earth happened?" Mrs. Powers asked, a trifle irritably. Actually, of course, you could hardly blame the girl; she'd been building up to something of a dramatic climax, only to have the whole mood wrecked by my clumsiness.

"Went faint," I said. "Happens every now and again." And instantly cursed myself for a fool unable to leave well enough alone, for her expression lost its contempt and became wholly sympathetic as she—and as I should have known she would—put two and two together and came up with some preposterous war wound sustained in God knows what remote Balkan valley.

"Here," she commanded, holding her glass to my lips, "drink this." I sipped delicately, uncertain what effect another jolt of straight hooch might have. It helped. In all fairness to Diana Powers, I should have permitted a thin trickle of the stuff to escape from one corner of the twisted mouth that was a raw gash in the seamed yet curiously sensitive face, and then died very quietly, very bravely and well. We had blown the goddam bridge and that was all that mattered, now or ever.

My head cleared rapidly under the beneficent influence of the spirits, and becoming aware of the dangers involved in having my skull cradled not only by a pillow but by the dear nearness of Diana's gently swelling bosom as well, I struggled to a sitting position—survived—and heaved myself up onto the sofa, where there was what we military tacticians call room for maneuver. I deemed it essential to emulate Sherman and keep moving lest the situation deteriorate, and deteriorate it threatened to do within seconds, as indicated by the now melting tenderness that suffused Diana Powers's expression. For now she understood all: the steel shell splinter deep within the gray matter, warping the thought processes, confusing the moral values to the point where I, poor shattered darling, saw nothing amiss in trafficking in filth.

"Look," I said firmly, "perhaps I'd best be getting along. The shakiness won't last, you know. I think you mentioned fifteen hundred dollars, and that you wanted to sell only half of the material now. Well then, suppose I give you my check for seven-fifty, would that be satisfactory?"

"A check?" Diana's voice was dubious. She, too, had regained her seat upon the sofa, still eyeing me solicitously. "Is that wise?"

This was a time to display the iron fist within the velvet glove —to demonstrate that the old steel splinter had done uglier damage than she had imagined. "Look here," I snarled, knowing full well how this high-spirited Irish colleen hated us Black and Tans, "you don't suppose I'm going to carry a great wad of notes with me in my line of work! It's got to be a check or nothing, and there's an end on't." I don't think George Sanders could have brought it off any better. Cold and nasal.

"You needn't be beastly," she snapped back. "I'm not in the least worried whether or not your check is good, but a check has a name on it, and I shouldn't think you'd want to involve names in a business like this." She hesitated, and when she resumed, her tone was softer. "I'm only thinking about your safety, you know."

More beastliness seemed in order, the first lot having obviously failed in its intended effect. I was finding it almost impossible to carry on being horrid to Diana Powers, but there appeared to be no other alternative. Given the slightest encouragement now, she would be directing the conversation back to the Polaroid camera and herself in something comfy, and that must *not* be allowed to happen.

"Suppose you let me worry about my safety," I rasped nastily. "Now let's get on with it." I produced my checkbook and dashed off, with what I felt was a kind of sinister recklessness, an order upon my bank to pay Cash the sum of seven hundred and fifty dollars, boldly signing it George Burnley. I ripped it smartly from the book and laid it on the coffee table atop one of the leather-bound albums.

"If that's the way you want it," Diana said quietly, allowing it to lie there. "I'll let you know when I'm ready to deliver the rest of the collection." Impulsively, then: "That woman who answered your telephone, is she—I mean to say, she didn't sound quite the type to be involved in . . ."

I chuckled unpleasantly, giving it the old rich, throaty note that Sanders does so well. "Gaby will be delighted by your comments," I said, leering. "Most of her compliments are reserved for her other talents." That, I felt, ought to do it nicely. And, for the time being, so it did. Diana froze.

"In that case, perhaps I shouldn't be delaying you from getting back to her." She arose from the sofa, very much the mistress of Peace and Plenty.

I gathered up the albums in silence and accepted in good (good, hell! magnificent!) heart this haughty dismissal. She did not accompany me to the hall, where I regained hat and raincoat. But as I heaved myself into my coat, she appeared at the library door, her face still stony. She was holding my check.

"I hadn't realized you lived in Washington," she observed icily. "I thought that Federal number was simply a—what do you call it, an accommodation? Next time you come, you must bring your Gaby along—I'd so love to see her demonstrate her—other talents."

"I beg your pardon?"

"Why settle for mere photographs when you can have the real thing?" inquired Mrs. Powers sardonically. "Perhaps you and your Gaby might cooperate in a display of your mutual skills. It might be terribly amusing to watch."

"Good night," I said, and got the hell out of there.

XXIII

Never has the pure, cool night air smelled better.

Tooling back along the Zulla Road toward Middleburg, I inhaled mighty gulps of the stuff, as if it could have purgative powers. The rain-bathed Virginia night was as a healing balm to the scarred soul, after its fashion, but by the time I reached the main road the initial effects had worn off and massive waves of mental agony were once more sweeping between the temples.

My foremost worry was, as it should have been, the problem presented by Mrs. Davis Carter Powers. That she was something of a moral oddball was indeed a facet of the problem, but of far more moment was the possibility that she might at any time discover my real identity. Thus far, to my knowledge, she had never appeared at Youth House or at any of its annual rites, such as the Christmas cocktail wake for the editorial staff, at which the top brass were generally present, dispensing kindly, Dickensian smiles to the happy tenants. Why this should have been the case was not clear. Perhaps Davis Carter Powers (whose personality had suddenly assumed a complexity I had never suspected) felt that it might not look well for one in his position and of his mature years to produce such a young and smashingly attractive wife. Or—having gained some knowledge of her unexpectedly free-wheeling views as to what constituted amusing entertainment—I wondered if she had simply declined to take any part in her husband's patently stuffy business life lest she be bored to tears. In any event, there seemed to be no readily evident reason to suppose that this situation might continue to obtain. She might, upon a whim, decide to visit Youth House to see with her own eyes where dear Davis worked his fingers to the bone.

She might appear at the next retirement banquet to listen to dear Davis mumble his allotment of platitudes about good old Clarence Whatsisname and the great days in Accounts Receivable. And there, face to face, she would encounter George Burnley in the person of Frederick W. Lazenby.

And there would be the very devil to pay.

Or would there?

I could, of course, simply deny being George Burnley so firmly, yet so graciously and with such charm, that we might all have a hearty laugh at this mistake in identity. "Whah, bless yoh haht, Miz Powuhs, Ma'am, Ah've neavuh hud of a Gawge Bunleh, but ef he looks lahk me, he showleh has mah entiah sympatheh, yuk, yuk, yuk. . . ."

On the other hand, I could counterattack in the manner of young Rupert of Hentzau dealing with Antoinette de Mauban: "Granted you have unmasked me, Madam, yet would I have you consider the consequences were it to become known in certain quarters which I shall forbear to mention that your husband is a collector of erotica. Rest assured, dear lady, that I shall have not the slightest hesitancy in making good this threat, cost what it may, nor shall your entreaties have the least effect upon my determination in this affair." (It would mean wearing a monocle and beautifully polished black boots. Prussian accent, naturally.)

I rehearsed this splendid scene all the way to Aldie, where it dawned upon me that if anybody was in a worse position than I, he was Davis Carter Powers. What, in point of fact, had I to fear from Davis Carter Powers or his wife? Nothing. For if they threatened me with exposure they would, in effect, threaten themselves. I was worrying myself needlessly.

Having decided this, I immediately felt my morale pick up and was consequently enabled to address myself fully to the business of exercising maximum care in driving back to Washington and the Gerlacher Building, where the night watchman could no doubt be persuaded to admit me and my squalid burden. It would not do to be stopped by some Virginia State highway patrolman. Not that I was concerned about the albums, which were effectively concealed under a blanket in the VW's forward baggage hold, but Joby might wonder if, by some stroke of absent-mindedness, I were to leave a Virginia traffic ticket lying about loose, dated at a time when I was supposed to be sipping sherry at Judge Brackett's.

Suddenly, just as I was pulling up to the service entrance of the Gerlacher Building, I remembered the photograph which had slipped from the album I'd knocked off the coffee table in the Powers library.

It couldn't have been. Not Eleanor Alice Horvath! My mind had played me a trick, probably in that split-second of impact. And yet I could have sworn that such was not the case. It would be simple to check, of course. Indeed, I owed it to Eleanor Alice to expunge this impression from my mind.

A mere five minutes of heavy pounding on the service door, accompanied by a steady ringing of the bell, sufficed to bring up from his lair in the bowels of the building the night watchman, shuffling on ruined feet and in a filthy frame of mind. I was in no mood to trifle and when he began to whine about the goddam way a man couldn't sit down for a minute without the goddam bell ringing, I quieted him swiftly and effectively with a folded buck. If he had kept his big mouth shut, I would have given him two bucks for running me up in the elevator at that hour.

"Don't worry, I'll walk downstairs," I told him. "I can let myself out, can't I?"

"I gotta check you out, friend. Orders say everybody comes in gotta be checked out."

Clutching my armload of albums, I was in no small degree of fear that another photograph might slip out at any moment, and I did not desire to prolong this discourse. I agreed that I would let him know when I left, and then, finally, I was safely inside the office of the Old Dominion Genealogical Researchers with the door locked and the blinds drawn.

Seated at my desk, I inspected my purchase. Of Davis Carter Powers's tastes it must in fairness be said that they were catholic; all was grist, as it were, to his mill. Unlike the clientele to whom B. J. Tombes undoubtedly catered, Powers apparently felt that reading was a waste of time and that one picture was indeed worth ten thousand words. And while mine has not been what could in full honesty be described as a more than normally sheltered life, I confess to having been unaware, until that moment, that certain practices even existed. I had gone through three of the Powers albums before I found Eleanor Alice. Not just one Eleanor Alice but a whole cycle of her, each tableau more astonishing than the last.

It had to be Eleanor Alice, for there upon her wrist was, beyond any possibility of mistake, her charm bracelet. It constituted her sole adornment.

Physically, she was even more fantastic than I had allowed myself to imagine, and I had allowed myself to imagine much. She was, to put it tritely, the beloved of Solomon in spades, and then some.

Even more incredible to me was her very obvious enjoyment of what she was doing. Here was no young and innocent maiden, drugged by drink or drugs and photographed in a stupor; here was the paragon among Baptist Young People having herself a whale of a time, now beaming unabashedly into the camera lens, now leering joyously at her partner or partners of whichever sex. In one situation where her face was not visible, she signaled her satisfaction by making a thumb and forefinger circle. And it was clear that with Eleanor Alice, anything went.

My secretary—and there was no other possible conclusion to be drawn—was not only a raving nymphomaniac but a bisexual and an exhibitionist as well. My secretary! The chaste and virginal worker for the Thropplestance Memorial Baptist Church; the attendant at young people's encampments and gospel feasts; the dutiful daughter to her widowed mother; the capable and devoted worker in the interests of *Youth Outlook* loved nothing better, it seemed, than stripping down to the buff and giving free rein to her libido, of which there was an apparently inexhaustible supply.

I tell you, it gave me to think.

B. J. Tombes I could understand, and even the repulsive Pig Eyes. They were biological sports. But then there had been the revelation that By Stephens owned a small but, in his view, stimulating collection of erotica, disclosed as he calmly discussed the possibility that his wife might have latent Lesbian tendencies. Then there were the Powerses; he an aging voyeur, she with an already demonstrated ambivalent attitude toward convention. And now Eleanor Alice Horvath. Were Joby and I the only two reasonably normal people left? Was the whole world, as some novelists have argued and many psychiatrists insist, sexually unbalanced?

It was an absurd, an impossible line of reasoning. I was absolutely certain that I entertained no secret desire to leap into bed with a naked Boy Scout, just as I was equally positive that Joby did not lust for the nubile among the Girl Guides.

No, it was simply that since my involuntary (more or less) association with Dumbo Savoury's collection, I had been led into association with people who were sexually weird. I was losing my perspective, to put it another way.

The thing was to get home. I suddenly felt as I had often felt before on those assignments which had taken me from Joby's side to some exotic shore in some foreign clime—Get Home! To hell with the scenery, the carefree natives, the curious rites and all that jazz—Get Home to Joby!

I stashed the albums safely away in one of the filing cabinets and made my way down the dimly lit stairs to the street floor. I gave a yell for the watchman at the door to the basement, but that surly guardian of the night had either died or gone to sleep or was out on his appointed rounds. The hell with him; let him worry about whether or not his check-out record was straight.

But the matter of Eleanor Alice Horvath, I thought, as I navigated homeward, would require further study. A great deal of further study.

Joby was reading in bed when I finally urged the weary body upstairs, clutching a loving cup for the two of us. The great beast, Rafael, was sprawled, tummy up, at the foot of the bed, and acknowledged my presence with several massive thumps of his tail.

"Hi," said Joby gaily, looking up from her book which was, I perceived, one of John O'Hara's novels. "How was Judge Brackett?"

"Judge who?" I asked stupidly.

"Your party, how was it?"

"Oh. Oh, that. Oh, pretty dull. Everybody being terribly polite; pretty much as you'd expect, but the sherry was good."

"I hope you didn't overdo."

"You know me, kid. Freddy the Wino. How's the book?"

"Terrible. I honestly don't know why I read John O'Hara—all these terribly rich, middle-aged, swanky people . . ."

"The old Vogues at home," I interrupted brightly.

". . . carrying on with everybody else's wife, all this sex. You can't tell me, Eff, that real people really act like O'Hara's people do—not all of them anyway." Joby amended. "If I thought people really were like that—you know what I mean—I mean if a person actually believed that morals didn't mean anything at all, if *every*body thought that way—I think I'd take a gun and shoot myself."

"Have a drink, Joby," I said, feeling one of those enormous gushes of tenderness for her, wild syntax and all, and the lovely, clear way she saw life from so sweet and pure a mind.

"We'll never be like that, will we, Eff?"

"Never, Jobe. Never."

"Umm—that goes down well."

"Good. I thought we deserved it. Make us sleep like babes."

"I love you, Eff."

I just couldn't answer, because I would have started blubbering.

XXIV

Monday.

What sort of a day was it?

A day like any other day, filled with those events that . . . but let it pass, let it pass. Suffice it to say that Monday was a rough one.

To begin with, there was the still unplumbed problem of Eleanor Alice, and when she tripped in bearing the ritual morning coffee, I found myself hard put to know how to act. She wore a severely simple dress of heather-toned spring tweed and looked the very model of the discreet, efficient, loyal secretary. But gazing at her over the top of the *Times*, I could not but acknowledge that I knew what that harsh tweed concealed; I had seen those superb breasts bared in ecstasy, those magnificent thighs outflung in wildest passion, the ripely sensual mouth giving and receiving the most curious of caresses, the voluptuous body contorted in the throes of lust.

"Have a nice weekend?" Eleanor Alice asked cheerily.

"So-so," I replied. "Usual thing; chores around the house. And you?"

"Our study group went on a field trip to West Virginia."

"Oh? What study group is that?"

"Self-improvement, I guess," Miss Horvath said with a deprecatory smile. "A bunch of us at church are learning photography. You know, shutter openings and focal lengths and light meters; that sort of thing."

I damn near spilled a cupful of boiling hot coffee on that one.

When she had gone, I found myself unable to concentrate on the crossword puzzle. It was impossible, I found myself thinking, that Davis Carter Powers was unaware that the Bacchante of his photograph collection was that nice Miss Horvath who worked for Mr. Lazenby on the editorial side. Davis Carter might not be too sure just who I was, but in view of his appreciation of the feminine form divine I would cheerfully bet my last dollar that he knew who Eleanor Alice was. Given such knowledge, would a man of his stamp simply let it go at that? Would a man of my stamp, for that matter? I was obliged to concede that it was most unlikely, given a similar set of circumstances.

It followed, then, that Powers knew about Eleanor Alice, and further, that he had probably put this knowledge to his own use. But how? And what sort of use? Would it not be the better part of wisdom on my part to discover the answer to these nagging questions, if for no other reason than my own protection?

With an unpleasant start, I realized that this sort of thinking was nothing more nor less than a rationalization of blackmail. So, too, I realized now, had been my Rupert of Hentzau scene with Diana Powers.

This would not do. We Lazenbys have, in years gone by, committed many errors—an Alpheus Lazenby was seized, duly tried and hanged by the neck until dead for his activities on behalf of the British Crown shortly before Cornwallis surrendered at Yorktown—but we have never descended to blackmail.

Nevertheless, the character of the relationship between Davis Powers and Eleanor Alice presented a veritable feast for thought.

How long these musings continued is difficult to say, but it seemed only a few minutes before Miss Horvath returned to my office, her eyes flashing indignation as she thrust a carbon-copied flimsy across the desk toward me.

"Here's something you'll want to see," said she, unobservant of my involuntary twitch (for such was the delicate condition of my synapses). "Mr. Walsingham's sent you a carbon of his opinion of that German thing you liked so much."

"Good or bad?" I asked, reaching for the paper in her trembling fingers.

"You'd better read it for yourself."

So I knew.

Reading Nat Walsingham's memo, I forgot all about my own problems and did a slow burn that increased in intensity with every line. This time Walsingham had gone too far. Of the content of the von Eggar piece he had no valid criticism save for some inconsequential nit-picking at the style and organization. But then he got around to the author. . . .

The mood changed from boiling anger to one of cold implacability as I picked up my phone and bade Eleanor Alice, who had withdrawn to her desk as I read, get me the office of the Cultural Attaché of the West German Embassy. After the usual brisk exchange of secretarial rank-pulling (which Eleanor Alice won by the simple expedient of declining to give my name, rank and serial number, and using instead the majesty of the institutional name: "This is Youth House calling . . ."), I heard Heinz Hohenlohe-Furtha's cheery tones and Eleanor Alice's triumphant "Mr. Lazenby to speak to you, sir."

"Hello, Lazenby. Nice to hear from you. Wanted to have more of a chance to talk with you Saturday at the Lampreys'."

My God! Was it only two days ago?

"What can I do to be of service to Youth House?" he asked. I got right to the point.

"Nat Walsingham says you told him that a writer, a German newspaperman named Horst von Eggar, used to be a wheel in the Hitler Jugend, and I'd like to find out a little bit more about the situation if I can."

"Von Eggar . . . von Eggar," Hohenlohe-Furtha murmured as one who runs through the files of his memory. "Of course! Horst von Eggar; Munich, I think. Why, yes, as a matter of fact he was a member of the old Youth Organization, although I don't think he was ever what you could call a—what is it, wheel? Why, if I may ask?"

"Well, maybe you can tell me this: What exactly was he, or what did he do? Can you fill me in on that?"

"Do? Why, so far as I know, nothing. That is, nothing more than any other kid in the organization. You know the sort of thing they went in for—marching, playing soldiers, that sort of thing. And then, at the end, not playing any more."

"You mean he actually got into the fighting?"

"So I understand. In one of those militia outfits—they called them People's Grenadiers, if you recall. Old men, boys, anybody who could carry a gun."

"I seem to remember them," I observed with my customary tact. Hohenlohe-Furtha chuckled. "But what about that last-ditch outfit they tried to put together?" I persisted. For the life of me I couldn't remember what it had been called. H-F chuckled again.

"You mean the Werewolves? No, that I can tell you definitely. In fact, I'm certain that his experiences as a babe-in-arms—did you know, by the way, that he managed to get himself wounded rather badly?—left him with no illusions about militarism, and for a German, that's a pretty rare thing." (I decided that even if he couldn't help clicking his heels, old Heinz was a good sort and the West German Federal Republic deserved more like him.)

"May I ask how come you're so well up on von Eggar?"

"He was one of the reporters I helped select to come over here, back when I was in the foreign office in Bonn."

"Let me boil it down, then," I said. "In effect, von Eggar being in the Hitler Jugend was, considering the time and the circumstances, not too different from some American kid being in the Boy Scouts, let's say?"

"Considering the time, the place, and the circumstances, that's pretty much the way it was. But for God's sake, don't ever quote me to the Boy Scouts."

"I can't thank you enough." I meant it. "And since I can't, I'd like to buy you a drink."

"Now that I'd enjoy. Seriously, I hope I've been some help."

"You have, friend. Believe me."

We parted with further expressions of mutual esteem, and I began girding my loins, a process roughly three-quarters completed when my phone rang and the dulcet tones of Mrs. Oradean Nonnenmaker advised me that, if I were not otherwise engaged, the Senior Ass would be graciously pleased to receive me at my earliest convenience. I signified my immediate availability, and our little chat closed with that stately courtesy so typical of all our intercourse at Youth House.

Walsingham was in the sanctum when I arrived. Samuel K. Nurney's hawklike visage bore the expression of a Cardinal about to rebuke an Archbishop for permitting Catalonia to go Presbyterian. Walsingham's look was that of a newly elevated Junior Vice Commander of the American Legion who has just unearthed a card-carrying member of the Newspaper Guild. And I, if I may be allowed to say so without creating an impression of unseemly vanity, attempted to comport myself in much the same manner as was recorded of Martin Luther preparing to begin the Reformation: stern, firm and righteous. Carved in rich pearwood, we would have made one hell of a fine panel for a triptych.

The proceedings were conducted initially with the same solemnity alleged to have attended the negotiations looking to the Treaty of Vienna. I will not interrupt the heady pace of this action-packed, fun-filled narrative of A Boy and His Dirty Pictures (2 vol. boxed. Privately printed, Milano) with a transcript of our discussion but, in sum, it rapidly developed that Samuel K. had decided, in view of Horst von Eggar's unfortunate affiliation with the Hitler Jugend and the potential repercussions involved and despite the patent validity of his article, that it would be best to forget the whole business so far as *Youth Outlook* was concerned.

I thereupon countered with Hohenlohe-Furtha's comparison of the Hitler Jugend and the Boy Scouts, and noted that von Eggar had been cleared for his visit to the United States by the West German Foreign Ministry. To this, Walsingham observed it was widely known that the Germans were either at your feet or your throat, a platitude he delivered with a pomposity of which I had not thought him capable. Further, he added, it was more than likely that von Eggar, seeking German-style to protect himself whichever way the wind veered, had secretly sold out to the Communists and that this supposedly anti-Nazi article was in reality a subtle effort to discredit the West German government. Which was, I said, pure guilt by association, coupled with baseless supposition. We were, I vow, almost as good as a high school debating society's annual competition.

It was at this point, however, that Walsingham committed

his reserves—prematurely, for the fact was that I didn't yet realize this was at last war to the death, and if Samuel K. Nurney had brought forward any other reason than von Eggar's membership in the Hitler Youth—if he'd said simply that he didn't like the writing or the story's organization, I would probably have backed off. After all, our Senior Ass did not arrive at his present journalistic eminence without some small degree of savvy, and if he had discarded von Eggar on purely professional grounds, I would have been among the last to argue his decision. And as a matter of fact, I'm reasonably certain that SKN himself didn't realize that this had suddenly become a no-quarter-asked contest, or that Nat had determined to use this story as the lever which would jack me right out of the running for the job we both coveted.

But, as I say, Walsingham sent the Old Guard thundering into the line with the suggestion—actually a flimsily veiled threat—that a columnist, say Pearson or Sokolsky, George—especially Sokolsky—might have a field day with the information that a magazine of the high moral tone credited to *Youth Outlook* was publishing an article by an ex-Nazi who might very well be a current Communist.

It was at this juncture that I got the message.

"It would be even more of a field day," I declared grimly (Cemetery Ridge burst into flame and the Emmittsburg Road was hell), "if Pearson got the idea that the contents of *Youth Outlook* are selected by blackmail, by God."

"And just what the hell do you mean by that crack?" Nat demanded nastily. His face was flushed and it was possible that he realized he had just stepped overboard.

"I think I understand what Frederick is driving at," Samuel K. Nurney put in coldly. "And I also think that if the German Embassy people see nothing wrong with this von Eggar, then we're pretty well in the clear so far as our responsibility to our readers is concerned. I think his piece is sound reporting. I don't think it's disguised Communist propaganda. The Germans have an unfortunate tendency, and we're all aware of it, toward authoritarian government. Von Eggar argues that the present democracy is still a thin veneer, and I'm inclined to think he's probably right. We'll buy his article and we'll run it, and," he concluded, speaking now directly to Walsingham, "I personally do not give a damn what Drew Pearson or George Sokolsky or the Lord God Jehovah says about us. The contents of *Youth Outlook* are not about to be selected by blackmail, not now and not ever.

"That's all, gentlemen. Frederick, will you instruct the accounting people to make out a check to von Eggar; standard starting rate. Get off a letter to him, carbon to me; say we'd like to look at some more of his material, too, while you're at it."

So there it was. Victory.

Walsingham left the sanctum without another word, aware that he had been routed. And who had short-fused him? I, Honest Freddy Lazenby, Defender of Truth and demon Boy Editor. From here on in, I realized, we would be able to dispense with the bogus cordiality, for Nat would be openly out for revenge and the opportunity to put himself once more in what the sports writers call hot contention for the pennant. It would be best in future not to stand with my back to any open windows whilst Nat Walsingham was in the immediate vicinity.

Back in my office I found a note from Eleanor Alice reminding me that I was supposed to meet Sam Ball at the Press Club for lunch at 12:30. I glanced at my watch and noted with mild surprise that our go-round in SKN's office had blown the morning. It was time to be on my way. The walk downtown would do me no end of good.

XXV

Since the day was fine, I elected to go straight down Fifteenth to F rather than cut over to Fourteenth and then down. Fourteenth below K is splendid for window shopping, but Fifteenth is, next to Connecticut Avenue between L Street and Dupont Circle, the city's finest for girl-watching. The brokerage offices and law firms clustered there turn their secretaries out to feed between noon and 1 P.M., and the spectacle is one to rejoice both eye and spirit, as well as to raise the question of how the brokers and barristers ever manage to get any work done. The secret of the proper enjoyment of Fifteenth Street is never to overhear the conversation of these frolicsome career girls. This precaution observed, the stroll constitutes an admirable prelude to lunch.

Thus, spiritually refreshed, I arrived at the Press Club in splendid fettle and swiftly made my way into the Members' Bar where I found the journalists packed three deep as they discussed the vital issues of the day in hoarse yells. Intermingled with the scriveners were assorted public relations men, lobbyists, lawyers, naval and military types, administrative assistants to Congressmen, Congressmen, former Congressmen, and others willing to foot the bill for nonvoting membership for the privilege of rubbing elbows with the movers and shakers of American public opinion. As a general rule it is possible to tell the working press from the nonvoting membership by the manner in which they order drinks. The nonvoters always specify brand names: "Jack Daniels Black on the rocks, Sam," say, and, "Beefeater with a twist." The working stiffs content themselves with whatever the bar brand is, except in the case of bureau chiefs and other dignitaries who order *obscure* brand names: "Discovered this at

St. Andrew's last month; not bad stuff," or "Got used to it in Moscow."

I saw Sam Ball huddled at the far end of the bar by the space reserved for the waiters, his expression inscrutable as always.

Sam is an old friend from the days of my youth when we twain battled against the forces of evil for the Good, Gray Baltimore *Sun* and for peanuts. Then he found The Money Window. In his case The Money Window turned out to be the Civil War. He started off with a biography of Turner Ashby, the Confederate cavalryman who got killed before he had a chance to hit the big time. Sam wrote it more or less as a labor of love and, much to his astonishment, saw it snapped up by the first publisher who read it. That was seven years ago, and Sam has been quietly raking the stuff in ever since. What with all the hooraw about the Civil War Centennial, Sam has played it cagey. He leaves the big set-pieces to Bruce Catton, Allan Nevins, Burke Davis and such like eminences, and concentrates on the minutiae. Let Clifford Dowdey or Fairfax Downey refight Gettysburg and Vicksburg; Sam does a minute-by-minute study of the cavalry skirmish between Stuart and Kilpatrick at Hanover, Pennsylvania, titles it "Forgotten Turning Point," proves (to his satisfaction, at any rate) that it actually determined the outcome of Lee's Pennsylvania Campaign, and damned if it doesn't sell as well as a major work by Earl Schenk Miers. The Money Window.

"Hail," I greeted. Sam beamed down from his great height. "Hail."

"How's the silver war?"

"The issue is in doubt. How's the nation's youth?"

"The issue are in doubt. Let's grab a table."

The object of this lunch with Sam was to sound him out on the possibility of his doing a piece on the War of the Rebellion for Y.O., but first things first. We accepted a couple of bourbons from the barman and found a table well removed from the sullen thunder of the barside discussion group. Our waiter roused himself by a mighty effort of will and dropped a couple of menus between us, sighed and relapsed once more into catatonia. Not that we needed menus; the Press Club bill of fare is as immutable as the

Talmud, and the food is prepared according to ancient rituals believed to be derived in part from the Code of Hammurabi. But the waiters feel better if you pretend to inspect the list of dainties and rich viands. We did so.

"My God," said Sam, moved to the depths of his being. "Chop suey! What kind of chop suey would they turn out here?" It was one of those golden moments that live in the memory:

"Chop *sui generis*, no doubt," I said triumphantly. I was feeling that bonny.

"Ever considered vaudeville?" Sam inquired coldly.

"Vaudeville you think of next?" I riposted, hotter than a two-dollar pistol and twice as shiny.

"You will be the death of me, Frederick, I vow and declare."

"Death," I quoted, "Nature's way of telling us to slow down."

"Will you shut the hell up? More to the point, what're you doing about a book?" Sam asked. He has been bullying me for the past couple of years to join the line at The Money Window; at this stage of the game, he alleges, a coherently written account of Confederate ammunition procurement policies in the Trans-Missippi would find its author fighting off the publishers. He snorted at my silence. The harsh fact is that I simply do not give much of a damn about the Late War for Southern Independence except to wish, from time to time, that the Confederacy had won, in which case we wouldn't have to worry about such jewels in the national crown as Georgia and Louisiana where, by now, the spiders would be in charge and much easier to deal with.

"In time, in time," I said defensively. Then, remembering the object of the lunch: "What are you working on just now, come to think of it?"

"Ahh," Sam's large, amiable face sagged with pleasure. "This time, Buck, old Sam is headed for the real jackpot country. Mind you, I'm not saying it's pure genius, but it ain't bad for a country boy. I'm working the shady side of the Sooth." I looked appropriately baffled. "The side the history books don't tell, Buck. Never been done, really. Maggie Leech touched on it in her book but, being a lady, she didn't go into the gory details, and she was mainly concerned with our fair city. I mean, we know approximately how many cat houses there were in Washington before Bull Run, but what about Richmond, say, and who were the high-class call girls? See what I mean? Why, Buck, some of those gallant old bastards used to carry whole harems right into the field."

I stared at Sam for some moments in silence. Was there no escape from it anywhere? "It sounds terrific," I finally said dully. "Maybe the United Daughters of the Confederacy would pay you not to write it."

"All I ask is that they pass a resolution condemning it."

"Not the sort of thing we could condense and use in *Youth Outlook*," I suggested. Sam shook his head. "We were more or less casting around for a piece on the part young people played in the war," I went on hopelessly. "Boy colonels, maybe. It was pretty much of a young man's war, after all."

"You don't say."

"Well it was, dammit. We'd pay fifteen hundred."

"Fifteen hundred?"

"Cash money."

"How soon?"

"No later than September."

"What the hell?"

"What the hell?"

"Let's order," Sam said, and the deal was concluded to our mutual gratification. I was prepared to go to seventeen fifty, if needs must, and Sam's acceptance of fifteen hundred had saved Y.O. a tidy little chunk of change. And Sam could turn the piece out in a couple of weeks without seriously interrupting his work on the sinful side of the South. Good deal all around.

"Telephone for Sam Ball, Mr. Sam Ball," boomed the speaker set into the ceiling above our table. Sam arose and made his way toward the house phone in the foyer. Idly, I picked up the early edition of *The Star* which some early eater had abandoned on the leather cushion beside me. Casually I scanned it. And then my heart came surging into my throat and a thin steel band began to tighten with incredible swiftness around my skull. "Police Make Record Obscenity Haul," a local headline announced. Vice Squad officers, the story disclosed, had arrested a man tentatively identified as B. J. Toombes, of Los Angeles, California, and charged him with possession and sale of pornographic material. "Veteran Vice Squad members told reporters that they had never in their experience seen so much obscenity as was found in Tombes's hotel room. The California man is believed to have an accomplice who has so far escaped apprehension. Police are continuing their investigations in an effort to discover where Tombes marketed material prior to his arrest. 'This case,' said Inspector William Rutwig, 'is by no means closed. We are working very closely with federal authorities and with California law enforcement agencies.'"

"Anything wrong?" Sam asked, returning from his phone call and observing my forehead beaded like wampum with perspiration.

"Wha—? Oh. No. No, not a thing," I said shakily. "But I'm going to have another bourbon. With a twist of adrenalin."

If I were not to go mad, I must unburden myself.

"Hoo ha," Sam breathed thoughtfully when I had finished pouring out my piteous tale. "Of course, you could simply go to the cops and explain the whole situation; how you come to have all this crap and what you were doing buying stuff from this Tombes character and so on."

"Do you think they'd believe a word of it?"

"From my limited experience in dealing with our local gendarmes, no. In fact, hell no."

We sat for some moments rapt in silent thought.

"Does Joby know anything at all?" Sam inquired finally.

"Nothing," I replied, and explained about my Central Intelligence Agency cover story. Sam's face was grave when I stopped talking.

"As far as I can see," he declared heavily, "there isn't a single angle in this whole mess you haven't played 100 per cent dead wrong."

"You've been a great help," I said, not without bitterness.

Sam's face brightened. "There's one cheery spot, though. Maybe your boy Tombes will observe the harsh code of the underworld and keep his big yap shut."

"Yeah," I said in a voice dead to hope. To my disgust, Sam's face slowly turned an astonishing shade of scarlet and his large shoulders began to quiver. Two large tears formed at the inner corners of his eyes, and he snuffled alarmingly as they coursed down each side of his nobly proportioned nose. He buried his ugly face in his hands, shoulders still chugging away, and from the depths of his palms arose the disgusting snorts and gaspings of helpless glee. From the depths of this horrid maelstrom there emerged the single word: "Sorry."

"Balls," said I succinctly, and summoned our waiter to fetch us food.

XXVI

Monday had by no means finished with me.

Were I of the Presbyterian persuasion, I would be constrained to say that long before I was born it was fated that I should visit my office in the Gerlacher Building that day. But I am not of the Presbyterian persuasion, and I put it down to plain bad luck. Or bad judgment. Or both. With a dash of panic. The news of the arrest of B. J. Tombes had to a certain extent unnerved me. I felt it was imperative to conduct a discreet reconaissance of the place to ascertain whether the Vice Squad had not already descended upon the Old Dominion Genealogical Researchers.

"If you find out anything nasty about Jeb Stuart, I don't want to know about it," I cautioned Sam Ball as we left the club after what had turned out to be a somewhat strained lunch.

"I'll keep you posted on the youth piece," Sam said. "I'll come and sit in your cell with you and tell you all about the world outside."

I conducted my approach march with my customary skill. The police were not in possession. Locking the door of my lair, I sat down to ponder what my course should be in the light of the latest developments. It was clear that the Old Dominion Genealogical Researchers was no longer a safe cover, for if B. J. talked, I was in the soup. The police would establish what is known as a stake-out and the next time I appeared in the Gerlacher Building the trap would be sprung; George Burnley would be identified first as a major purchaser of pornography, and second as Frederick W. Lazenby, and after that the only decent solution would be to leave me alone with my Webley, a cigarette and a last glass of brandy. Indeed, I reflected, it was not impossible that even as I sat there the police were quietly taking up their positions on the fire escape.

I'd paid a month's rental on the office and filing cabinets and other equipment. What would happen if I simply took Dumbo's collection and vanished away? Nothing, probably. I could telephone the office equipment people and tell them to pick their property up at their earliest convenience. And when the rent became overdue, the building management, assuming the Old Dominion Genealogical Researchers had gone bust, would simply scratch the name from the door and await the next victim. Then what? Renting another office and more filing cabinets would involve the use of George Burnley's name again, unless I went through another session with the Maryland State Police and emerged with another identity so that I could start still another bank account. The whole prospect was absurd. I had, in all likelihood, already placed myself in violation of Maryland law by securing a driver's license under a false name, and there seemed to be little point in repeating the offense.

What, then, was the alternative?

Had I, perhaps, grossly exaggerated the danger inherent in storing Dumbo's cartons in my own attic? And now that I had concluded my negotiations with the unspeakable Tombes, was there really a valid need to maintain a clandestine hideaway? Was not the sensible thing to do, in truth, to haul the whole ruddy mess back home again? But this smacked of low comedy, the sort of thing Charley Chase used to do so well, or Buster Keaton. With steamer trunks, if memory serves. Nevertheless, home it would have to be, for time was of the essence. The important thing was to act decisively and swiftly before B. J. Tombes softened up and sang to the Vice Squad. In the matter of Joby's reaction to the sudden reappearance of the cartons (which I had had the foresight to have caused to be stored in the Gerlacher Building basement), I would simply have to rely once more on the magic of the C.I.A. and take my chances.

As always, I felt better with a decision reached. I would forthwith rent a station wagon for the evening, and with any luck at all have seen the last of the Gerlacher Building before midnight.

I wondered, suddenly and inexplicably, how Snaveley of Loudon County was making out in his quest for Revolutionary antecedents.

It was at this precise moment that there came a tapping as of some one gently rapping, rapping at my chamber door. Stifling a scream, I realized that the door was locked and that, if I kept quiet, whoever was applying for entrance would probably go away. Or come shouldering straight through, Police Special drawn and blazing. I was trapped. The only thing to do was open the door. If it were some lost soul seeking its ancestors, I could tell it I was too busy to accept any new clients. If it were the law, at least I should not be involved in any unseemly scuffling. The charge of resisting arrest and obstructing an officer in the performance of his duties could not be added to the long list of my other offenses against society.

Rising on gelatinous limbs, I surged octopus-like to the door where some last remnant of the blood that once sent Sir Giles de Lazenbye into battle against the Saracen managed to brace the sagging spine and lift the quivering chin, and still it. From all I had heard, Grant was a decent chap.

I opened the door and there stood Mr. Johnny Salvi, lately aide-de-camp to B. J. Tombes. His manner was, if possible, even more furtive than upon the occasion of our first meeting. Wordlessly he slipped past me into the office. "Shahdadah," he muttered, once safely inside. I complied. He stood uncertainly in front of my desk.

"I goddah blow town," he announced, "owney . . ."

"Only what?" I asked coldly.

"Owney 'at bassard Tombes gahdawdahdoh."

"So?"

"I figger you'll loan me a C." Mr. Salvi's hitherto uncertain manner vanished, now that he was approaching familiar territory: blackmail. "Or relse mebbe I make mebbe a li'l phone call to the cops." He smirked evilly at the cunning of his scheme. "You doughwad I mead?"

Now this was really too much to be borne. Added to all the hazards and worries I had suffered since accepting custody of Dumbo's collection, and to the frustrations of this day, Mr.

Salvi was simply more than should be, in all fairness, required of mortal man to sustain. That he would not hesitate to place an anonymous telephone call to the police, advising them of George Burnley's dealings with B. J. Tombes, there was not the slightest doubt. That he should be permitted so to do was impossible of toleration. This wretched man must be silenced for the nonce. Now it was that instinct took charge. I composed my features in a placatory smile.

"We wouldn't want that to happen now, would we, Johnny?" I asked, winking horridly. "And I'd like to see that day when I couldn't spare a few bucks to help out a friend in need." I started to reach into my breast pocket for my wallet, but ceased abruptly when Mr. Salvi's right hand darted into his coat pocket and pressed into prominence against his shoddy suiting the unmistakable outline of a gun barrel. "Just getting the bills out for you, Johnny," I said hastily.

"No fuddy stuff, pal," he cautioned. I produced my wallet and then appeared as one struck by a sudden and happy thought.

"I picked up some new stuff over the weekend," I said, nodding toward the filing cabinets. "Real hot, man; crazy. You want to take a look before you go?"

Mr. Salvi's little eyes gleamed.

"Take a look in that right-hand file, bottom drawer," I urged. "I thought the stuff you and Tombes were peddling was good, but wait 'til you get a load of this. Might give you some brand new ideas to take back to the Coast, man."

"Yeah?" Mr. Salvi's professional interest was aroused.

"Would I kid you, Johnny?"

"'At wunt be smaht, pal," Mr. Salvi observed, and walked over to the file cabinet I had indicated. He bent and tugged at the drawer handle. "'Slocked," he grunted.

"I forgot," I apologized, moving to stand beside and over him. "Here's the key." I handed it to him and awaited the moment when his eyes and attention were focused on the keyhole. And then I gave him what I devoutly hoped was a nonmortal rabbit punch. I confess to a certain primitive satisfaction as the side of my hand clobbered the back of his neck, and to a soldierly satisfaction when I observed that the job was well and neatly done, just as we had been taught at Fort Benning in the dear, dead days. Emitting only the faintest of grunts, Mr. Salvi collapsed face down upon the floor, and now to my compendium of crimes was added assault and battery. I waited for several seconds to ascertain that he was still breathing, and then it occurred to me that I hadn't the foggiest notion of what to do with him.

First things first, I told myself with a calm I would have believed myself incapable of commanding in the circumstances. I couldn't sit there indefinitely, rabbit punching Salvi every time he showed signs of returning to consciousness. He must be immobilized. The echos of that ancient commando course kept growing stronger as I set about gagging and roping my victim, dredging up from the well of memory knots and expedients designed to hogtie whole platoons of German outposts or Japanese sentries. When I had finished pushing and hauling at Salvi's unhealthy bulk, his hanky was tucked into his mouth and his ankles were bound to his wrists behind his back in such a fashion, by means of a combination of his belt and shoelaces, that the slightest movement would produce a most excruciating pain. It was a job that would have brought a shout of admiration from the late Colonel Anthony Drexel Biddle, though I say it myself.

At the last minute, I recalled the gun in Salvi's pocket.

It turned out to be a ball-point pen, which somewhat diminished my victory. On the other hand, I should have known that Mr. Salvi had not really been carrying a gun. If he had, he would not have wasted time in explanation and the request for a loan; he would simply have held me up at pistol point. I was about to replace the pen in his pocket when I observed a tiny lens set into its upper end. Again, I should have known better; when I held the lens to my eye and turned it to the light, there was to be seen a microscopic female, caught by the camera in an act which is considered a felony in several states. Johnny wasn't missing a bet.

It is all very well, in the paper-backed mystery novels, for the sturdily amoral private eye to clobber some one who displeases him. The author simply lets the victim lie there, and moves the tale so swiftly that the reader forgets to wonder what ever happened later. In actual practice, the situation is fraught with problems. I had met the first of these by immobilizing Salvi through the use of his belt and shoelaces, but there was no telling how long these field expedients would retain their efficacy. I had now to ponder whether to reinforce his bindings, which would have involved a trip to the nearest drugstore and the purchase of large quantities of adhesive tape, or whether to trust to the teachings of the Infantry School. Next, there was the question of what was now to be done with him. It would have been unwise to haul him from my office, during business hours, to the nearest broom closet; I knew of no empty offices on my floor in which I could have dumped him, assuming I could have gained entrance. The sensible course, then, was to let him stay where he was for the moment.

It was then that I perceived that Salvi had regained consciousness and was glaring at me with baleful eyes. From behind the handkerchief stuffed into his mouth came a series of outraged grunts, and as I watched, he tested his muscles against my knots. I was pleased to observe his face turn red and perspiration appear upon his forehead. He immediately ceased his efforts.

He would be, I concluded, all right where he was, at least for as long as it took me to get to the nearest drugstore and back. "If you lie still, you'll be all right," I told him. "But if you try to get free, I've got the knots arranged so you'll break your arm first." And for all I knew, that might be true; in any event, he appeared to take my warning to heart, for he lay quiescent. "Now just take it easy," I said. "I'll be right back."

You see, the main thing was to keep him away from a telephone until I could remove Dumbo's collection and myself to safety.

I was still operating pretty much automatically when I left the office and rang for the elevator.

It shuddered slowly upward and right past me, bound for the misty heights. Far overhead it clanked to a stop for a few moments, the folding gates crashed open and shut, and then it descended with the speed of a man sinking into a quagmire to halt uncertainly before me. The gates banged open and I stepped quickly inside. To come face to face with Nathaniel Walsingham.

"Gurk," I said, by way of greeting.

"Fred," Nat replied curtly, and nodded.

We completed the descent in stony silence as I fought an almost overmastering urge to offer some—any—sort of explanation for my presence there. For that matter, what the hell was Walsingham doing there? And why should I feel obliged to explain anything to him?

All might have gone well if that malign cretin of an elevator operator had kept quiet. He had never spoken to me before except to utter sulky snorts of acknowledgment when I called my floor. But today was his day to babble. As we sank to rest at the street level he turned from his controls and gave me a toothless grin before he opened his gate.

"Guess you thought I wasn't going to stop for you, ain't, Mr. Burnley?" he sniggered. Then, thank God, he opened the way to freedom.

"I guess that's right," I gibbered. "Thought you missed me for sure that time." And fled, grimly conscious of Nat Walsingham's bemused stare. But my boy was not finished wreaking his havoc. "That Mr. Burnley," I heard him cackle behind me. "Always rush, rush, rush."

"Going back to the office, Fred?" Nat called out after me, and I ground to a halt just outside the entrance to the building.

"Dentist's appointment," I replied hastily. "Late already. See you."

"See you," Nat said carelessly. But from the gleam in his eye I knew the evil was done. The Walsingham brain was already busy gnawing at the question of why an elevator operator in a rundown office building should address Frederick W. Lazenby as Mr. Burnley, and if I knew the Walsingham brain, it would not rest until it found the answer. I hastened off in the direction of the nearest drugstore in the sure and certain knowledge that another rent had been made in the fabric of my pathetic little attempt at subterfuge. But there was no time to worry about that now. There was the problem of Mr. Salvi to be dealt with.

XXVII

Again, the mystery writers make it sound so simple. They never, for instance, go into the messy details of *how* the hero gets hold of enough adhesive tape to bind up the villain; he just happens to have it lying around his trench coat, presumably.

"You said *ten* rolls of adhesive?" the drugstore clerk kept asking me. "That's one hell of a lot of adhesive, you know."

"I want the wide kind," I kept telling him.

"I mean, if it's like for a broken rib or something, you wouldn't need no more than say six; seven at the outside."

But you get the point. Buying ten rolls of adhesive tape, it turned out, created much the same impression as might have been left by a man stepping into an automobile dealer's and ordering two Rolls-Royces.

And as for putting the stuff to use—well, sir! It certainly makes a boy understand the continuing popularity of rope. But by the time I finished, Salvi looked like a badly wrapped mummy. And the drugstore clerk had been right. I could have managed with only six rolls. The only real unpleasantness came when I removed the handkerchief from Johnny's mouth. His tongue momentarily freed, he gave vent to a stream of what I assume must have been Sicilian blasphemies, switching briefly to Anglo-Saxon when his native language failed him. In the end, I encased his entire head in adhesive tape, leaving only a small opening for purposes of ventilation. Then, in a moment of devilment, I took out my pen and wrote across the lily whiteness of his forehead, "I am Johnny Salvi and I am wanted by the police, who may be reached by dialing NA 8-4000. Thank you."

Then I went out and arranged to rent another station wagon.

Perhaps the less said about the return of the Savoury Papers to the wee hoose in Georgetown that evening, the better. I played the C.I.A. angle for all it was worth and then some, and Joby, though quietly furious at this further evidence of the agency's highhanded methods, again accepted my story.

"But I just don't understand why they don't keep the papers right there with them," she complained bitterly. "They say they've finished looking at them; what's to stop them from deciding they want to have another look day after tomorrow? What then? Do you pile everything back in a station wagon and trot it back to them?"

"Joby," said I, simulating tolerant patience, "who can explain how the C.I.A. operates? This is the way they seem to want the thing done, whether you and I like it or not, and rest assured that I don't. But I'm sure the thing's over now, so let's forget about it. Maybe when Dumbo gets back to the States he can explain the whole business."

I make no pretense whatsoever that this line of argument had any merit to it, but it was the best available. Then, too, with my mind momentarily divested of its most pressing worries, I was able to put a good deal of sincerity into it. The Savoury Papers were safely back in my attic, and I felt reasonably certain that Johnny Salvi would be discovered in the morning by the first visitor to the fourth floor gentlemen's room, where I had deposited him. A night on a cold marble floor could do him no great harm and might indeed prove morally beneficial.

Exhausted by my labors, I had suggested an early retirement, but the soothing effect of the prebed bourbon so warmed and rejoiced me that I decided on a small refill. With this end in view, I descended below, glass in hand, and was in the very act of pouring when the telephone rang. Calmly, I set bottle and glass down and calmly I made my way into my study to respond. Only to discover that for the first time in living memory Joby had remembered to haul the damned thing upstairs. From above, I heard her answer.

"Yes. Yes, that's correct. What! All right, all right; I'll tell him." Joby's voice held a well honed edge of irritation, and the little hairs on the back of my neck assumed the position of the soldier at attention. Her next words were uttered in a tone of utter bewilderment. "But my name's not . . . hello! Hello! Well, damn you!" The phone crashed back into its cradle.

Oh, God.

What was it Ferdinand Foch, Marshal of France, said at the Battle of the Marne in 1918? "My center is giving way, my right is pushed back—excellent! I'll attack."

Swiftly I withdrew to the kitchen, stoutly braced the lately weak second nightcap, secured equipment, put the show on the road and flung myself once more into the breach, dear friends. Briskly I marched upstairs and into the bedroom to discern Joby sitting straight up in bed, wearing the expression of a faithful wife who is going to get a couple of straight answers out of her husband or bloody well know the reason why. The Guards will fix bayonets and move in quick time.

"I heard," I said brightly. "The check-up call."

"The which?" Joby asked evenly.

"The check-up call. You know. Routine check to make sure everything went off smoothly. That was," I added confidentially, "a Peter Rabbit call, wasn't it?" Joby nodded, her expression unchanged.

"It was that English female again," she said, her voice betraying no readily definable emotion. "She said to tell you the second half would be ready next Sunday."

All right, men, do we die here on the beaches or do we die inland?

"Good," I declared heartily.

"Why good?" Still toneless.

"That's the code acknowledgment; means they're satisfied everything worked out. They told me about it downtown."

"She said something else. She said, 'I'm looking forward to meeting you, Gaby.' And then she hung up before I could say a word."

"You're quite sure she said 'Gaby'?" I asked earnestly. Joby nodded, and now the faintest glimmer of uncertainty flickered in her eyes. "Good," I repeated, this time heavily and with an air of heart-felt relief. " 'Gaby' was the word they said they'd use if the whole thing were over and done with. Officially, we're all finished with the blasted C.I.A., thanks be to God."

"Eff." Joby's manner had that intensity about it which invariably marks the presence of a crisis in our marriage, of which, again thanks be to God, there have been only a few.

"Yes, Jobe." I matched her manner with a sincerity that rang deep and true as a Prudential Life commercial.

"Are you telling me the truth?"

"Yes, Jobe."

"This Englishwoman really is with the C.I.A.?"

"Yes, Jobe."

Wordlessly, Joby slipped down between the covers and turned her back. I gazed down at her helplessly for a few seconds, wanting to add something more, but certain that this was not the time for further talk. For one wild instant I thought of a burst of simulated indignation at Joby's suspicions, then decided against it. Instead, I finished my second nightcap standing up, enjoying it fully as much as a cup of hemlock laced with cooking sherry. Then I turned off the lamp on the bedside table and eased the weary frame into bed, grimly aware that sleep was probably a long way off. I sensed, rather than felt, the rigidity of Joby's body and knew that she was not asleep but wide awake and thinking deeply. She was reaching some sort of decision about my story, but whether she would communicate it to me before dawn—or ever—was something Joby alone would decide. Meantime there was naught to be done but wait.

Of one thing I was positive. No matter what happened, there would be no return to Peace and Plenty and Diana Powers. She had apparently recovered from her pique and was now consumed with curiosity about the obscure talents of George Burnley's gaudy paramour, Gaby. Which meant that if I failed to turn up the following Sunday, she would probably—nay, undoubtedly—call again. And, if my estimate of her was correct, come straight out with a proposition, should Joby happen to answer the phone. Which would, in turn, blow my C.I.A. story sky-high and with it—assuming this were not already the case—my marriage. Somehow the woman must be prevented from making another Peter Rabbit call. Sometime the next morning, George Burnley would have to phone her; warn her that his wire was being tapped by the police, and forbid all further communication, save from his end. That should do the trick, especially if the warning were to be accompanied by a none-too-subtle threat of exposure. George was turning out to be even more a cad and bounder than I had anticipated.

Now, beside me, I felt Joby relax into sleep. She had evidently decided not to tell me her decision, and there was nothing left for me to do now but try and get to sleep.

So ended Black Monday.

XXVIII

When I awoke the next morning, Joby was gone.

A bleary look at the clock-radio indicated that the hour was past 9:30.

So this, I reflected, was what Tom Eliot was talking about—the bangless end. Joby had left me. Doubtless she had seen through my idiot maunderings about the C.I.A. from the very beginning. Perhaps at this very moment she was emulating Anna Karenina down at Union Station, staring dull-eyed at the approaching wheels of the morning Congressional. Or maybe she had the Volkswagen out on some winding Maryland road, wide open, her eyes unseeing, her auburn hair streaming behind her in the fierce wind of speed, an impossible curve dead ahead. Any second now the phone would ring and a grave voice would be asking me whether I was the next of kin of a Mrs. Jobiana Lazenby. . . .

There came from beyond the bedroom door a small, sad whimpering. I heaved myself out of bed and admitted man's best friend. Rafe shambled in, unspeakable woe writ large upon his great, shaggy face, the crumbs of his morning dog biscuit depending from his drooping dewlaps.

They say dogs Know.

Rafe gathered himself and sprang heavily onto the bed and lay sprawled, his enormous face between his paws, his eyes twin pools of misery.

Damn, damn, damn!

A scrap of paper was propped against the small mirror on my bureau. With the lithe stride of a panther I was across the room to get it. "There is some Taylor pork roll in the meat tray for your breakfast," the note said.

Now that I was on my feet, thought became a little more coherent. A woman contemplating self-destruction under the morning Congressional would hardly be likely to think about Taylor pork roll. On the other hand, it might be just the one insane detail she would think of.

At this point you may be tempted to ask just how the hell I was so certain Joby had gone; why I didn't dash downstairs to ascertain her absence? In the first place, my Jobiana would never have allowed me to sleep so late. In the second place, if she had risen early and been up and about below, Rafe would have been out in the fresh air of the back yard and there would have been the bracing aroma of brewing coffee in my nostrils. Thirdly, there was this note.

A cup of strong, black coffee seemed indicated. I wasn't getting anywhere simply standing there in the bedroom trying to figure out what had happened. Struggling into my bathrobe, I descended and started the kettle heating. Reaching into the cupboard where Joby kept the instant—I smiled a brave, infinitely sad smile at the thought that this familiar, beloved routine was shattered now: No more to come down early of a Sunday and prepare to wake Joby with a steaming cup; no more midnight cups to be shared while we dissected a party—I came face to face with the Memo-Minder (Best Xmas Wishes from J. C. Gault, Registered Plumber, "Whatever Your Woe, We'll Flush It Out") upon which Joby was accustomed to jot down her shopping needs, odd telephone numbers (for two years there a simple legend which said, "Concrete men will call," which Joby had hastily scrawled on the Memo-Minder's border and which conjured up such visions as I will not harrow you with at this time. We were having the patio (ha!) finished off, as I remember. It always reminded me of Thurber's splendid, "They are here with the reeves." Joby finally erased it, having suffered just about all the Lazenby wit she could stand) and sundry engagements. There, in the square reserved for that Tuesday, was the notation: "Dr. Riegelsnider, 10:30."

Dr. Riegelsnider? Who the hell was Dr. Riegelsnider?

Then I remembered. Dr. Riegelsnider was Joby's dentist. A couple of years back he had removed himself to practice his ghastly art in Baltimore, and faithful Joby had stuck with him. On my urging, she'd tried my boy Jordan, but Jordan was an ex-Navy man and, according to Joby, lacked the Riegelsnider touch when it came time to drill. I could understand and sympathize with her views; Jordan is a bully, but when it comes to having a tooth drilled, I need a bully.

So it was that simple. Joby had risen early to drive to Baltimore in time for her appointment. Probably she had mentioned it to me before today, but my mind, filled to bursting with my clandestine concerns, had not absorbed the information. So she was not gone away, really. She had not seen the C.I.A. rigamarole for the tissue of lies it was. She had decided I was telling the truth about Diana Powers, which I was, although not strictly speaking. But the main thing was, Joby would be back.

The kettle began to keen.

I cannot remember ever having enjoyed a cup of coffee quite as much. When Rafe came lumbering morosely down the stairs, I presented him with a second, wholly undeserved dog biscuit and he seemed to catch my lightsome mood as he crunched it slowly into damp fragments on the kitchen floor.

It was now much too late to try and make the office. I would telephone Eleanor Alice and tell her not to expect me until after lunch.

Eleanor Alice. . . .

Usually, when Joby drove to Baltimore for a dental appointment she spent the whole day there, following her siege under the drill with a restorative tour of the antique emporiums on Read Street, from which she customarily returned bearing an exquisite example of the Read Street merchants' eerie skill at disposing of junk.

Suddenly bright, the remainder of the morning stretched luxuriously before me. With Joby in Baltimore, might this not be the occasion to probe the enigma of Eleanor Alice? Without fear of interruption?

I come now to a portion of this narrative which honor bids me write, but in which I can take no proper pride. Nor can I attempt to explain or excuse the workings of my mind that morning. Maybe I was simply lightheaded with relief. That would be the charitable view, but in this instance and in all honesty, I don't think I deserve the charitable view. Putting it bluntly, the ugly truth is that I wanted to have another look at those orgiastic photographs of my secretary.

Fie, for shame!

How is it possible, you have every justification for asking, that a man who alleges that he is deeply in love with his wife, who has just recovered her after thinking he has lost her forever—how is it possible that he should suddenly develop an urge to gaze upon the flamboyantly naked body of his secretary?

A glandular reaction, perhaps? A tiny malfunction of the brain? The Fundamentalist Satan? God knows.

Like a miser creeping off to his strong room, so crept I up to the attic and there, hunched beneath the rafters I searched for and found the pictures of Eleanor Alice in action.

But why, I mused, be content with mere photographs? And was Eleanor Alice's avocation really so outrageous? Was she not —if we really faced the facts—simply enjoying freely and without shame, as the ancient Greeks did, the fullest pleasures of the bodily senses? Was it not, to carry the argument a step further, puritanically narrow—nay, bigoted—to view her shenanigans as sinful? A merry romp with Eleanor Alice would constitute nothing more than an exuberent adventure of the flesh; it would have no real relationship to the spiritual love I bore for Joby. Except in the strictest Judaeo-Christian theological view, it could not even be considered adultery. And indeed, any sound anthropologist will subscribe to the view that man is basically polygamous, I told myself; that the sexual strictures imposed upon him by a society hag-ridden by the fear of a Baptist Hell are unnatural and therefore, in the truest sense, evil.

Then, too, I was not getting any younger; youth, what there was left of it, was fleeting, fleeting and so why not gather rosebuds while we may? Everybody in Gibbsville, Pennsylvania, did it; why not me?

Thus I rationalized, squatting amid my cartons.

I gazed down at a photograph of Eleanor Alice cavorting riotously with another young woman of only slightly less voluptuous proportions but equally bizarre tastes. What Eleanor Alice needed, I thought, was to learn the delights of heterosexual lovemaking. But the next photograph indicated clearly that she had little to learn, and the next after that brought proof that this wanton child could teach me much. Amid what unlikely circumstance had these photographs been made? At the camera outings sponsored by the Thropplestance Memorial Baptist Church? Was that amply endowed young man embracing Eleanor Alice the Youth Director? And why should it be he in those superbly rounded arms, amidst that warmly glowing flesh, cradled between such hospitable thighs? Why not me?

Moving as one who walks in a dream, I tucked away the photographs, shut the cartons and descended to the second floor where, absurdly, I decided it would not be fitting to telephone Eleanor Alice from the bedroom. Unplugging the phone, I lugged it downstairs and dialed Youth House.

It was simpler than I'd expected.

"I thought you were probably working at home," Eleanor Alice said sympathetically when I explained my absence. "Nobody's called except a Mr. Julian, and there was nothing important in the morning mail."

Julian? What did he want?

"There are a couple of manuscripts I've been running through this morning," I lied casually, "and I was wondering whether I could go over a few points with you at lunch."

"Why certainly, Mr. Lazenby. Shall I order something sent up to your office from the canteen?"

Youth Director—ha! A petty, ill-made lout, e'God, ill-matched to such a wench, By Our Lady! Ho! Lass, give us a buss.

"Actually," I cooed, "I thought about getting away from the office. How about meeting me at 12:30, say, at Le Tricorne?"

"That would be lovely," trilled Miss Horvath. "I'll be there on the dot."

"That would be fine," I said. "See you then." And hung up the telephone with a hand that trembled ever so slightly. Frederick W. Lazenby was committed. For the first time in his married life, he was deliberately setting out to dally with a woman not his wife in the almost certain knowledge that the dalliance must inevitably reach its climax in bed.

Now you tell me why.

XXIX

Impeccably attired in my best bib and tucker, I cabbed to Le Tricorne at the appointed hour and bade the Captain show me to a table in one dim corner, partially hidden from the rest of the dining room by an ancient Norman armoire of astonishing ugliness and possibly the only authentically French item on the premises.

"You wunt be a Mr. Lazenby, maybe?" this proud Gascon inquired. I admitted that such was my name, at which he fumbled in the pockets of his seedy black jacket and produced a crumpled piece of paper. "Yuh sekkuhturry lef' word you was to call Ballimur oprateh nummuh twenny-two. You finnah phone inna foy-yay, onna lef'."

This could only be, I reflected as I made my way toward the telephone booth amateurishly disguised to resemble a kiosk, a call from Joby. Doubtless she wished to have me stop by the grocer's on the way home and pick up some item for this evening's dinner. I slipped a dime into the center slot atop Mr. Bell's device, told the operator my desires, got my dime back and, in the fullness of time, secured the ear of Operator 22 in the Queen City of the Patapsco Drainage Basin. She, efficient girl, manipulated her connections with such verve that my eardrums rang, and then there came the sound of Joby's voice: "Eff?"

"What ho?" cried I right gaily.

"Listen, Eff, could you manage dinner all right tonight by yourself? Because here's what's happened: Dr. Riegelsnider thinks one of my wisdom teeth should come out, and then he wants to do some other work, and all in all what it boils down to is that he thinks I ought to stay overnight and get everything all finished. Would you mind terribly, because it's perfectly all right, all I've got to do is pick up a toothbrush, and I've already called Sally and she says they can put me up but I'm worried because I haven't got a thing ready for you I was going to cook a curry but then Dr. Riegelsnider came up with this idea of his and so promise you'll go out to a restaurant and buy yourself a steak or something or if you want me to I'll tell Dr. Riegelsnider I just can't make it and come on home and let him finish up another day."

"Now you stay right there and let Riegelsnider do the job right," I said firmly. "And don't worry about me and dinner. I can grab a bite downtown and still get home in plenty of time to feed Rafe."

"Don't give him too much of the horsemeat. It gives him gas."

"Okay. Not too much horsemeat. Now listen, will you be able to drive back all right tomorrow, or do you want me to catch a train over and drive you back?"

"Of course not. I'll be perfectly all right. Did you get my note? About the pork roll, I mean."

"It was delicious. Now you relax and give my best to Sally and Howard, and I'll see you sometime tomorrow."

"Will you miss me?"

"Of course I'll miss you, silly."

"I'll come straight home; won't even set foot on Read Street."

"You just take care of yourself, that's all I ask."

"Love you, darling."

"Love you, Jobe." And we hung up with a verbal kiss.

Bless her heart. (Oh, Janus Lazenby! Mouthing the sweet nothings of happy domesticity whilst awaiting the siren's step . . .)

But was there not, I mused, as I returned to the dining room, to be discerned in all this the sure hand of some whimsical Fate?

"You like maybe a cockt'l?" the Captain inquired as I gained my table.

"Gibson, House of Lords," I specified. In a place like Le Tricorne it is wise, harsh experience has long since taught me, to stipulate a brand name. Otherwise you get some vile fluid which has been mixed by trolls and allowed to stand for several weeks in a warm room. The Captain's swarthy face darkened as he departed to place my order; I believe the profits to be derived from a custom-mixed Gibson are considerably below those received from the house concoction.

For some reason, Washington seems to have more than its share of the nation's vast stock of fifth-rate hash joints masquerading as restaurants, and probably Le Tricorne is not worse than the majority of them. As I say, it has the advantage of wretched lighting, and if matters proceeded along the general lines I anticipated this could be important. In point of actual fact, there had been little or no anticipation of what tactics should be employed, as I now suddenly realized. It is probably not far from the truth to declare that in my experience few precedents existed for the situation in which I now found myself.

Would bluntness be best? All is known, wanton child. But enough of this persiflage—take off your clothes . . .?

Such shock measures might, on the other hand, precipitate a burst of hysterical outrage. It was possible, as recent psychological studies have taught us, that Eleanor Alice had one of those totally split personalities: one day she was plain, dutiful Eleanor Alice; the next she was Madame La Zonga, who despised plain, dutiful Eleanor Alice.

The subtly leering approach, then? "Do I understand, my dear, that you take your French lessons from Dr. Birch?"

These meditations were interrupted by the Captain, who had fetched my Gibson from the bar and turned it over to the imitation garçon who would attend our messing. This latter shuffled slowly over, his ancient, wicked face a mask of contempt, and set the glass down before me, carefully slopping a portion of its contents onto the cloth. Like all Le Tricorne's merry men, he had attended Surly School and mastered such arts as tunnel vision and plate-slapping. I took a precautionary sip and found the potion reasonably palatable. In the bottom of the glass lay a red onion, which is Le Tricorne's idea of a real howler. I removed this regrettable object by means of the plastic spear upon which it was impaled. The bartender's smug smile, glimpsed from a corner of my eye, faded into a sneer as his jape fell flat on its face.

And then Eleanor Alice was amongst us. Suppressing an oath, our waiter moved leadenly to pull out the table to permit her to seat herself on the banquette beside me as I succeeded in heaving myself partially to my feet. The artful fellow had jammed my end of the table smartly into my groin.

I must say my secretary did me proud. Her glossy tresses shone darkly; her eyes held hidden fires. She was wearing, to my intense satisfaction, a dress of tan jersey, very simply cut to adhere sternly to the superb outlines of her body. There was a glow about her, and I noted that outside the office, in the great world, she carried herself differently, more proudly and less diffidently.

"Hope I'm not late," she murmured, settling herself.

"Not a bit," I hastened to assure her, and offered her a cigarette. "What about a cocktail?"

"I wonder if I really ought to." She accepted a cigarette and the flame from my instantly presented lighter. "Maybe just a little glass of vermouth."

"Oh, come now," said I jovially. "You can do better than that. Join me in a Gibson. They do them fairly well in here."

"Well," she replied dubiously. "Maybe just this once."

"Wonderful," I declared with great heartiness, and lifted my hand to signal our waiter, extending two fingers to indicate that he should double the order.

"Gosh, I don't know how long it's been since I had one of these at lunch," Eleanor Alice murmured when she had taken her first sip and half the contents of her glass. "It tastes just terrific." And tossed off the rest.

"I really shouldn't," she said with a winsome smile when her second arrived. "You wanted to talk about some manuscripts, and oh! Did you get the message to call Baltimore? I thought you probably wouldn't want to be disturbed at home, so I got the operator's number and then phoned here."

"Worked out fine. And let's not worry about manuscripts. To be perfectly honest with you, I thought that for once we should simply forget about the office for a little while and have lunch. You know what Dr. Mountain always says: A good executive should never forget to let his secretary know when she's doing a good job."

"Gosh, thank you, Mr. Lazenby."

"And I also think we've been working together long enough for you to forget that 'Mister' routine. Makes me feel like my father. What say we make it just plain Freddy?"

"Well, you're the boss—Freddy," replied this glorious creature, giving me a cheery smile.

Le Tricorne was gradually filling with victims, and around us rose the genial hum of iron-willed diners briskly fortifying themselves against the horrors of the cuisine ahead, as well they might. The effect was to isolate Eleanor Alice and me nicely behind our armoire. Catching our waiter's eye—no inconsiderable feat—I gave him the nod for another round.

All was moving, I felt, with the smooth precision of a German General Staff exercise: tanks rolling swiftly in the van, heavy infantry moving close behind to consolidate the gains, the enemy ready to be knocked out by a masterly flanking sweep. As calculated, the arrival of the third Gibson produced only a murmur of remonstrance which I countered effectively with the statement that the afternoon offered no really pressing business at the office and so, what the devil, why not reward ourselves with a little outing to counterbalance the many Saturday mornings we'd put in when deadlines pressed?

We chatted, then, of this and that. "How's the photography course coming along?" I inquired at length, magnificently casual.

"I'll just never learn all there is to know about light meters," Eleanor Alice said with a maidenly giggle.

And now, as I end the refrain, thrust home!

"I take it," I said softly, "you have more fun modeling . . ."

Eleanor Alice was in the middle of taking a sip of her drink. For a long moment she gazed at me over the rim of her glass before putting it down on the table in front of her.

"So you know," she commented calmly. "Did you like what you saw?"

"Who wouldn't?"

"Do you want to go to bed with me?"

Humbert Humbert had nothing on Frederick W. Lazenby when it came to the abrupt disclosure of feminine bluntness in matters of sex. "There's nothing I'd like better," I replied in a voice that shook slightly. She gave me a slow, infinitely knowledgeable smile.

"I'm glad of that. I'll bet you're awfully good in bed."

My God! Just like that! I stared at her, words failing me.

"You look so beautifully shocked," she said, and her smile broadened. "Can this be *your* Miss Horvath? But the point is, Freddy darling, why pretend? I'm oversexed, and there it is. Maybe I'm a nympho for all I know, except they say a nympho is never really satisfied. But I adore sex. I like men. I also like girls. I try to keep all that out of my business life, and I do pretty well at it, too. But you've come barging into the private part of my life, whether I like it or not—and mind you, I do—and I'm simply being honest about it. Or am I going too fast for you?"

I shook my head, still dumb. I mean, what do you say? Reaching for my hand, Eleanor Alice took it and placed it firmly on her thigh under the tablecloth. "I've wanted to feel your hand there since the first day I walked into your office," she announced. "There and elsewhere." She was not, my nerveless fingers somehow communicated to the staggered mind, encased in a girdle.

My throat was dry and my voice was parched and cracked: "When?"

"You've got to get back to the office. I forgot to tell you this morning, but I took the liberty of putting you down to see that Mr. Julian at four o'clock. He just said he wanted to drop by and get better acquainted."

"Damn!"

"So let's make it at five, then, at my apartment."

"But—" What the hell? Was this one of those incredible families of sex maniacs? "I thought—I mean, your mother . . .?"

"Not my home, you silly. Davis keeps an apartment for me over on N Street just off Connecticut."

"Davis? You mean Davis Carter Powers?" Great God in the foothills, what next? Eleanor Alice nodded happily.

"He's an absolute bunny, really," she said. "We've had an

arrangement, I guess you'd call it, for the past year. He got hold of some pictures of me and made me a straight-out proposition that made so much sense I couldn't turn it down. And all he really wants to do is watch Joan and me."

"Joan?"

"Joan Blanchard from the office," Eleanor Alice explained, and I instantly remembered Miss Blanchard as a petite but nobly proportioned blonde who worked somewhere in the accounting department. Eleanor Alice smiled at my pretty confusion, which was beginning to feel like the onset of hysteria. Debauchery in the accounting department too? "You probably didn't recognize her in the pictures you saw; Joannie always wears a black wig when we pose."

"And you two cavort for Davis Carter?"

Eleanor Alice nodded. "It's more fun when you have an audience."

"But those photographs?" I asked. "Where did you—I mean?"

"Next summer you'll have to come up to our Blue Ridge Encampment. Actually, I suppose, the police would be down on us like the wolf on the fold if they knew, but who ever investigates an old rustic lodge that's supposed to be a Baptist youth retreat? It's more or less like a club, only we all feel the same way about sex, and it makes everything so much simpler."

"I see what you mean. Sort of a nudist colony in a clerical collar."

"Well, we do have to be careful."

"Society taking the dim view it does of the old-fashioned orgy these days," I observed, a trifle tartly.

"Do you know," this amazing young woman asked, "that we haven't even given a thought to food?"

"Who needs food?" I permitted my hand a tentative exploration.

"Umm, nice," murmured Eleanor Alice. "I like you when you're randy, Freddy. By five o'clock you ought to be a perfect terror. Promise me you'll be a perfect terror."

"Always provided I don't explode before then."

Eleanor Alice giggled. "And you thought you were going to

have such a terrible time assaulting my virtue. Now do be a lamb and order some lunch for us. By the time we've finished you'll have to be getting back to the office to see your Mr. Julian, and I'll just go on over to the apartment and get ready for you."

Somehow, in an absolute fog, I got through the remainder of that luncheon. Eleanor Alice tucked it away with good appetite, but I barely managed half a dozen forkfuls of what Le Tricorne was palming off on the public as scallopine of veal. My mind, you must understand, was not wholly on the subject of victualing; indeed, it was racing at full speed as I envisioned what lay ahead, delayed only by that fatuous jerk, Don Julian. An All-American Ouled Naïl, by the Lord Harry! At the same time I felt a certain amount of unease at the prospect of matching my somewhat limited talents and abilities against a girl of Eleanor Alice's demonstrated prowess. There was always the haunting possibility that I might fail to meet her standards of performance, a humiliation too ghastly to contemplate.

But what really had me stunned was the fantastic ease and calm with which the whole affair had arranged itself. It was almost frightening. Let me rephrase that. It was frightening.

I mean to say, I had never before encountered a girl who was, sexually speaking, totally amoral, and her frankness had put me off balance.

"Time for you to be going," she announced when I finished my coffee. She gave me another of her electrifying smiles. "You know, I think I'll get into a costume for you; mesh hose and all that. I think you're probably a black mesh hose type, deep down."

"You do that," I husked.

"Okay."

"I'll grab a cab and come as soon as I can," I promised, summoning our check.

"Not *too* soon," protested Eleanor Alice Horvath archly, and I took my departure with cheeks that blushed bright crimson.

XXX

My emotions, as I hastened back to Youth House, were as frothy as something out of a Waring Blender. What normal American lad has not dreamed of happening upon a lascivious wench, even more anxious than himself to pursue the pleasures of the flesh? But to find one! And so far as the marriage vows were concerned, might it not be proper to compare Eleanor Alice to one of those temple prostitutes of old, whose function it was to purify the priests by draining them, so to speak, of their baser desires? I would doubtless be a better husband to Joby, rid of my less attractive urges. (Frothy, you comprehend.)

There was a certain piquancy, too, in the thought that I should be satisfying my lusts courtesy of Davis Carter Powers. The situation had definite overtones of Restoration Comedy, and if I hadn't chickened out on Diana Powers, I vow it were such a farce as would have rejoiced Congreve. Which reminded me that I must make my call to Mrs. Powers. Stopping by a drugstore, I did.

Slipping on my James Mason accent like a well loved smoking jacket, I gave her the word, having first wasted a few dozen of the pear-shaped on the Aunt Jemima type who answered the phone.

"I can't say definitely if I can make it," I told Diana in the underplayed, tense voice of a man calling from a foggy Dublin street corner while I.R.A. lads searched the adjacent public house and Victor McLaglen betrayed me for a ball of malt.

"Just as you please," Mrs. Powers replied coolly.

"But for God's sake, don't be calling me again," I said, watching the Hitchcock-type shadows grow long as they closed in on me. "I'll call you."

"Are you all right?" She asked swiftly, a gratifying note of alarmed solicitude in her voice.

"It's yourself that mustn't worry," I said gruffly, yet with gentleness (I might last another hour, with that damned slug in me chest; Mary Mother, give me strength . . .). And hung up as the house came to its feet with a thunderclap of applause ("Sir Frederick Lazenby's maudlin yet oddly touching Captain 'Himself' O'Rafferty recalled the young Olivier to this reviewer. . . ." —Kerr, *Herald Tribune*. ". . . Lifted a mediocre production occasionally to the heights."—Taubman, *Times*).

Well pleased with myself, I returned then to Youth House.

Bang on the button, Julian showed, high black shoes, white socks and all. He came in and gave me a real Junior Chamber of Commerce handshake ("Hell-*lo* there!") and sat down in the armchair facing my desk.

"First time I've ever been in Youth House," he began. "Gosh, I can't tell you how many years ago it's been since I used to subscribe. Or rather, since my parents used to subscribe for me. Got a whole closetful of old *Youth Outlooks* in my attic right this minute; saving them for my kid when he's old enough to appreciate them. Wonderful, wonderful magazine for young people."

"Always nice to hear that kind of praise," I replied.

"Well, you folks certainly deserve it. But I know how busy you magazine editors are, so I'll get right to the point and tell you that I'm here simply to get a little better acquainted. I try and make a point of getting to know all the people on the various committees and groups I work with because I feel that once you know a man, you can really plan your teamwork, and teamwork is what counts these days."

"That it does," I replied. "Teamwork gets the job done."

"Exactly my theory; teamwork gets the job done every time."

Oh, for God's sake!

Julian crossed one plump little thigh over the other and gazed upon me with immense satisfaction.

"Of course, you fellows are doing all the real work," I said heartily (anything to break the silence). "And never getting the credit for it. But that's the way it goes, I guess."

"That's pretty much the way it goes," Julian laughed gaily. "Yessir, that's about the size of it."

Fellowship, that's what we had. All we needed were fezzes.

"How's it going, anyhow?" I inquired, seeking to keep the interview afloat. Julian's face became instantly solemn and he rutched around in his chair to check the door to my office. Not an enemy spy in sight. His voice was conspiratorial.

"Well, sir, mind you, I haven't even had the chance to tell Judge Brackett yet, but—and this is in the strictest confidence, of course—the fact is that we're on to one of the biggest operations ever uncovered, right here in Washington, D. C. You've probably seen the story in the papers."

"Probably did. Yes, come to think of it, yes, I did."

"Ah." Julian's smile was smugness itself. "Well, you being a journalist yourself, you understand that the papers weren't putting out everything they knew. And there's a lot more they don't know."

"Oh?" (The senses were alert, but the manner was that of Herbert Marshall discovering that the Countess Maritza was actually in the pay of the Kaiser—suave, detached. . . .)

"One hell of a lot. This fellow Tombes, it turns out, is a very important figure in the pornography racket; probably one of the biggest of the West Coast operators. And smart, yessir, smart. Haven't been able to get so much as a single word out of him."

Hosanna! So give three times three and a long locomotive for B. J. Tombes!

"But," Julian went on, dropping his voice even lower, "it also turns out that we—and by we, you understand, I'm talking about all the agencies interested in this situation—well, sir, it develops that we don't need to worry whether Tombes ever talks or not."

"How's that?" But I knew the answer. Oh, how I knew the answer to that one.

"Goddamnedest thing." Julian shook his head in wonderment. "Bright and early this morning, a janitor in a building downtown calls up the police to say there was this guy all trussed up in the crapper with—now get this—a note on his forehead. So they haul this poor son of a bitch down to headquarters in a squad car and spend about an hour unwinding damn' near ten miles of adhesive tape off him. And who does he turn out to be but Tombes's goon, a punk named Salvi with a record as long as your arm."

Oh, idiot Lazenby. *Why?*

"So, anyhow," Julian continued, "it seems this Salvi is so mad at the guy who tied him up he can't wait to unload his story, and, by God, he had quite a story to tell. Apparently Tombes had sold a whole hell of a lot of stuff to a man named Burnley who was running his operation behind a front called the Old Dominion Genealogical Survey in this same building where the cops found him—Salvi, that is. And according to Salvi, this Burnley is probably one of the biggest distributors in the East, judging from the amount of stuff he bought. So anyhow, when Tombes got caught, Salvi had gone to Burnley, see, and tried to nick him for some cash to blow town. So Burnley clobbers Salvi and gets the hell out himself. Although—" Julian paused and shook his head again, "I can't figure out anybody being so stupid as to make sure that Salvi would get turned over to the cops. I mean, if he had simply tied him up for long enough to get away, Burnley ought to have known that Salvi wouldn't talk. Any guy that dumb won't stay loose long, that's for sure."

"Yeah," I agreed in a voice devoid of timbre. "That's for sure. Anybody know where this Burnley might be now?"

"Hard to say. They know he loaded all of his stuff in a station wagon the night he bopped Salvi, but the night man at the building didn't catch the license number. They've got the F.B.I. checking out the prints they found in the office itself, though, so it's just a matter of time."

Just a matter of time.

As long as it took until some sharp-eyed fingerprint expert at the Bureau observed that some of the prints collected from the offices of the Old Dominion Genealogical Researchers exactly matched those appearing on the identification form filled out by Second Lieutenant Frederick W. Lazenby, Army Serial Number 0-430124, Infantry, United States Army Reserve, upon his entry on active duty on 4 November 1942 at Fort George G. Meade, Maryland. They do it by some kind of mathematical formula, so they don't have to know your name. They just send some men around with handcuffs.

Surely even the stupidest lout would have seen the necessity of thoroughly wiping clean all surfaces whereon a fingerprint might have been impressed. But this is not the case. Speaking as the stupidest lout, I can talk with some assurance. I had, true, done a superficial job with my breast pocket handkerchief, and had thought of returning to finish the job once I had achieved the transfer of the Savoury Papers. But by the time I had accomplished the job, fearful every moment of a Salvi freeing himself of his bonds or the determined entry of one of Washington's finest, wild horses could not have induced me to spend another minute in the Gerlacher Building. Humphrey Bogart in his prime might have done it. Not me.

"Well, sir, I've got to be running along," said Don Julian, rising to give me his manly handshake. "Can't tell you how much I've enjoyed getting together for a little chat. I'm looking forward to working with you, believe me."

"That'll be just fine," I mumbled, giving him a death's head grin and a hand that could not have grasped so much as a pencil at that moment. "Glad you could stop by. Topped off my afternoon."

"See you soon," Julian promised, tripping toward the door.

"Yes, indeed," I called after him. He would, too.

XXXI

It was, then, a mood heavy with Gotterdammerungish overtones that enveloped me as I set out for the address on N
Street . . .

My career was rapidly drawing toward a disastrous close, and
with it, in all probability, my marriage. There might be refuge
among the faceless millions in New York, but my profession
would be closed to me, unless I accepted the final degradation
of a job writing photo captions for one of the less reputable girlie
magazines. And what right-thinking man could blame Joby for
refusing to share the bed and board of a notorious pornographer?
Washington was full of right-thinking men, and perhaps she
would find a real and lasting happiness with one of them.

But . . . drink a highball at nightfall, tonight let's all be
gay . . . for tomorrow may bring sorrow, be good fellows while
we may. Maybe those aren't the exact words, but what the hell?
Tonight we live and *gaudeamus igitur*.

I stopped by the Jefferson for a fast belt of bourbon, which
helped lighten the burden of gloom Julian had left with me, and
I took a second by way of insurance. There was the usual table-
ful of staffers from the *Geographic* across the street, refugees from
reality and the great crested grebe, cheerfully damning their
fate over Martinis. A sultry-looking blonde seated alone at a
table across the dimly lighted cocktail lounge gave me a sympathetic smile, but I pretended not to notice; tonight I had other
fish to fry. Finishing my beverage, I continued upon my sinful
progress, carrying myself stiffly erect in the manner of the late
Conrad Veidt, my face set and grim. I was rather hoping to

leave the sultry-looking blonde with the impression of a tragic, remote and mysterious figure, bound upon some gallant, hopeless quest.

The apartment I sought was in one of those tall, narrow, converted town houses. Miss E. Horvath and Miss J. Blanchard, their neat calling cards advised visitors, occupied Apartment 4-D, which put them on the topmost floor, accessible by means of a coffin-sized elevator. I stepped into this contrivance and was hoisted slowly aloft. Midway between the second and third floors the damned thing abruptly stopped, and I nearly burst into high, maniacal laughter at this fitting blow. What further absurdities could the Weird Sisters pile upon my head? I looked for the emergency bell and pushed it at precisely the same instant that the infernal machine gave itself a jerk and resumed its upward course to the clangor of a bell fit to sound the tocsin for a third-class city—Buhlang! Buhlang! Buhlang!

Slowly from above there descended into view the porthole of the third floor elevator door, a mad-eyed face pressed against the glass. There was no place to hide in my self-propelled sarcophagus, nor could I make myself heard over the tintinabulation of that giant gong. I could only grimace and shrug as the face slowly receded from view and disappeared beneath the elevator's doorsill, and then as I arrived at the fourth floor, the bell suddenly ceased. The door slid open and I emerged, my self-confidence severely shaken, to find Apartment 4-D to the right of the elevator shaft. The residents of the fourth floor were, apparently, accustomed to the sound of the emergency alarm but took the view that they were too high up to be of much help in a crisis. I lifted the small brass knocker on 4-D's door and let it fall.

"Door's open; come on in," came the voice of Eleanor Alice Horvath from within. I inhaled deeply and entered. "I'm in the kitchen getting the ice out," she called as I found myself in a tiny foyer. "Make yourself at home."

God knows what I was expecting, but it wasn't what I found.

What I mean to say is that most men, if they think about the problem at all, have formed a fairly well detailed idea of what ought to constitute a proper love-nest. The dimly lighted apartment of my former fantasies with Eleanor Alice had been just such a place, subtly but significantly decorated with a few indiscreet nudes on the walls, filled with the haunting fragrance of some exotic oriental incense, equipped with a bar fully stocked with all the standard aphrodisiacal liqueurs, and furnished throughout with low, deep, incredibly soft furniture.

But this! Out of *Mademoiselle by Better Homes & Gardens,* with an assist from *Woman's Day* and *McCall's.* I can see the titles now: "Little Cash, Lots of Chintz Make a Career Girl Comfy," say, or "Fun with Foam Rubber; Simple Frames and Smart Fabrics Spell Furniture with a Flair," not to mention "Don't Scorn Those Rummage Sales; Somebody's White Elephant May Solve Your Décor Problems."

Over the tiny marble-arched fireplace, the Utrillo street scene, reproduced right down to the brush strokes. Over the sofa, the Van Goghs, reproduced by the same miraculous modern methods, "so real your friends will say they *must* be originals." The sofa itself, black corduroy catafalque for a robot, was flanked by two end tables cunningly contrived of squares of stained and waxed plywood resting on upended concrete blocks painted black. At one end of the long, narrow room, between two tall chintz-curtained windows, stood a small record player; at the other end, an early 1921 rolling tea table, daringly painted Chinese red and bearing an array of bottles and glasses, the single note of debauchery. Over all, the warm, homely glow from the two converted coal-oil lamps on the end tables, their shades made up of parchment paper replicas of Our Nation's Historic Documents, including the Declaration of Independence.

More than a little bemused, nay, baffled, I had started to inspect the contents of the bookshelves—need I note that they were simple pine boards supported by stacked and unpainted bricks? —when Eleanor Alice entered from the kitchen, bearing a hammered aluminum ice bucket and adding immeasurably to the feeling of unreality which had begun to steal over me on little cats' feet.

She had kept to her threat, and the spectacle was one to stagger the imagination. She was wearing a black negligee of a transparency I had hitherto assumed to exist only in the more costly grades of women's hosiery, but artfully gathered here and there to conceal and to emphasize. On her feet, spike-heeled shoes richly sprinkled with sparkling rhinestones. On her wrist, the charm bracelet.

The effect was much as if Miss Marlene Dietrich, garbed for her celebrated role in *The Blue Angel*, had strolled into the living room of, say, the Kappa Alpha Theta House at State and asked for a stiff brandy.

Eleanor Alice advanced sinuously across the room and put the ice bucket down on the tea cart. Turning, she leaned against this object and grinned at me brazenly—Lilith incarnate among the White Elephants; Jezebel of Sunnybrook Farm.

"You like?" she asked, her voice husky in a fashion I had not heard before. I nodded, momentarily unable to speak with anything remotely resembling the human voice. "Good," she purred. "Do you want to kiss me?"

"Merry vutch," I croaked hoarsely. She held out her arms and I shambled toward her, drugged by the sight of her billowing femininity. She came into my embrace like the Great Boston Molasses Flood engulfing a fireplug, pressing herself hard against me, and wow! When she kissed, she kissed all over, and I found myself thinking, not without a degree of alarm, that if she could put this much of herself into a kiss, what might follow in later and more complex activities would be well-nigh incredible, like the three-minute mile. After some moments, during which my knees were restrained from buckling only by the pressure of her thighs, she drew her mouth away. "Nice?" she murmured. "Now mix us a drink, please." And stepped away from me.

I mixed us each a veritable bomb of a highball. Unable to manage the little silver jigger, I simply held the bottle over the glasses and sloshed, and even that took every ounce of muscular control at my command. When I turned from the tea cart, Eleanor Alice was at the far end of the room, bending over the record player, from which presently emanated the soft, insistent throbbing of a small orchestral ensemble playing J. S. Bach for

drinking espresso by. She came away from the record player and
accepted her drink, taking a grave sip from its potentially lethal
depths. The transparency of her attire became even more astonishing, and I fear my eyeballs may have bulged.

"You're looking shocked again," she said softly. "Now don't
tell me you've never seen a girl in a negligee before."

"Very few like you," I said sincerely.

"It's nice, isn't it?" she agreed happily. "I guess that's why I'm
an exhibitionist along with everything else. Do you mind terribly?"

"I'm all for it," I babbled. "I mean, after all, look at the ancient
Greeks. The Greeks knew how to appreciate the body. They
worshiped it, as a matter of fact. And the Romans—"

"The Romans were sexier," Eleanor Alice noted, disclosing
a facet of her education which might have come as a blow to the
classical languages faculty of her college. Goucher, I think it was.
"Just read Petronius Arbiter for instance. You *have* read Petronius
Arbiter, haven't you?"

"Not in the original, of course," I replied, feeling the quality
of unreality growing stronger apace. I took a long swallow of my
drink, and then another, longer one as Eleanor Alice draped herself along the sofa and leaned back against the black cushions
Inexplicably, my glass was empty and I walked to the tea cart
and refilled it. I now observed on the wall directly above this
cabinet maker's whimsey a small picture which had escaped my
notice before. It was, so help me, the *Youth Outlook Creed*
("Suitable for framing, sent to you with your renewal"), written
God knows how many years ago by Dr. Walter Van Meter Mountain in an effort to codify the ideals which should serve to inspire
the young readers of his magazine.

> "I will keep the faith of my fathers,
>   for their strength is my country's strength,
> I will keep myself firm for the right,
>   for the right is our debt to our God,
> I will keep myself pure in body and mind,
>   for without purity there can be no future,

I will hold high the torch of learning,
for without learning there can be no liberty.
These things I will do for my God, my Country,
   and my parents.
                    —Walter Van Meter Mountain, 1925

Moody and Sankey couldn't have phrased it better, but it was hardly the sort of thing calculated to inspire lust. I returned, even more bemused, to the vicinity of the sofa.

"Or look at Pompeii," Eleanor Alice resumed. "Davis gave me the most marvelous book of illustrations of those paintings they won't let the tourists see. You wouldn't believe some of the things they did. I keep it in the bedroom, in the bottom of my bureau, along with some other things. I'd keep it out here, but—" She shrugged her magnificent shoulders. "That's why this place looks like a girls' dormitory—we have to think about the cleaning woman." She extended her glass and giggled. "Davis always says he feels like he's seducing the Bobbsey Twins."

I poured her another bomb, feeling somewhat relieved to have learned the reason for the apartment's unlikely décor. In the love-nests of fiction and my dreams, the problem of what to do about the cleaning woman never arises—these petty details are always seen to by a superbly discreet Filipino houseboy as played by Keye Luke.

Then too, there was a certain piquant depravity in the concept of this innocent snuggery as a passion pit, and this doubtless had some sort of obscure appeal for Davis Carter Powers. I confess, however, that it left me unmoved.

"Davis keeps a dressing gown in the bedroom," Eleanor Alice said calmly when I brought her drink to her. "You could slip into it and relax, if you want to. Joannie won't mind."

"What?" I yelped.

"Joannie," murmured this smoldering volcano of sex, her eyes hazily amused as she looked up at me from her recumbent position. "She had some shopping to do downtown, but she shouldn't be too much longer."

"You mean—" I stopped, aghast at her implication.

"Really, Freddy," she said with just the faintest note of asperity in her voice. "I thought you said you wanted to party. Well, you can't party with just two people, now can you?"

I realized, with a heart that had turned to stone, that my Miss Horvath contemplated nothing less than a small orgy *intime*, and that I should be expected to conduct my forthcoming amorous adventures in the presence of Miss Blanchard and, for that matter, with her. It was an eventuality for which I was utterly unprepared, for unlike Davis Carter Powers, whose participation was allegedly purely visual and passive, I was clearly slated to take an active part in the evening's riot. I sat down heavily in one of the armchairs adjacent to the sofa, and imbibed another enormous quantity of my drink.

To say that the situation had changed drastically would be to give no hint of the mental turmoil which now assailed the embattled brain. For while I had rationalized away the moral objections to a romp between the sheets with Eleanor Alice, I was unable to repeat the performance when it came to a romp between the sheets with Eleanor Alice *and* Miss Blanchard. A line, I felt, had to be drawn somewhere.

I observed that my second drink was far gone, and moved to replenish my glass, adding no dilutent to diminish the full-bodied flavor.

"And then, a little later on, there'll be Davis," Eleanor Alice said casually when I regained my armchair. Happily, I was fully seated when she released this information.

"Davis!" I bleated. "You mean Davis Carter Powers?"

"Honestly, Freddy!" Had she not been sprawled at ease on the sofa, Eleanor Alice would have stamped her rhinestoned foot. "After all, he does pay the rent. And he's never any trouble; I mean, about wanting to butt in or anything. Nobody else has ever made a fuss about Davis being here. Sometimes he brings champagne."

Now this was absolutely beyond the pale. I might have succeeded in readjusting my thinking to accept the idea of Miss Blanchard as a fellow participant in the occasion, but that my debauchery should provide an evening's entertainment for Davis

Carter Powers was unthinkable. And while Davis might welcome me with open arms into his clandestine society of freethinkers, I did not care to have him privy to my appearance in circumstances best described as curious. A slow, knowing wink from Powers in the corridors of Youth House would be too grisly to be suffered.

The coffee table before the sofa—a slab of slate supported by a spidery wrought-iron frame—was too low for another self-immolation, even had I been in position to attempt it.

And besides—let the whole truth be told—I did not want to sabotage the whole business. Given time, thought, and another luncheon, I might be able to explain some of my bourgeois prejudices to Eleanor Alice, in which case I might yet be able to enjoy her sumptuous charms under conditions more nearly normal. At the same time, the thought struck me that normal sexual relations had about as much appeal for Eleanor Alice as a bowl of cold mashed potatoes. At any moment now, she might produce a bull whip.

But hold! A bull whip—there was the germ of an idea there.

As these reflections occupied my mind, my physical self was occupied with doing severe damage to my third block-buster. This, on top of the firm foundation already laid down, brought about one of those brief periods of dazzling lucidity during which to think is to act. My course suddenly lay clear before me: If Eleanor Alice admired the Romans for their promiscuity, then it behooved me to be Byzantine.

"Damn," I said, feigning irritation. "I wish I'd known what sort of a party you had in mind. I could have come prepared."

"Prepared?" Eleanor Alice inquired, then gave me a knowing smile. "But darling, I've got everything we'll need right here."

"Not that sort of thing," I told her, chuckling evilly. "I mean, if I'd known, I'd have brought along some rope." (Something B. J. Tombes had mentioned had suddenly and happily surged upward from the bottom of memory's mires.) I leered at her with what I hoped was an expression of unadulterated lubricity and limitless depravity. "You see, I'm a bondage man myself."

"Oh?" Eleanor Alice took a deep gulp of her drink. I moved

swiftly to refill it, topping off my own glass at the same time. The record player had switched from J. S. Bach to something in the Afro-Cuban manner and the room was boom-a-laying with the sound of throbbing drums. "I had no idea," she said as I handed her her glass, and there was no mistaking the fact that the disclosure of this aspect of my character had given her pause. "I'm not sure Joannie would go along with that sort of thing . . ."

"I'm sure she's a girl with imagination," I replied sunnily. "I don't suppose you'd happen to have any rope around the apartment? Or a good, heavy twine would do almost as well. . . ." Eleanor Alice shook her head. Her expression was betraying the first dim traces of alarm. "Or tire chains," I went on, affecting not to notice the effect of my remarks, the last of which produced a definite nervous start, as well it might. I glanced at my watch. It would be fatal if Miss Blanchard were to turn up within the next few minutes. For all I knew, she might be a latent bondage girl, God help us all.

"Listen," I said hastily, "before we start partying, why don't I grab a cab and find a hardware store still open somewhere where I can pick up a few things. Hell, they always stock chain and clothes line. We can have a real ball." I shot from my chair eagerly.

Eleanor Alice stared up at me, a disturbed glaze clouding her eyes. "We-ll," she said hesitantly, "if you really think . . ."

"A real ball," I reassured her, edging toward the chair upon which lay my hat and topcoat.

"Freddy?" This faintly. "Couldn't we just—just party?"

"That's the whole idea," I replied enthusiastically, seizing my coat and hat. "Now you just relax and mix yourself another noggin while I run out and round up what we need."

I slipped quietly out of the door. Eleanor Alice was sitting upright on the sofa now, staring fixedly at the opposite wall. Just as the door closed, I caught a glimpse of her raising her glass to her lips and draining it.

The casket-shaped elevator bore me slowly earthward, and the snickerty-snacking of its inefficient machinery seemed to mutter over and over as we descended "cowardly-cowardly-cowardly-

Lazenby-cowardly." "Chicken-chicken-chicken," it snapped as it halted at the first floor and the door clacked open. I fled. As elevators go, this one might properly have been called Truthful Otis.

I fled, but with what mixed emotions, all compound of craven fear and offended middle-class morality and regret. For of course I had no intention of returning. I would find a telephone somewhere and call back to the apartment, saying that I had come all over faint or had been arrested for purse-snatching or walked under a bus. Some plausible excuse would present itself. As to how I could nerve myself to face Eleanor Alice again after this evening's debacle—that problem would have to be resolved when it arose.

With luck, I thought, with such a stroke of luck as only the gods might deliver, she might pass out and never be the wiser. Those drinks I had fed her had been of a potency to fell a Russian field marshal in midtoast.

What a hell of a way to conclude an assignation.

XXXII

If I had gone to Eleanor Alice in the twilight of the gods, I came away in the dark night of the soul.

The fresh air of N Street did nothing to revivify the wretched shell of a man who had crept away, beetlelike, from his rendezvous with Venus. God alone knew how I could face Eleanor Alice again; I knowing what I knew about her, she knowing the unsuspected depths of depravity to which I was prepared to descend, as attested by my own lips. Yet the memory of that magnificent body was a well-nigh unendurable goad as I walked blindly toward Connecticut Avenue. Not for me now were such comfortable thoughts as the preservation of my marriage from the ineradicable stain of adultery, of the true faith I bore for my Jobiana, and the moral strength which had enabled me to overcome my baser instincts. These would come later when I sought to justify my conduct to myself. But right now my only thought was that I had just loused up the juciest opportunity ever to come my way.

The exercise of walking served to circulate through my system the formidable quantity of bourbon I had taken on earlier and this, swiftly concentrating its effect on the higher brain centers, in turn dimmed the lucidity which had brought me to this pass. I toyed with the idea of returning to Apartment 4-D and smothering my Eleanor Alice with burning kisses and passionate entreaty. I would tell her that my suggested adaptions from the Gothic were but the workings of a mind unhinged by the sight of her ravishing flesh; that she, Miss Blanchard and I would make such revel as might cause the Olympians to flush with envy.

Perhaps Davis Carter Powers wouldn't show up after all. It might still be managed.

Too late, too late, sighed the sad spring breeze that carried a wisp of old, tired sandwich wrapping rustling down the empty tree-lined street.

Fool, fool, murmured the branches overhead.

You need a drink, blinked a neon sign over a bar at the intersection of N and Connecticut. In the light of the sign, I looked at my watch. Not quite seven o'clock. I had spent perhaps an hour in Apartment 4-D; the night was yet young, there was yet hope.

> *"Missed my chance,*
> *Not a backward glance,*
> *And you walked out of my life,"*

sobbed the juke box from a far corner of the bar as I entered and settled myself into the first empty booth I came upon. I had never happened to patronize this establishment before and, God willing, I never will again. Long and narrow it was, with indirect lighting that was intended to produce a warm and cheerful glow but succeeded only in giving all present the appearance of persons in the grip of some raging fever. The air-conditioning advertised boldly on the door was not yet in operation, and the atmosphere was foggy with the commingled bouquets of stale tobacco, staler beer and ancient whisky stains, with powerful overtones of some kind of pine-scented disinfectant.

Seated at the bar were Burke and Hare, Jack the Ripper, Dr. Crippen and Lizzie Borden, moodily sipping beer and light wines, which are the only beverages the District's hate-inspired laws permit to be served to patrons not seated at tables. Seated at a table, you can get drunk as a lord in Washington on any potion you may select. You can get drunk as a lord seated at a bar, for that matter, provided you have an infinite capacity for beer and light wines. Logic has no place in the governance of the Federal City, whose affairs are directed by the Congress, Heaven help it. The city, that is.

"Yeah?" queried a slattern in the employ of the management who had torn herself away from an exchange of sallies with the Ripper to attend my wants.

"Double bourbon."

"Bringya two singles don' serve no doubles," she intoned. There were no reductions for bulk orders where Stavros Agranopolous, the licensee, was concerned, I gathered.

The two singles, served in those maddening, thick-walled little glasses which appear to hold a pint and actually contain about a third of an ounce, were duly set before me. I drained them off one at a time and looked for a public telephone, even as I signaled for a repeat order. At the back of the room, adjacent to a door cleverly labeled "Bucks," hung a wall-type pay phone. I made my way thence, inserted a dime, and recalled that I did not know Eleanor Alice's number. A battered Metropolitan Directory depended from a chain attached to the bottom of the instrument, and I spent some minutes fumbling through its crumpled pages searching for Horvath, Miss E. A., or Blanchard, Miss J. without success. Had it not been for my somewhat fuddled state, I should have realized that the phone in their little home-from-home would be unlisted. I cursed myself for not having taken the elementary precaution of securing the number from the phone in the apartment. It had stood on a small table just beside that record player.

I returned to my booth and two fresh tots of bourbon. Perhaps the hand of destiny was in this, I reflected morosely; it was never intended that I should return to Eleanor Alice. Were I to try, a cornice would topple inexplicably, a taxi swerve out of control. . . .

From the booth behind mine, where two couples were seated, came a raucous hoot of female glee, followed by a masculine snigger. "Honus to Gawd, Leon, you are the freshus man I ever." "C'mawn, Glorya, ya know ya liked it." "For Gawd's sakes, Leon, sumbuddy's gunna *see* you."

To listen to this sordid badinage while only a block or two away sweet Eleanor Alice. . . . I found myself staring, unseeing, at the reflected image of Lizzie Borden, the frowzy, full-buttocked blonde who was the sole female patron at the bar, systematically destroying the remnants of what might once have been a fairly fine figure by a single-minded dedication to tap beer.

She must have, in turn, observed the reflection of my steady stare in the grimy mirror behind the bar, and mistaken its empty intensity for invitation. She swung around on her bar stool, which screamed piteously and thus brought me out of my dismal revery. To my horror, she slipped down from the stool and advanced, a trifle unsteadily, toward my table.

"Hiyah, honey," she said amiably as she swung herself onto the bench opposite mine. "Ya look lonesome." She leaned her large and all-too-obviously unbrassiered bosom upon the table, her chin upon her hands, and gazed at me with eyes full of beery concern.

"Oh, I wouldn't say that," I replied hastily, prepared to flee. But my waitress blocked my escape, materializing like a witch.

"What'll ya have, hon?" she asked the blonde. "The usual?"

"Gennulmun hasn' offered buy me a drink yet," the blonde said archly.

"Well for Chrissakes," snorted the waitress, outraged.

"By all means bring the lady whatever she wants," I said wearily. The waitress snorted again and returned to the bar.

"Ya know, you're a swee' guy," the blonde confided. "An' swee' guys got no business bein' lonesome, ya know what I mean?"

"Well now, that's nice of you to say," I mumbled, starting to ease out of the booth.

"Here y'are, hon," said the waitress, who had been moving with the speed of light, blast her soul. She placed a long, dark, evil-looking drink in front of the blonde and two more single bourbons before me. "Chocolate coke and a rum, like you always have," she added. I fought down a wave of nausea.

"You'd better bring me a check," I said, giving my witch a fetching smile, which she rewarded by a sneer as she turned on her heel and left. The blonde took a hearty swig of her hell brew and giggled happily.

"I get so goddam tired of beer," she told me. "You know what I mean. Makes me perspire." She unbuttoned the top two buttons of her dress to reveal a cleavage capable of engulfing a man.

Again this forward lass misinterpreted the startled gaze I had given the natural phenomenon thus disclosed. She unbuttoned the third button. "How's about you pick up a bottle and we go on up to my apar'mun," she suggested with a winsome wink. "Mebbe have a li'l fun, you know what I mean?" She winked again in a manner calculated to bring me panting in her wake.

God knows what might have followed save total moral collapse —for my mood was so richly dark that I might well have cast one last defy at Fate with a wallow among those mountains and valleys of blowsy flesh—when Dr. Crippen loomed suddenly over us, breathing heavily. He was, I noted with alarm, crocked to the ears.

"You getta hell outta here," he advised the blonde brusquely.

"Aw, fuh Chrissakes, Harry," she protested.

"Stannup, you sunnabitch," Harry said to me, ignoring the blonde, who had started to water at the eyes. "Stannup, goddamit! Knock ya sunnabitchin' teeth out, try'nd lay my date."

"Now take it easy, pal," I said, keeping firmly seated. "You got this whole thing wrong."

"Honus to Jeezus, Harry," wailed the blonde, fumbling ineffectually with her buttons. "Tha's the God's own truth."

"Stannup, goddamit!" roared Harry in a voice to shatter glass. "Try'na lay my goddam date, wouldja!" Drawing his arm back, he delivered himself of a punch which would doubtless have fractured my skull had it landed as intended, but it did not. Instead, it clobbered the blonde, who had started to rise and whose fluffy coiffeur thus came directly onto a collision course with Harry's fist. The hair-do saved her skull. She bounced back onto the bench again, cracked it loose from its moorings and crashed with it to the floor beneath the booth, screeching bloody murder. The booth adjacent exploded into action as the girls added their cries to the blonde's and the gentlemen, with the madcap Leon in the van, burst forth to protect and defend Womanhood, uttering cries of rage. Harry turned to defend himself against this flanking attack even as the barman, an agile and muscular fellow apparently not unaccustomed to contretemps of this nature, hurtled his counter, brandishing a policeman's baton and backed by the combined forces of Burke, Hare and Jack the Ripper. A beer bottle, trailing foam like the tail of a guided missile, hurtled past my head to shatter the round mirror over my booth.

Other tables farther down the long room swiftly began dispatching reinforcements and I seized the occasion to slip from my booth beneath the straining figures of Burke and Hare, who had traitorously switched allegiance in midbattle and were now endeavoring to restrain the barman while Harry hit him in the stomach. Moving at a fast crouch, like Groucho Marx on mischief bent, I made for the door.

I was just about half a block distant when I heard the mounting shriek of sirens as the officers of the law approached to quell the riot, clearly audible and rapidly mounting in decibels as its participants warmed to their work. I hailed a passing cab and gave the driver my address. As we drew away from the theater of war, I remembered that I had neglected to pay the bill, and the thought briefly rejoiced me. The loss would probably go unnoticed in the general havoc, unfortunately.

What a mockery I had made of this day. To end thus, involved in the most squalid sort of barroom brawl.

There remained yet a few dregs to be drained from my bitter cup. Two great, moist, dark eyes met mine when I admitted myself to the house, luminous with reproach. I had forgotten all about feeding Rafe. How low, I wondered, how low can a man sink? I felt pretty sure I knew the answer.

I dished out an enormous supper for my faithful Argus, but this was no sop to a conscience swiftly assuming the weight of Pelion piled upon Ossa. The noble dog, quick to catch my mood, nibbled his repast without enthusiasm, gave me a despairing glance and shambled heavily off to collapse into his favorite corner. He sighed gustily and went to sleep, leaving me alone with my thoughts.

Sleep for me would be a long time knitting up the ravelled sleave this night. The debacle in the bar had sobered me to a certain extent, but sobriety was not, perhaps, the best solution. I poured myself a stiff one and took it into my study. There I turned on the radio and tuned it to one of the local good music stations, as the trade terms them.

Suddenly, more than anything else in the world, I wanted to hear Joby's voice, to reassure me that I was, for the moment at least, escaped from my nightmare world. I reached for the phone and employed the direct dialing system to call the home of the friends with whom Joby was spending the night. After some minutes a voice, unfamiliar in timbre, answered.

"Is this the Gossage residence?" I asked.

"That's right."

"Well, could you call Mrs. Lazenby to the phone please?"

"Mrs. Lazenby?"

"Mrs. Frederick Lazenby. She's a house guest."

"They're all out for the evening. I'm the sitter. You want to leave a message, I could write it down for when they come in?"

"No, that's all right. Just tell Mrs. Lazenby that Mr. Lazenby called. Nothing important. Just wanted to say hello."

"Tell Mrs. Lazenby Mr. Lazenby called, nothing important, he just wanted to say hello, is that right?"

"Thank you very much."

"No trouble at all."

Hell!

WGMS was pouring its heart out in a spate of Brahms. Rafe whimpered in his sleep and scuffled his absurd paws as he dreamed happily of slow rabbits. I arose and refilled my glass, a gaunt, tortured figure, wrapped in melancholy, and weaving ever so slightly. Brahms gave way to a commercial, and the commercial to the eleven o'clock news of the international and local scenes. The world was going to hell in a bucket, and a twelve-year-old boy somewhere in Texas had taken a shotgun to all eight of his little brothers and sisters, scoring a possible. "And finally in the local spotlight," the announcer said, "police have spread a city-wide dragnet for George Burnley, key figure in the current sensational vice probe which has shaken Washington with its disclosures. Detectives told reporters today they have reason to think the wanted man is still somewhere in the city, but they declined to give reasons for their belief. In sports, local baseball fans received some slight encouragement in their hopes that the coming season will show—"

I switched the thing off and sat staring at the wall.

> *"Missed my chance,*
> *Not a backward glance,*
> *And you walked out of my life,"*

crooned memory's juke-box softly, as Eleanor Alice's eyes narrowed lasciviously and her arms came up.

> *"How I prayed*
> *I'd make the grade,*
> *But you walked out of my life . . ."*

And so from verse to bed.

XXXIII

I awoke like a ruined cathedral in whose soaring, bat-hung towers great gales have set the mighty bells to bonging out such a peal of sounding bronze as to split the skies with their dissonance.

My God, what a hangover.

To complete this living death, I had failed to make it to bed and had, instead, slept fully clothed in my armchair. The lights glowed dimly in the full daylight against which, one at a time, I tried out the oysters which were doing temporary duty as my eyes. The effect was like catching the full impact of an atomic blast, and I was obliged to sprawl quite still for several seconds after each attempt. At some time during the night I had apparently consumed large quantities of asphalt, traces of which remained lodged in the teeth. It had turned to lead in the stomach, in surly defiance of the laws of chemistry, yet even as I considered this unlikely development it turned to liquid soap and began to foam turgidly. I just managed to make it to the bathroom.

Afterward I brewed myself a giant's tankard of Alka-Seltzer, but in my extremity even this sovereign specific could accomplish little, especially after I had unwittingly caught a glimpse of myself in the bathroom mirror.

It would have been simple to have called the office and told them I'd come down with the Bulgarian crud and was confined to my bed. Normally, my roseate health helps to keep the group insurance rates for Youth House well down, and I am entitled to several years of sick leave. But the Lazenby conscience, submerged as it was beneath liquid soap and total recall, was ticking over smoothly, like the generators in a sunken submarine after the last surviving crewman had tapped out his final message against the dripping hull. I had to get down to the office. We Lazenbys knew how to play the game.

I fed Rafe, and had to withdraw to the bathroom again. Even the zestiest, tastiest, vitamin-rich horsemeat ever packed for fun-loving dogs has an aroma and appearance not warranted to dispel the screaming meemies from the physically delicate. The consequence of this was to make me feel like a bass drum. Had I tapped the tum at that moment, I would have resounded like the percussion section of the New York Philharmonic under the direction of Leonard Bernstein.

The hangover, medical authority tells us, is generally the result of that dehydration of the body fluids brought about by the effects of alcohol upon the digestive system. And it is widely received that alcohol is a depressant. The inhalation of pure oxygen has been suggested as the most efficacious remedy, but it is your rare average family which keeps a tank of pure oxygen about the premises for Daddy's mornings-after. Folk medicine offers various alternatives, ranging from a tablespoonful of honey, to replace sugars lost through alcohol's work on the bodily chemistry, to the hair-of-the-dog. None work. Or at least, not for me they don't work. Emptied as I now was, I was consumed by a monstrous thirst, and this I proceeded to quench in part by another tankard of Alka-Seltzer, coolly ignoring the manufacturer's dosage recommendations and slipping four tablets into the water. Belching like an armored cruiser bombarding a coastal fortification, I attempted further temporary repairs (only a dockyard could make me fit for sea again) by subjecting the wreckage to a cold shower, the sole effect of which was to make me turn blue.

Somehow I managed to get dressed and then like God's own fool, I determined to eat something. That was it; eat something. Preferably bland and soothing to the tortured interior. A soft-boiled egg, say.

Securing an egg from its rack on the inside of the refrigerator door, I placed it in a small saucepan of water and set it to boiling. Then I made myself a triple-strength cup of instant coffee, by which time I'd forgotten the precise moment at which I'd set the egg. Breakfast, then, consisted of a cup of black coffee thick enough to support light armored vehicles moving at speed, and a hard-boiled egg which I rendered only just palatable by a couple of dashes of soy sauce, which I mistook for Worcestershire—not that it made much difference. Before I had tasted the final spoonful of this rubbery delicacy, I knew that my selection had been unwise. The egg simply turned to stone and joined the asphalt with a thud.

Alternately rumbling and gurgling, swept by massive waves of cold, nausea and fever, I made my way to Youth House by means of a cab whose keen-eyed driver had espied the feeble gesture from the glassy-eyed figure on the sidewalk before my house. I had thought of asking By Stephens for a lift uptown, but By was inclined to be heartily cheerful o' mornings, and this I was not prepared to endure.

Youth House that morning had a certain tragic poignancy for me. If I have, in the course of this narrative, seemed from time to time to take a wry view of my employers, it must not be mistaken for contempt. You may tramp the editorial rooms of magazines the world over and find none more generous, none more courageous, none more reputable than *Youth Outlook*. Admittedly, many of its practices seem to derive from the best thinking of the tenth century, but this is a small price to pay for the personal satisfaction to be derived from the knowledge that one is, in the best and truest sense of the word, informing and shaping the minds of the best part of the country's youngsters. Of office politics there was a minimum; of favoritism, none. Dr. Walter Van Meter Mountain has been widely caricatured as a stuffed shirt and the epitome of that crass American culture so repugnant to the pseudo-intellectuals, but when the late Senator McCarthy was at the apex of his curious career, *Youth Outlook* carried an editorial series which makes me proud to this day for its detached, impartial, utterly fair damnation of the philosophy that guided the man. Nor did the Senator from Wisconsin, or any of his adherents, dare to cry "Communist," lest the benumbed nation be shaken from its mesmerized acceptance of this legislator and burst into hoots of laughter.

Granted that we cannot be as waspish as *Time* (and as often wrong), and that our tone is not designed to emulate the brain books like *Harper's* and the *Atlantic*, we manage to put out a magazine that hits the anthologies with equal regularity.

It is not too much to say that *Youth Outlook* is an institution. That I had stumbled upon a couple of moral termites in its sturdy timbers signified nothing, for gnaw as they would, they could not affect the basic integrity of the structure. Davis Carter Powers had no say in matters editorial, and the fantastical tastes of Eleanor Alice Horvath and her playmate, Miss Blanchard, could in no manner affect the content of the magazine.

All this, I reflected as I made my way into Youth House, I was about to lose. It was no small thing to be able to stride, as one in his own home, across this vast reception hall, beneath the vast portrait of Dr. Mountain attired in the academic robes which signified his status as a philosopher, *honoris causa*, of Oxford University, past the scores of framed citations that included, among other honors, two Pulitzers won by the Senior Ass when he was, like myself, a lowly junior associate. Nor was it a small thing to know that, armed with no more than a passport and a *Youth Outlook* identity card, I could be sure of a friendly reception anywhere in the world, with the possible exception of the Chinese mainland. The tale is told of a *Youth Outlook* writer finding a complete file of *Youth Outlook* among the personal effects of the Paramount Phoum of the 'Ngruba, a little known tribe in the far western region of Nigeria. The Shah of Persia is a regular subscriber, on behalf of his children, as is the Maharajah of Johcundahar.

From this friendly and imposing place I would shortly be cast out, a moral pariah. I arrived in my office awash in self-pity and down by the head.

Eleanor Alice was, thank God, nowhere to be seen, and shortly after I had eased gingerly into my chair, not wishing to send the stone in my stomach crashing against my spine, a Miss Nordlinger, from the stenographic pool, appeared at my desk. Hers, she told me, was the unhappy duty of advising me that Miss Horvath would not be at work today, having been detained at her home by a migraine. I received this intelligence with murmurs of sympathy and a great lightening of the soul. There was, after all, some balm in Gilead. My egg brought me back to reality, and I barely managed to suppress such an exhalation as would have blasted Miss Nordlinger through the wall had it gotten launched a moment sooner. The child left blithely, unaware of her narrow escape.

My telephone rang. I picked the instrument from its cradle and held its incredible weight against my ear. Over the roar of the surf pounding inside my head, I heard the voice of Samuel K. Nurney's private secretary, Mrs. Oradean Nonnenmaker. She sounded worried.

" I just can't tell you what an imposition you're probably going to think this is," she babbled, "and if there were any other way out I'm sure Mr. Nurney wouldn't have dreamed of putting you to so much trouble at such short notice." My shirt collar began to test its strength against my neck muscles.

"If there's anything I can do, you just name it," I said, mustering up from some hitherto unrealized reserve a heartiness that would have done credit to a rising young chiropracter just nominated to Kiwanis.

"Well, bless your heart, Mr. Lazenby," cooed Oradean. "I wonder if you could drop by the office here for just a second. I can explain it so much better in person than over the phone."

"Be right there," I replied briskly. Heaving myself to my feet, I waited for several seconds until the room stopped swaying. Then I set out in the direction of the office of the Senior Ass, placing each foot gently before me and settling the weight slowly to avoid needless shock. In due course I reached Nurney's anteroom. Oradean had stepped out momentarily, and as I sat waiting I was once more reminded of the career that might have been mine if Dumbo Savoury had dropped dead before setting foot in my house. Ranged along the wall were mementos of highlights in Samuel K. Nurney's pursuit of journalism; SKN shaking hands with Admiral Byrd; SKN receiving the Legion of Merit from Franklin D. Roosevelt; SKN wearing the Order of the British Empire (". . . for his outstanding contributions to the cause of Anglo-American understanding . . ."), with the then British Ambassador grinning toothily at the camera. Here were the honorary degrees, some in Latin, others in English, from the Universities of Pennsylvania, Vanderbilt, North Carolina and Bob Jones; the membership certificates in the Royal Geographical Society, the Pilgrim Society, Sigma Delta Chi, and various other professional and learned societies. With them hung the elaborately illustrated testimonials tendered by the Board of Directors on the occasion of various anniversaries and a letter from Dwight D. Eisenhower, thanking our boy for his selfless efforts as a member of the United States delegation to the Geneva Conference on Freedom of the Press.

What was there ahead for me? Writing double-entendre captions for a girlie magazine . . . "Bettye LaFlamme says she's fit to bust if Hollywood won't give her career a leg up." . . . Or turning out books for the Priapic Press: "MADCAP MODELS, a novel which tells the real TRUTH about what goes on in New York's studios, sent to you in a plain brown wrapper."

Great!

What ever happened to Fred Lazenby?

"I'm so sorry to keep you waiting," chirped Oradean, tripping in. And then, as her eyes took in the total picture: "Are you feeling all right?"

"Never better," I laughed, and wanted to keep right on laughing. Steady, lad; none of that now, not in front of the men. I choked back my manic glee and stared with such concentration at Mrs. Nonnenmaker that I felt my eyes beginning to cross.

"Well now, I'll tell you what this is all about," she began, settling herself for a nice long chat. "SKN has had to make a hurry-up trip out to Chicago; there's been some trouble about the July plates, I think, but anyhow it simply wouldn't wait, so he's gone to Chicago and what it amounts to is he was scheduled—in fact he's had it on his calendar since last fall, October I think it was when they wrote—to give this speech before this big meeting of librarians, you know the ones I mean, they always hold their annual convention here, and well, the speech is due today, and last night when he called me at home—the whole Chicago thing came up so suddenly he had to call me away from television—why he asked me to ask you to stand in for him, although there's really nothing to it because SKN has the speech all written and ready to go and all you actually have to do is read it. They're meeting at the Mayflower, and you're supposed to be there no later than two or two-fifteen at the latest."

Had this earnest and good-hearted woman taken dead aim and hurled a grenade at my head she could not have wrought more devastation. It took a few seconds for the full horror of it to be absorbed as I filtered the sense of her message from the spring torrent of her verbiage. By that time, she had shoved a Manila envelope across the desk toward me. Scrawled in red crayon across the front of the envelope was the single word, "Librarians." A formal invitation on stiff parchment paper was paper-clipped to the flap, and this Mrs. Nonnenmaker seized and examined with a small exclamation of impatience.

"That man! Really! He didn't say a blessed thing about attending the opening luncheon. I guess you'd better figure on getting on over to the Mayflower by noon then, Mr. Lazenby. You'll be at the head table, of course. And I'm just absolutely sure you're going to do a wonderful job."

That sanity survived this latest blow is awesome testimony to the mind's resilience, but it was the empty husk of Frederick W. Lazenby that groped its blind way back to his office and sagged into his chair, eyes dead, breathing shallow and just this side of Cheyne-Stokes. I lit my first cigarette of the morning, careless of the fact that past experience had indicated that, in my case, the first cigarette during a hangover usually produced the sort of coughing fit that leads spectators to pause and wait fearfully for bits of backbone to appear amid the flying spray. I inhaled deeply and prepared to meet my Maker with an adenoidal roar. Nothing happened. I took a second, deeper puff. *Then* it happened.

Surprisingly, although the noise and vibration threatened to split the skull, my head felt considerably clearer after things quieted down, an experience I understand is shared by snuff-takers. The stomach was still locked in dubious battle about the flinty remnants of my egg, but the brain now felt capable of mild exertion. I dared not subject it yet to an examination of the ordeal that lay ahead, lest the good be undone, and for this reason I did not trouble to inspect the contents of Samuel K. Nurney's prepared text. Knowing SKN, I felt certain the speech was bound to be sound, neatly organized and logical, and pleasantly brief and to the point. Instead, I elected to make slow but steady progress toward a complete recovery, and thus began toying with the *Times* crossword puzzle. Home of Mt. Everest led off across, an Advocate of Anarchy vertically, and I was away with Nepal and nihilist.

Oddly enough, once the initial shock had been sustained, I gave no thought to ducking out. Even given the handicap of the hangover, I could probably have devised some means of weaseling out of the speech. I could have protested a sore throat, or the pressure of work for *Youth Outlook*, which would, of course, take priority over an extramural activity, no matter how deserving. But with the delivery of this, Fate's latest hammer stroke, I found myself soothed by an inexplicable serenity. All this, it seemed, was ordered when the universe was young and I, no longer captain of my soul, could do nothing but go quietly along, accepting each new development as it transpired. In pugilistic circles, I would have been described as punchy.

In the wings, Fate was working the last bugs out of a thunderbolt before the stagehands hauled it high up into the flies.

Miss Nordlinger poked her pretty head in at my door to announce that, having been apprised by Mrs. Nonnenmaker of my schedule, she had summoned a cab to transport me to the Mayflower. I glanced up from City of S.E. France and split my face in what I sincerely meant to be a smile of great charm as I prepared to thank her for this kindly service when that goddam egg got in one last stroke of deviltry and there surged up from the depths of my being a belch fit to frighten lions.

I fled past her, the expression on that innocent child's face forever burned into my brain.

"Haul away handsomely, lads," Fate called to the stagehands.

XXXIV

At my bidding, my cab driver paused briefly outside a pharmacy to permit me to dash inside and purchase emergency medication. I had no wish to disgrace myself at the head table, and by the time we pulled up to the Mayflower I had swiftly munched my way through a whole roll of Tums. The effect, as I descended from the cab and made my way into the hotel's lobby, was a kind of numbness about the middle, as if that part of me between the rib cage and the knees had ceased to exist as a working segment of the whole. I mean this in no disparagement of Tums, the manufacturers of which strongly recommend against the practice of gulping down their most excellent palliative by the fistful. By now, as well, I was once more ravaged by thirst.

A glance at the "Today's Events" board sufficed to inform me that the Annual Convention of the Future Librarians of America would open with a luncheon in the Main Ballroom at 12:45 P.M., this to be preceded by a Reception for Distinguished Guests in the Cabinet Room, a smaller chamber designed to accommodate such lesser functions. Thither, then, I made my way, clutching my Manila envelope. The vasty corridor was thronged with young men and women, all wearing great round badges bearing the open tome and the lamp of knowledge of the F.L.A.

A towering female with the expression of one of the fiercer Roman goddesses spotted me as I entered the Cabinet Room and swept alongside, bearing with her, like a sloop of war caught in a frigate's lower yards, a small, plump, bald man with a ferocious little black beard. These twain, it developed, were Dr. Antonia Biedermeier and Dr. Heygood Weymiss, respectively the senior advisors of the young women's and young men's divisions of the Future Librarians of America. The ever-efficient Oradean Nonnenmaker had already advised them that I would be substituting for the Senior Ass, and we spent several minutes telling each other what a fine fellow Samuel K. Nurney was and what a shame that the stern demands of duty had dictated his absence.

"This would have been his first address to the junior group," Dr. Biedermeier said regretfully. "Of course, he's talked to the senior convention several times, and all of us were so impressed we felt we just must have him speak to our juniors."

"We in the National Congress of Library Administrators feel that our junior group is far and away our most important long-range program," Dr. Weymiss added in an astonishingly deep voice. "This is our fifteenth year in the field, and while we're nowhere near the Future Farmers, we feel we're doing pretty well. We get a much smarter kid, too, as a general rule."

The two of them were herding me gently but firmly deeper into the crowded, conversation-loud room, pausing from time to time to introduce me to such dignitaries as Brig. Gen. Harrison T. Minafee, director of library services for the Armed Forces Information and Education Command; a Miss Ardythe Chasm (at least that's the way I heard it), executive secretary of the American National Red Cross Book Procurement Program; a man whose name I failed to catch but who did something about libraries for the Veterans' Administration, and several others of equal stature in the stack-and-catalogue card field. Around me I heard snatches of professional chitchat—glue was still rising and rebinding contracts these days, my God! Max Feinberg's got the Huntington made, but he won't leave the Folger. Who'll take over the Fogg? Is it true about the Widener and Sam Schnitlauf? All pretty stimulating stuff.

Eventually we arrived at a long table whereon were set out the goodies calculated to delight the distinguished guests—plates of petits fours, dishes of palely glowing mints, and three huge silver punch bowls. Behind the bowls stood alert members of the hotel catering staff, wearing broad smiles and ready to dispense the unwholesomely pink fluid, upon the surface of which floated bits of garbage.

Under any other circumstances I would have recoiled from this noisome fruit soup as from a girl whose skin is not Ivory-fresh or deodorized by Mum, but my tongue would shortly be so swollen as to render speech impossible unless I gave it some sort of lubrication. I accepted a cup from a grinning servitor and swallowed it as speedily as was possible without presenting an appearance of feral greed. It was ghastly, but it was wet. Dr. Weymiss, I noted, had also taken a cup.

"There's Gwendolyn Seep," Dr. Biedermeier whispered huskily from her gray-crowned heights. "She's done the most marvelous things with her group at Smith."

"Wonderful school, Smith," I allowed, and passed my cup back for a refill. Nodding vigorous assent, Dr. Weymiss did the same, giving me a conspiratorial little smile.

"Hope all this isn't being too dull for you, Larrabee," he said, taking a gulp of punch. "Haven't I seen you around the Cosmos?" He finished his cup and went back for more.

"Sorry, I'm not a member. Fine club, though, I understand." I followed the Weymiss example. The taste continued foul, but it was doing the job, by George.

"Stuffy, though," Weymiss observed. "Oops! There comes Doctor Fenstermacher. He's from State." And with a murmur of apology, he hauled alongside Dr. Biedermeier and together they sailed off to greet the State Department's representative to the assemblage, leaving me alone by the refreshments. I finished my third dose of punch and returned my empty cup to the waiter, in whose eyes I thought I detected a certain mild amusement. Quite possibly, it occurred to me, he had been among those present when they stirred in the newts' eyes.

Suddenly a very pretty girl was amongst us, deftly pinning to my lapel one of the saucer-sized roundels of cardboard which made us all one big happy family. Printed upon it were the words "HELLO THERE. MY NAME IS FREDERICK T. LEATHERBEE of YOUTH OUTLOOK MAGAZINE. WHAT'S YOUR'S?" Mine and my organization's names had been inserted in capitals with a fountain pen.

"I do hope I've got the name right, Mr. Leatherbee," the lass said anxiously. "Dr. Weymiss was in such a rush this morning. I'm Nancy Furlong, from Sweet Briar. I'm chairman of the Collegewomen's Division—we're the older members of F.L.A." She giggled, dimpling nicely. I beamed upon her.

"Happy to meet you, Miss Furlong," I said warmly. "How about joining me in a cup of punch?" She giggled again, although this invitation had not struck me as being especially witty.

"I wouldn't dare," she stage-whispered. "I've had two already. Can't you tell?"

"Tell? Tell what?" I inquired, draining the dregs of my fourth cup.

"It's spiked like crazy," she hissed. "Doctor Biedermeier doesn't know about it or she'd have a fit, but Doctor Weymiss had them add two quarts of gin to every bowl they mixed. That Doctor Weymiss." She shook her pretty head whimsically. "He's a one, all right. But I must dash. Can't tell you how much I'm looking forward to hearing your speech later on, Mr. Leatherbee." And she was gone.

I remained strangely calm upon the receipt of this grim intelligence, like the captain of a dreadnaught which has just taken a couple of torpedoes below the waterline amidships, who sends his damage control officer below to ascertain conditions. I had taken aboard four cups of this potentially lethal fluid, approximately the equivalent of a Martini-and-a-half by gin content, which, in my condition, was sufficient to sink me. Balanced against this, like a bulwark protecting the combat control center, was the fistful of Tums. If the bulwark held, all would be well. If it gave way. . . .

Still numb below decks, though vaguely conscious of a distant sloshing, I followed the distinguished guests who were now moving slowly toward the Main Ballroom, walking with great precision so as to avoid being jostled. As we entered the great hall, my ears were assaulted by the thunder of roughly eight hundred adolescent voices raised in conversation. There was a momentary silence as Drs. Biedermeier and Weymiss led our procession in single file behind the long, flower-bedecked table on the dais overlooking the assembled multitudes at the tables set out on the ballroom floor, below the salt. Then the whole mob rose to its feet and gave us a nice round of applause. We responded by milling about nervously as we tried to find our places.

A Reverend Doctor Somebody delivered an invocation of inhuman length, beseeching heavenly approval for the great work of the convention, for the selfless devotion of the organization's adult sponsors and advisors, for the wholehearted dedication of the fine young people gathered here in this room and for greater public recognition of the vital part the librarian plays in the life of the whole community. The fine young people gathered here were getting as restive as natives after the rainy season before he amen-ed us to our seats. The Tums were still holding fast.

I found myself seated between Brig. Gen. Minafee and Miss Chasm, who appeared to be sharing a private joke.

"General, you really are a shocker," Miss Chasm caroled demurely.

"Prior planning, my dear," rumbled the General, one of your beefier types and clearly the despair of his military tailor. He raised his glass of water and took a slow, appreciative sip. Miss Chasm also took a sip of hers, very tentatively. "Ummm," she murmured. "That helps."

"Better have a sip of water, Leatherbee," said the General, winking heavily at Miss Chasm. "I thought Sam Nurney would be sitting here, but I guess you won't object. Go ahead; have a drink of water." He chuckled as I lifted my glass to my lips. "Little understanding I have with the banquet manager. Man's got to get through these goddam luncheons one how or another," he concluded jovially as I took a mouthful of purest vodka.

Below, the boiler room was a steam-filled hell as the black gang made for the ladders.

Fumes from the inferno thus unleashed began seeping into the superstructure. Curiously, the effect was to further enhance the strange euphoria that had encompassed me earlier. I surveyed the ballroom and its chattering inhabitants with increased interest, as the criminal on his way to the gallows enjoys with heightened perception and razor-keen appreciation his last sight of the sun. Waiters began placing dishes of one sort and another before me, but I recall little of their nature or flavor. Not a criminal on his way to the noose, I decided, after giving the matter a great deal of thought, but an early Christian, eyeing the tiered ranks of humanity above him in the arena as he awaited, meekly calm, hearing the clangor of iron gates thrown wide and the measured tread of the approaching lion. Into thy hands, O Lord. . . .

Indeed, I recollect but little of the gay conversation I enjoyed with General Minafee and Miss Chasm, for overcome by the we-who-are-about-to-die feeling, I continued to sip at the General's little joke. My stream of mots, anecdotes and ironies kept them in stitches, as I recall, although from time to time I seemed to catch a note of alarm in Miss Chasm's eyes.

"To the farsighted," I declared, as we nibbled through our sherbet (orange, I think, and not at all bad with vodka, by the way), "books are the curse of the reading glasses." "What," I inquired as the coffee arrived, "is a bibliophile but a man suffering from tome-main poisoning?"

"Better ease off on that stuff, Leatherbee," the General muttered uneasily at one point, nodding almost imperceptibly toward my now nearly empty glass.

"Oh ye of little faith," I chided him. "Wine is a mocker, but vodka I?"

"It's your funeral," he said, displaying a childish rancor I had not believed him to possess. Miss Chasm, for her part, had partaken sufficiently of her glass to side with me.

" 'Tisn't," she declared stoutly, in rather too loud a voice. Several heads up the table turned disapprovingly in our direction. " 'Syours, tha's whatitiz." She attempted to wink at me, but could manage only a blink. I perceived that her eyes were slightly out of alignment and glazing rapidly.

What might have developed into a first-class brouhaha between the General and Miss Chasm died aborning when Dr. Biedermeier rose to her feet and moved to the lectern set squarely in the middle of the high table.

"HEEEEEEEE," she began, her voice amplified to a Valkyrie's

scream through the miracle of modern electronics. "HOOOOOOOO," she added, fiddling in panic with the microphone which leaned its reptilian head at her. There followed the sound of an avalanche hurtling down upon some sleeping Swiss village, several sharp reports, as of musketry, and then, very loud and clear, "Will somebody for God's sake fix this thing?"

I thought General Minafee would have a conniption, and as for the Future Librarians of America—Well, sir! They like to have raised the roof, they just mortally like to have raised that old roof, the way they took on. Beside me, Miss Chasm was weeping fit to die. "Poor Antonia," she kept repeating. "Poor Antonia. She will never live this down, never, never, never." Ever conscious of what Youth House expects of its representatives, I maintained dignity of a sort by burying my face in my napkin.

After several minutes, a small man in the livery of the hotel appeared, fiddled knowledgeably with the microphone and set matters aright. Order was restored, and I could not but admire Dr. Biedermeier's iron courage as she apologized for her *lapsus linguae* and brought the proceedings firmly back on the rails. With truly magnificent aplomb, she then introduced the guests of honor, and each of us rose slightly in our chairs as our names were intoned, to be greeted by a wave of polite applause.

It was when I rose to acknowledge my introduction that I realized that the Tums had given up the fight. From here on in it would be *sauve qui peut*. Barely had I regained my chair when we were all asked to rise again while the entire group recited the Future Librarian's Credo, a not altogether successful adaption from the Nicean. Standing there, I realized that other and nameless forces were at work upon me. I was coming down with one of those bugs that periodically sweep through the Federal City. Euphoria was beginning to give way to nightmare.

"Before we hear our speaker of the afternoon," Dr. Biedermeier declared over the great rustling and scuffling as the convention reseated itself, "I know you are all dying to learn the winner of this year's Lola Smiley Winship Trophy for Chapter Accomplishment, and it is my sincere pleasure to announce that this year's trophy has been awarded to the Middleburg, Virginia,

Chapter. Will the Chapter President and Sponsors please come forward."

In the rear of the banked tables there was a stir as a young girl, a man and a woman arose and began to make their way through the furiously clapping Future Librarians.

"Our foun'er," muttered Miss Chasm by way of identifying the trophy's donor, but I had no ears for her. I was transfixed.

"I want to introduce to you all," Dr. Biedermeier boomed over the dying applause as the trio reached the center of the table before the lectern, "Miss Margaret Goodspeed, a member of the senior class of Middleburg High School and president of the Middleburg Chapter of the Future Librarians of America, and the chapter sponsors, both members of the board of trustees of the Middleburg Memorial Library Association, Mrs. Davis Carter Powers and Mr. Lewis Cochran."

I was dead and in hell.

I was not dead, but mad.

I am not naked in the middle of Pennsylvania Avenue, because this whole thing is a dream from which I shall shortly awake to find myself safe in bed at home. All I have to do is open my eyes.

I did. Diana Powers was staring straight at me. But there was not the slightest sign of recognition in her cool gaze. Now Dr. Biedermeier was handing over an enormous golden trophy to Miss Goodspeed, and now Miss Goodspeed was responding with a pretty speech of acceptance. Now Mr. Cochran was bowing, and now he was saying something into the microphone, which Dr. Biedermeier had passed down from the lectern. And now Diana Powers was fumbling in her purse and extracting first a small piece of paper and then a pair of horn-rimmed glasses.

Saved, by God!

Saved, saved, saved!

". . . and thank you all very much," glorious, short-sighted Diana was wrapping it up. And smiling benignly. And taking off her glasses. And I was shaking like an aspen.

The Lazenby fabric could survive few more such jolts, if, in fact, it had survived this one, for it was becoming increasingly evident that the bug, whatever it was, was rapidly taking charge. I felt by turns clammy and as one who has wandered by mistake into a crematorium, and there was now a certain difficulty in bringing the eyes to focus upon objects in the middle distance.

"And now," Dr. Biedermeier resumed command, "we come to the traditional keynote speech of our annual convention. Every year, as you first-timers may not know, your Senior Advisory Board seeks to find a speaker who will bring you a message of significance for our times; a message upon which we can base our thinking and our programs for the future.

"Last year, as those of you who were here will remember, we received an inspiring and wonderful talk from Senator Hoopes, of Maryland, who told us that our duty to our country and to posterity was to press ever onward toward those goals which make this nation great." There was a brief smattering of applause. "This year, we were to have had as our speaker one of the truly great editorial voices of our generation—Mr. Samuel K. Nurney, the Senior Associate Editor of *Youth Outlook Magazine* and one of this country's outstanding authorities on the problems confronting youth today. Unfortunately—" there was an audible murmur of dismay at this disclaimer "—unfortunately, Mr. Nurney cannot be with us this afternoon, due to an unforeseen emergency which called him out of the city, but—" and now there was another murmur, as of mildly reviving interest "—knowing Samuel K. Nurney, I knew he would never let his young friends down, and he has not. We are, therefore, fortunate in having with us Mr. Frederick W. Leatherbee, Editorial Associate of *Youth Outlook Magazine* and alternate member of the President's Commission on Juvenile Correction. He will, I know, have a message for us all. And now, Future Librarians of America, it is my privilege and pleasure to introduce to this fourteenth annual convention our keynote speaker, Mr. Frederick W. Leatherbee. . . ."

Clutching my envelope and Nurney's speech, I inhaled deeply and heaved myself to my feet. With marvelous precision I made my way to the lectern. I dared not, after the "for God's sake, fix the microphone" bit, correct my name, and it would be much too involved to launch into an explanation that these were not *my* remarks and that I was simply reading a prepared speech. At the lectern, I withdrew the manuscript from the envelope and laid it down.

"All set up there?" cried Fate, peering upward into the flies. "Then let 'er rip, lads."

XXXV

Possibly as a result of the miasmas arising from that broad open sewer which is presently the Potomac River—thanks to the far-sighted legislators of the Congress and the State of Maryland—the Federal City seems to be afflicted by a greater than normal number of minor plagues, ranging from the relatively simple trots to the blind staggers. So prevalent are these lesser murrains that the city's residents have come to take a peculiar sort of pride in them. "John's down with this latest bug and had to cancel out his appointment with the Secretary of Defense," a Washington wife will say smugly. And, indeed, the bugs are not without certain benefits. John can knock off from work for a day or so and loaf around the house, sipping strong toddies to recover his strength. Undesirable invitations may be declined with honor. The point is that the bug is an accepted part of the Washington way of life. I mention this only to put you into the medical picture, lest you feel I exaggerate the effect of these petty pestilences.

I took a deep breath and gazed earnestly out over some eight hundred pink blobs, for by now vision was on a touch-and-go basis, just prolonged enough for my nostrils and tear ducts to get together. Then the pink blobs disappeared behind a shimmering wall of water and my stomach rolled slowly over on its beam ends, cargo shifting like molten lava. I had gulped into my lungs God knows how many cubic inches of cigar smoke, rising as from a burning ghat on the banks of the Ganges. Someone—it must have been Dr. Weymiss, since he was sitting closest to me—had cast good manners and human decency to the winds and, despite the presence of ladies, set afire his Perfecto.

My eyes cleared during a brief burst of wheezing and snorting that I trusted would pass as the usual preliminary throat clearings, only to disclose another wave of pale blue smoke curling in sinister fashion across the first page of my speech. Then I began to read, speaking in what I hoped was a clear, firm voice with suitable expression. The introduction was no trouble at all, and the customary opening joke, although not up to my own exacting standards, succeeded in eliciting an appreciative titter from my young friends. And still the smoke of that hellish cigar drifted slowly upward from somewhere behind me to gather itself in a small, still, stubborn nimbus that hovered about my head like the cloud that is said always to conceal the peak of Mount Everest. The aroma was unspeakable, as if Weymiss had somehow got hold of a stuffed grape leaf instead of a clear Havana. Or as if something had got into his cigar and died there. Horribly.

Clearly, Samuel K. Nurney had spared himself no effort in preparing this address, and my fingers, laid alongside the thickness of the manuscript, transmitted the information that the damned thing was of enormous length. I cannot recall one word of it, but SKN and I seemed to be covering the whole history of the library from the dawn of civilization to the present day, with a wealth of detail customarily reserved for doctoral theses and legal statutes.

Minutes after I had got past the opening joke my physical condition was such that had the small lectern been suddenly removed, I would have fallen face downward across the table. Only my arms braced against it, hands grasping its edges as the drowning man is said to clutch his bit of flotsam, seemed to be propping me more or less erect. My digestive system had now set up a slow, steady thumping, and to my other concerns was added the nagging worry that this might betoken the birth of yet another massive belch which, magnified and distributed by the public address system, could conceivably loosen the plaster of the ceiling. In actuality, this internal disturbance marked the further progress of the bug, although of this I was not, of course, aware. Nothing, from this point on, remains very clear in my memory. In effect, I became an automaton, operating purely by reflex.

On we droned, SKN and I, past Alexandria and through Rome's Silver Age, headed relentlessly for the Renaissance amid the stench of burning cabbage, innards bubbling like a brewery's mash vat. I had got to my first Medici when I observed a small disturbance at the rear of the room, hard by one of the entrances. After some seconds, this was matched by some minor scufflings behind me, and presently I saw Dr. Biedermeier steaming resolutely toward the trouble spot like a gunboat dispatched to quell a native rising. It was, I thought dimly, probably a group of young librarians, maddened beyond endurance by the remorseless flow of rhetoric, making a break for freedom.

SKN and I were engaged in describing the founding of the Bodleian when I saw Dr. Biedermeier speaking with some agitation to a blue-uniformed officer of the law, which was, I felt, carrying matters a little far. Then I noticed that I was losing my audience. More and more of the pink blobs began to turn to peer at the tableau in progress by the entrance. Then, abruptly, the little company gathered there began to move purposefully toward the head table, and as they drew near I was astonished to perceive in their midst none other than Nat Walsingham. The pink blobs followed their advance with interest, and with a mounting murmur. To counter this, the technician in charge of the public address system, ever alert to his heavy responsibility, souped up his volume and so threw his electronic marvel into disorder as tubes and amplifiers vied with one another to do his bidding.

"NOR WAS ANCIENT CAMBRIDGE TO BE OUTSHONE," I thundered in the voice of Jove and echoed by the tinkle of a thousand chandelier prisms. "THUS WE FIND THAAAHOOOOAHEEEEEOOOEY. . . ."

I believe the phenomenon is called feedback, but it is what happens when the public address system takes over and starts screeching to itself. "WHEEEEEEEE," the speakers screamed at each other. My eardrums palpated and seemed on the verge of implosion. I felt a tug at my sleeve and turned to find Dr. Biedermeier staring at me, her mouth opening and closing in the manner of a stranded fish, and behind her loomed the Officer of the Law, wearing an expression of great sternness. Speech was, of course, impossible in that inferno of sound. At the officer's side stood Nat Walsingham, stabbing a finger in my direction.

". . . TO SPEAK TO YOU," Dr. Biedermeier howled as the feedback process suddenly ceased. The cop moved forward and took my arm in a decisive fashion. He opened his mouth.

"ALL RIGHT LAZENBY. YOU'RE UNDER ARREST FOR ILLEGAL POSSESSION OF OBSCENE LITERATURE. COME ALONG QUIET."

The Lord God Jehovah couldn't have improved upon it. And what followed sounded to me like a pretty fair approximation of the Judgment Day, when the multitudes of the dead rise to mingle with the living. There was one split second of stunned silence and then the young librarians let go, and as they did the feedback resumed and God save us everyone. Chaos.

Numbly, as one who moves through a nightmare, I allowed myself to be led toward the entrance of the ballroom, moving through a tunnel of noise. "HOOOOOOOO," roared the loudspeakers and "WHEEEEE" screamed the young librarians, and the enormity of what was happening to me was lost in that incredible din. Only the firm grip on my arm was real. Pink blobs, laughing hysterically, appeared briefly, like fiends from hell, and vanished, to be replaced by other pink blobs. Then we were out of the ballroom and heading down the long corridor that bisects the Mayflower's street floor. The tremendous sound fell to the level of distant thunder as the ballroom doors closed behind us. Around me were clustered Dr. Biedermeier and Dr. Weymiss, gabbling incoherently.

A step or two away, wearing his mantle of self-righteousness, stood Nat Walsingham, surrounded by several other of my former companions of the head table. All stared at me with revulsion. I drew myself up in what few shreds of dignity were left me, an effort marred by the sudden birth and successful suppression of the belch that had been abuilding throughout my speech. This twisted my face into what appeared to be a sneer of insupportable arrogance. "Officer," I then said firmly, "I am at your service."

With what I trust gave the impression of a certain grandeur in defeat, I strode through the now silent group, heedless of the manner in which they drew aside as at the approach of a leper, head high, tread steady, eyes forward. I made it for about six paces, cheered on by the ghost of Major André, and then the whole long corridor began to list unaccountably to starboard and I noted with dismay that the carpet was rising swiftly toward my face. The bug had conquered, aided and abetted by that unholy cigar. Blackout. Curtain.

"Bull's-eye!" chortled Fate in triumph.

XXXVI

Conscience returned in time. I simply opened my eyes and there I was, flat on my back in bed, tucked in as tight and tidy as you please, arms outside the coverlet, staring straight up at a high apple-green ceiling which seemed bathed in a not unpleasingly soft yellow glow. I felt fine, doubtless because—although I was unaware of it—I was as full of pharmaceuticals and biologicals as an egg is of meat. Fine but detached. I must have been conscious for a full minute before I realized that I was not in my own bed. Our bedroom does not have a high apple-green ceiling. I pondered this for some time, feeling neither alarm nor elation but rather viewing it as an intellectual problem, the solution of which presented no occasion for urgency. I heard the sound peculiar to heavy doors opening and closing gently. Seconds later the sound was repeated. It occurred to me that I might be dead and on view in the slumber room of some elegant mortuary establishment. Or perhaps I was sharing the experience of Abraham Lincoln who dreamed he saw himself being mourned by tearful, silent throngs as he lay stone cold upon his bier. Either way, it was a matter of indifference to me. I was comfy.

Two faces suddenly materialized directly above me, lighted from below like two characters in a horror movie. One was that of a hawk-visaged female of indeterminate years wearing a more than usually absurd starched nurse's cap—all pleats and points. The other was that of a young man, from whose neck depended a stethoscope. Their faces were completely devoid of emotion.

"We've come around, I see," the young man said, his tone businesslike and impersonal. The remark was not directed to me but to the nurse, who sucked in her cheeks judiciously. "Better ask Doctor Chernowith to step in. Tell the wife she can see this one as soon as Chernowith is finished with him."

"Yes, Doctor." The nurse's face vanished and I heard her leave the room. Now might be as good a time as any to put things on a friendly basis.

"Gik," I observed, pleasantly enough. This was not what I had intended to say, and I felt a mild annoyance with myself. I could do better than that. I tried again. "Gik."

The doctor paid me not the slightest attention. Instead, he grasped my wrist and stared intently at the watch on *his* wrist while he fingered my pulse. "Um-humph," he remarked at length, letting my arm drop. He reached out to what must have been a bedside table, secured a thermometer, shook it briskly, eyed it severely, shook it again, eyed it again, and then jammed it into my mouth. I accepted all this calmly. Obviously I was not dead, or he would not be going to all this trouble.

The heavy door opened and shut again. Without turning his utterly disinterested gaze from my face, the young man with the stethoscope said: "This is Lazenby, Doctor. You asked to take a look at him as soon as he came around. He's still pretty goddam foggy, so don't expect too much."

I felt obliged to protest this misstatement. "Nurn," I said firmly around the thermometer.

Now there swam into view above me the mild, round, bearded face of the excellent Dr. Chernowith, wearing an expression of parental concern. Wordlessly he reached out and gently spread the lids of my right eye wide open and peered intently into it. "Hmmm," he murmured, pursing his lips. "Iris seems regular enough. No signs of the needle." He let my eyelids snap back to normal. The younger doctor slipped the thermometer out of my mouth and inspected its mercury column.

"He'll be in shape for transfer tomorrow," he said. "One of these two-day virus things, although I will say he was running around with one hell of a dose of the stuff. Funny thing—you wouldn't think a guy in his racket would have that kind of stamina. I mean, you'd think . . ."

"Ah," Chernowith replied happily. "That's just what makes

them such fascinating types. They *seem* so normal, even to the average practitioner. Unless you've studied the deviation under clinical conditions, well . . . Here, let me demonstrate." He bent over me suddenly, placing his face quite close to mine. "Fanny Hill," he said quietly, his gaze intense. He seemed to expect a reply.

"Gik," I said endeavoring to be cooperative and with the intention of telling him that I knew no one by that name. Despite this additional demonstration of my inability to communicate, Chernowith looked enormously pleased. His large, dark eyes were moist with satisfaction.

"You observed the immediate response?" he asked the younger doctor eagerly.

"Fanny Hill?" asked the younger man irritably. "Where is that?"

"Free Association," replied Chernowith solemnly. "One of the recognized classics of pornography. Prompt reaction from the subject, indicating recognition. Ver-ry interesting. I'll want to examine him at much greater length later." Abruptly he turned away from my bedside, seeming to forget all about me for the moment.

"You've seen the wife," he resumed softly, as if he did not want me to overhear his words. "Pretty little thing; doesn't seem at all the sort to be mixed up in this kind of business. Might be an idea to keep an eye on her, Doctor. Just in case, you understand. The police seem to feel quite certain she had no idea what was going on, and I'm inclined to agree. Generally, the wives don't. Comes as quite a shock to them as a rule and with these deep types—well, it's hard to say just how they'll behave when something like this hits them.

"But now I must be running along. Thank you, Doctor." And Chernowith in his turn disappeared and finally, like a bear emerging from his winter's hibernation, the mind stumbled out of the blissful detachment with which it had accepted the high green ceiling, the cold stare of the nurse and the ministrations of the two medical men.

The police? The *police!*

And then I was with it, and a more sickening moment I never hope to confront. After the total fiasco of the afternoon and my collapse, they had brought me here to what I now knew to be a hospital (Casualty? Mental? Which?). Then they had notified Joby as my next of kin, and now she was here, and . . . but Joby hadn't planned to return until evening, which meant . . . but of course; that was the reason for the lamp on the bedside table. I must have been out for the rest of the afternoon, assuming that this was still the same day. Or was it? How long had I been out? And what was this transfer business the younger doctor had mentioned? To jail? Where else?

God!

"All right, officer, you can let Mrs. Lazenby and the lawyer come in now," I heard the voice of the younger doctor saying briskly, and then, *sotto voce:* "He's still a little groggy, you understand, Ma'am, and I wouldn't stay too long. He's really had quite a session, and a good night's rest is what he needs more than anything else."

And then, praise Heaven, Joby was there.

"Eff!" she cried in a voice that tore me to pieces. "Oh, Eff!"

"Jobe," I croaked, and it came out that way. I was back in touch again! But the main thing was Joby, who had thrown herself on the side of the bed and was kissing me and sobbing all at one and the same time. Between murmurs of endearment, I became aware of another presence in the room. When this materialized in the halo of light from the table lamp, I perceived it to be By Stephens, my neighbor, who looked suitably embarrassed at being a witness to the touching reunion before him. He gave me a vague wave and a sheepish grin.

Joby finally pulled herself together and sat down on the uncomfortable-looking straight-backed chair By had shoved up to the bedside. I clung to her small, warm hand like grim death.

"By's been wonderful," she said, her voice still unsteady. "He came over to the house the minute I called, after—after the police phoned to say where you were."

"That's something I'd like to know myself," I said, feeling the morale flowing back into me from her hand.

"D.C. General," By said cheerfully. "It's where the gendarmes take all you hardened criminals. And there's a nice, big Italian cop sitting just outside your door. He's got six kids and has passed his examinations for sergeant."

"How long have I been here?"

"Roughly six hours. Now the point is, do you feel up to telling us just what the hell this is all about, or do you want to wait until morning? And one other fairly important question: Do you want me as your attorney?"

"I can talk now," I said firmly. "I think you're out of your skull offering to represent me, but I'm damned grateful."

And then, interrupted frequently by By's questions, I told them the whole sorry story, leaving out nothing except my near-escapade with Eleanor Alice. I would tell Joby about that part later, when I got out of jail, I decided.

"Oh, Eff, if you'd only confided in me right at the beginning," Joby reproached me softly when I had completed my dismal recital. It was the only reproach she ever uttered in connection with the whole wretched affair. By looked grave.

"The saddest words of tongue or pen, or something," he muttered. "If you had simply sat still and done nothing . . ." He shrugged. "In any event, they can't hang you. After our little chat the other Sunday, I checked out the law and your offense is a misdemeanor, not a felony."

"But I haven't done anything, dammit," I said, feeling a faint glimmer of annoyance.

"Ah." By grew solemn. "Technically speaking, perhaps. The prosecution would have to prove that you had obscene material in your possession with the *intention* of exhibiting it, selling it or giving it away. Now *we* know you had no such intentions. The trouble is, your friend B. J. Tombes has already told the cops that you told him you were going to make a mint from the stuff you bought from him. That's enough to give the prosecution reason to believe that you did, in fact, intend to sell the stuff. Which is why you were arrested."

"But that's simply not true, By. I never told Tombes anything like that. The man's a bloody liar."

"So you didn't and so he is. And that brings me to my point, which you're probably not going to like. Tombes is caught; he's trying to spread the blame around and he doesn't give a damn who gets smeared. It's no skin off his back. But this thing could hurt you badly—worse than it has already. Now I think there isn't a doubt in the world that we could get the charges dropped, once we got depositions from this Heppinstall Foundation and your pal Savoury."

"Well, why in hell not get them dropped, then?"

"Because in the meantime your name will be mud. The newspapers will have themselves a field day if you plead not guilty and we ask for a continuance until I can get the depositions. Every day of delay will mean that much more schmear all over the front pages. Do you see what I'm driving at?"

I was beginning to, and it looked unappetizing.

"You think Eff ought to plead guilty to something he hasn't done?" Joby asked, her voice a fine blend of bewilderment and incredulity.

"That's exactly what I think," By answered earnestly. "For his own good, Joby. Sometimes it works that way. A simple hearing in front of a municipal judge, and with Freddy's clean record and the responsible job he holds—"

"Held," I put in, bitterly.

"He'll probably get no more than the minimum fifty-buck fine—even that could be suspended—and the whole business is over and done with in less than five minutes," By went on persuasively. "Otherwise—well, otherwise, Freddy will be the star performer in a three-ring circus and even if we go ahead and get the charges dropped, his good name is shot to hell. Look, friends, I know whereof I speak. People remember the headlines; they don't bother about the follow-up stories on the inside pages which say the poor guy is pure as the driven snow. Believe me, you two, I wouldn't recommend this if I didn't feel sure it was the best way out."

"I know, but dammit," I said feebly, feeling the layman's maddening futility in the face of the law's impersonal complexity.

"Short and sweet," By declared firmly. "That's the only way. Over and done with. My God, Freddy, if this were something like a hit-run and you said you were innocent, I'd fight it all the way to the Supreme Court. But in a messy situation like this, the first thing you've got to think about is your reputation, and the faster we can get you out of this the better."

"I see what By means," Joby murmured. "It doesn't seem right at all, Eff having to plead guilty to something he hasn't done, but—" her voice trailed off. "And then, too," she added faintly, "it might be what they'd want him to do at Youth House. I mean, all this publicity would bounce back on them, too."

Which was a thought. Not that I expected to continue my association with *Youth Outlook*, but I did feel a certain loyalty to the magazine's good name, and Youth House had been good to me. Sparing it the reflected glow of my tarnished reputation would be the last and least service I could perform. And after all, By was the expert.

"When does all this happen?" I asked in a voice that rang like lead.

"Tomorrow, probably, if the hospital releases you."

"And by tomorrow night, it'll all be over?" Joby asked.

"After which you can forget the whole business," By told her.

"Yeah," I said. As simple as that.

"I'm glad you see it my way, Freddy," By held out his hand.

"You're the lawyer." I spoke without undue enthusiasm, but with the awareness that he was probably 100 per cent right in his estimate of the situation. "Thanks, By."

"We'd better be going, Joby. I think we're tiring the patient. Let's let him get his beauty sleep so he'll look real pretty for the judge. And Freddy, old friend, rest easy. Everything's going to turn out all right. Trust old By, pal."

"Sleep tight, my darling," Joby whispered as she bent to kiss me good-bye. "I love you."

And weirdly enough for a man in my situation, sleep tight is just what I did. The psyche can absorb just so many shocks, the soma just so many land mines, and then the subconscious takes over with soothing lullabyes and harp music and the soul snuggles deep into the warm, velvet womb of mindless peace. Things were no longer in my hands, my destiny no longer my responsibility. So I slept, safe neither in the arms of Jesus nor Morpheus but deep in the embrace of a massive sedation the hawk-faced nurse slipped me minutes after Joby and By had left.

XXXVII

One of the more disquieting aspects of residency in the District of Columbia is the fact that when you transgress, you are up against the powers and pomps of no mere municipal government: You are smack up against the might and majesty of the United States of America.

In re the United States *vs.* Lazenby!

The judge who conducts your hearing is appointed by the President of the United States, with the advice and consent of the Senate. The Prosecutor is a United States District Attorney. The effect is awful and depressing. The trial chambers of the Municipal Court, as it is called, unlike those seedy halls which serve the magistrates of lesser cities, are large, conventionally arranged and imposing enough to serve as the settings for the judgment of high crimes against the State.

To one of these high-ceilinged, walnut-paneled courtrooms, reserved for the Criminal Division of the Municipal Court, I repaired with By Stephens the next afternoon, following my release from hospital under the small bond set by the police to ensure my appearance. I had initially resisted the idea of Joby's accompanying us to the ordeal, but she had firmly rejected my reasoned arguments with the appropriate passages from the marriage ceremony and the old wither-thou-goest rebuttal. We took our seats on one of the foremost benches, set aside for those about to submit themselves to the arbitrament of justice.

The press table just outside the barrier which separates the court's working space from the public was, I noted to my dismay, filled to capacity with representatives of the city's daily newspapers. Behind us sat a scattering of those ghouls who are always to be found in attendance in courtrooms, hands cupped to ears to miss no grisly detail, eyes agleam to see the sinful undone.

The sordid business of punishing the wicked went forward with what I felt to be almost unseemly haste, and the only reassuring facet of the proceedings was the utter boredom of the various minor officers of the court. They did not appear to be conscious of their status as representatives of the puissance of a sovereign nation, and conducted themselves with that casual, knowing and self-righteous air that distinguishes minor court officers the world over, sniggering softly among themselves and tapping their teeth with pencils.

The judge, By told me in a low voice, was the Hon. T. T. Bealing, whose avocation it was to serve from time to time as a lay reader to the congregation of the Protestant Episcopal Church of All Saints-in-the-Fen, one of the city's more fashionable holy places. This information momentarily heartened me, since it has been my experience that the clergy of the Anglican persuasion are, on the whole, a jolly, reasonable and tolerant lot. But only momentarily.

"A prismatic, revolving son of a bitch," By muttered behind his hand. "I was hoping we'd be lucky and get Judge Pardoe." His face creased into a worried frown.

The Hon. T. T. Bealing was bald, red, wattled and appeared to be sneering a good deal more than was really necessary. It occurred to me that he was by way of being a frustrated divine and such men, it is widely acknowledged, are, even associated with the jovial confraternity of the Episcopal priesthood, dangerous as vipers. Indeed, T. T. was dispensing his judgments with a fervor that might have become John Knox but sat, I thought, exceeding ill upon a spiritual colleague of Bishop Pike.

My sound night's sleep had fully recuperated me, and I had spent the morning in deep thought concerning my present and future, endeavoring to reach a few decisions. In retrospect, I suppose I owe a certain debt of gratitude to the Hon. T. T. Bealing, for I strongly suspect that had another, less viciously self-righteous judge been sitting on the bench I would probably have comported myself in the meek manner which By had suggested as my best approach to justice. "You've made a mistake and you're sorry, see?" By had advised.

Mistakes I had made aplenty, true, and there was no doubt that I was sorry for them, but a mistake is by no means necessarily a crime, and I hadn't committed any crime, so there was nothing to be sorry for in that department. Or repentant, like a miserable sinner come to confession. The more I thought of attempting to appear repentant before T. T. Bealing, the less I liked the idea. Indeed, I realized sitting there, it would be damned well impossible for anyone with a gram of self-respect to kowtow to this virtuous slob; to submit to the public humiliation of a tongue-lashing by this tub of smugness.

But it was not T. T. Bealing alone who troubled my meditations. There was the ethical problem involved. Would it not be a crime to perjure myself by admitting to something I hadn't done?

Most important of all, there was Joby.

If I followed By's advice and pleaded guilty, there would always be people who would leer knowingly at her . . . "Don't you tell me she didn't know about those dirty pictures, Edith. How couldn't she, for heaven's sakes? Why, it wouldn't surprise me one little bit if she wasn't in some of them herself. . . ." The innuendoes she would be subjected to, the thinly veiled suggestions—it was simply not to be tolerated. The pornographer's wife, in the public view, would be no less an object of contempt than the pornographer himself. And I was no pornographer, dammit.

So I pondered, growing more positive of my ultimate decision with each passing moment.

I was still thus engaged, so it came as a mild shock when By suddenly nudged me and stood up, indicating that the United States was now prepared to get in its first licks at Frederick W. Lazenby. We approached the bench, By with stately tread, I attempting a rerun of my Major André bit, as the door to the small holding-cell just aft the courtroom proper closed softly upon a tall Negro whom T. T. Bealing had just labeled, in a voice that rattled the chamber's tall, arched windows, a Menace to Society and a Threat to every Decent Citizen in consequence of his Vile and Unspeakable Habit of Stealing Hubcaps. I shuddered involuntarily.

A clerk read off the charge against me in the monotonous tones of the consummately bored and at the swift pace of a tobacco auctioneer dealing with a sluggish market. I noted that my arresting officer, of whom I had only the dimmest memory, had also materialized from somewhere, and essayed a shy smile in his direction. He cut me dead, turning to talk to the youthful Assistant United States District Attorney who would present the government's case against me.

By introduced himself to the court as my attorney. T. T. Bealing produced a pair of pince-nez from beneath his flowing black robes and placed them on a nose which *Time* would describe as cobshaped, beet-red, blue-veined. Had this man, I reflected, attained his ambition to save souls, his parishioner must be a fool who would dare to call him Canon. Here was a veritable howitzer of moral virtue and Christian rectitude.

"Hrrmph-nurrmph," he trumpeted through that monstrous nose. "Lazenby, eh? Lazenby, yesss. The obscenity case. Well, well, well. Is the arresting officer present? Other witnesses, if any? Splendid. We can get on with the case, then. Counsellor, how does the accused plead to the charge?"

"Your honor, my client pleads guil—" By started to say, when I found my voice and said what the higher thought centers had decided was the only thing I could say and still live with myself and Joby and have any slightest claim on her love and respect.

"Not guilty, Your Honor," I boomed, far more loudly than I had intended. "I plead not guilty!" I repeated as By grabbed my arm, still mouthing the rest of his sentence and staring at me with a combination of wrath and amazement. T. T. Bealing slammed down the gavel.

"Now wait just a minute!" he thundered. "Just one minute here, I say! Let's get this thing straightened out."

"Your Honor," By began frantically, still clutching my arm, "my client has just been released from hospital and—"

"Your Honor, I'm feeling perfectly all right, and I want to

plead not guilty, no matter what my lawyer says." I turned to
By. "I'm sorry, Bayard. I just can't go along with it."

"It's your funeral, Freddy," he said coldly, and then gave me
a brief, bleak grin. "But I'll stick with you. That's what I hired
out to do."

"All right, then," rumbled T. T. Bealing. "Apparently you wish
to disregard counsel's advice and enter a plea of not guilty. So
be it. And now perhaps you will tell me whether you wish to
be tried by this court or by a jury." His tone was growing nastier
by the syllable, and the thought of Bealing dispensing impartial
justice was one which, in other circumstances, I should have found
hilarious.

"I want a jury trial," I replied stoutly.

"Your Honor," By spoke out, "I am sure that if you would
grant a continuance, I can produce evidence in the form of depositions which will result in the dropping of the charges against
my client."

"Denied," snapped His Honor. "Your client has made his decision, apparently without any help from you, Counsellor. If he
wants a jury trial, he's going to get a jury trial. In fact, I am
delighted he asked for a jury trial, because in that way we will
have the opportunity to spread all, I say all, the facts upon the
record so that the entire community will be able to learn of the
filth and corruption in its midst. The accused is charged with
one of the most disgusting and despicable offenses against the
morals of society—the dissemination of obscenity without regard
for its hellish effect upon those who come in contact with it. No,
Counsellor, I am truly glad that the accused has elected to test
his innocence through a trial by jury."

"Do I get to say something now?" I asked.

"*Please*, Freddy," By begged.

"I'm listening" rasped the Judge. "Let him speak, Counsellor,
if he's got anything to say."

"Look," I said to the court and whoever else was listening, "I
am pleading innocent because I *am* innocent. I'm fed up with
running around in circles with the law, thinking I've done something when I haven't. That's what got me into all this in the

first place. All I did was to store some stuff for a friend. All right, so it was pornography. The fact remains that I didn't sell any of it, show it to anybody or give any of it away, and what's more I never intended to. I stored it because a friend asked me to store it, period.

"But has anybody asked what the real truth is? No. Everybody's gone ahead on the assumption that I'm guilty. Even my own lawyer advised me to plead guilty and get out of this mess in a hurry. To avoid publicity. And maybe that would have been the smart thing to do, except that it would also have been the dishonest thing to do.

"The trouble is, when you mention pornography, everybody sniggers and assumes the worst. They don't wait to hear the explanations. It so happens that there is a perfectly valid reason for the collection I stored, and I intend to prove it. If I pleaded guilty now, the whole unholy mess would probably be forgotten two days after the last newspaper story appeared. But there would always be people who thought that I was nothing more than some kind of oddball pervert who liked dirty pictures. And I would always know that I had sold myself out simply to avoid a lot of nasty, unwarranted publicity. And I'm the one who has to live with myself."

"Have you finished?" T. T. Bealing asked when I paused for breath, fixing me with a glare of such malevolence that his pince-nez appeared to be glowing white hot.

"No, sir, I haven't," I replied stubbornly, because by now I was well warmed to my theme and getting angrier by the minute. "Maybe what's happened to me will start people thinking seriously about this pornography business, instead of sniggering behind their hands and trying to brush it under the carpet (I make no apology for this last confusion, in view of the circumstances) and forgetting about it. We make a tremendous stink about *Lady Chatterley*, and do nothing about the real filth. And until I got mixed up in this, I didn't realize how much there was around, or how easy it was to come by. This may sound silly to you, Your Honor, but it boils down to the reason I've got to prove I'm innocent, and that's all I've got to say. Thank you."

And distinctly from the press bench, by God, there came a single male voice. "Good man," it said, and I knew I'd done the right thing. It was a lousy speech, but I felt good. Everything was out in the open now, and it was me versus the United States, for better or worse, and somehow I felt I could take on the United States and win.

"Very touching, Mr. Lazenby," sneered T. T. Bealing, outdoing all previous efforts. "I hope it impresses your jury. Remanded for trial in ten thousand dollars bail. Next case."

"Your Honor!" It was By's turn to thunder. "Ten thousand dollars bail! On a simple misdemeanor, Your Honor?"

"You're at liberty to appeal, Counsellor," snapped the Judge. "Right now, you're wasting the court's time."

By turned to me, fuming helplessly, his fists clenching and unclenching, his face white, as they say in the novels, with rage. "We'll by God well appeal," he said to me as one of the young Deputy U. S. Marshals approached for the purpose of leading me off to the holding-cell. "I've never heard of such a fantastic bail. Meantime, I'll see about getting a bondsman."

"Forget it, By. What's the point of spending a fortune on bail. I'm in the soup now, or at least until you can get those depositions, so the hell with it. If I'm going to be a martyr I'm going to do it right."

By hesitated, and then shrugged and grinned. "Okay, martyr, you're running the show." Suddenly he held out his hand. "And Freddy boy, I'm damned glad you decided to do it your way after all. Only next time, tell your kindly old lawyer about it beforehand, huh? Even when your kindly old lawyer has given you a bum steer. And keep your chin up, son. Ol' By's going to get you clear of this mess or damn' well get disbarred. And that I ain't about to get."

The Deputy Marshal took a gentle but firm grip on my arm, and I turned for a last look at Joby. I fully expected to see her hunched over, shoulders shaking as she wept salt tears. I should have known better. She was standing up, looking straight at me, her eyes shining, a proud smile on her face.

It was as good a way to go to jail as I could wish.

EPILOGUE

If there were no tribulation, there would be no rest;
if there were no winter, there would be no summer.
St. John Chrysostom, *Homilies*

And never, may I observe, has a saint spoken truer words.

As soldiers are said to recall only the less wretched moments of war—the mind savingly expunging the horrors—so my memory has succeeded in editing out some of the grimmer hours that ensued following my hearing before Judge Bealing. But I am glad that I elected to go to jail rather than accept bail; otherwise I would not have met Dr. Chernowith again, and thus would have gone through the remainder of my life bearing the mute burden of the true facts.

It came to pass as By Stephens had predicted. The charges against me were dropped after the Heppinstall Foundation, finally installed in its new quarters, had verified the scholarly basis of and need for the Savoury Collection (or the "Un-Savoury" Collection, as it promptly became known in the local press). The foundation's assurances were backed in depth by a long cable from Dumbo himself, whom By had located by some feat of trans-Atlantic, telephonic house-to-house searching in Rome, where he was deep in a study of the notable collection of illicit literature housed in the Vatican Library. Dumbo's cable cleared up as well the matter of my transactions with the reprehensible B. J. Tombes, and this in turn led to the discounting of the charge of assault and battery lodged against me by Johnny Salvi, who, together with his erstwhile employer, is presently engaging the attentions of higher legal echelons concerned with the interstate transportation of obscene materials.

My dealings with Diana Powers were not, of course, involved and remained unmentioned.

The local press, after an initial period of hilarity, comported itself with a fairness which made me proud of my chosen profession, carefully playing its accounts of my eventual exculpation as prominently as it had featured the fiasco at the Mayflower and my subsequent arrest.

Joby was magnificent throughout, and if there is anything at all in Ecclesiasticus XXVI: 1, my days will surely be doubled. She never wavered, never faltered, even after my recital of the details, only slightly edited, of my interview with Diana Powers. "I'm glad," she murmured when I had finished describing my ignominious flight from the temptations of the flesh. "I think we would have survived, but there would always be this thing and . . . well, I'm glad it worked out the way it did." (On mature consideration, I decided it would be best for all concerned if I made no mention of my escapade with Eleanor Alice. A man is, after all, entitled to reserve certain matters to himself, and what would have been the point?)

During this, the most dismal period of my life to date, one thought loomed second only to my concern for Joby. This was the interview I must eventually and inevitably endure with Dr. Walter Van Meter Mountain. Youth House had remained resolutely, monolithically silent after my arrest, save for a single statement issued formally by Samuel K. Nurney to the effect that, pending Dr. Mountain's return from Mexico City, where he had flown to attend the Sixth Pan-American Conference on Illiteracy Problems, judgment would be reserved. This same reply, I learned later, was made in response to the hundreds of letters which cascaded into Youth House after the Associated Press story on my arrest had appeared throughout the country.

The summons came the day after the charges against me had been dismissed and I was given my freedom back unstained and pure.

Joby and I were at breakfast, nibbling in desultory fashion on toast and Cooper's marmalade, wanting desperately to seem cheerful but both aware that an ordeal lay ahead. Joby kept insisting that Dr. Mountain was not the sort of man to bow to the mob by firing me regardless of the fact that I had been cleared. And surely his position on the board of the Heppinstall Foundation (of which, until this crisis, I had not even been aware) counted for something. I, on the other hand, was more deeply aware of Walter Mountain's abiding, overriding concern for the reputation of the magazine he had devoted his life to building. The Heppinstall Foundation was, after all, no more than an outside interest whose demands must always come second to those of *Youth Outlook*. How could it reasonably be hoped that the parents who subscribed to *Youth Outlook* for their growing teen-agers would tolerate the presence on the magazine's staff of a man who had trafficked in pornography, in no matter how honorable a cause?

Joby answered the phone, and returned to the breakfast table with a strained expression that required no explanation. "That was Mrs. Strangeways," she said, her voice tight. "Doctor Mountain would like to see us both in his office at eleven o'clock this morning." She sank into her chair and lit a cigarette shakily.

"Both of us?" I lit a cigarette myself.

Joby nodded grimly and exhaled a cloud of smoke. "What do you think it means, Eff?" she asked, gazing at me bleakly.

I was momentarily baffled, and then it all became clear. Dr. Mountain would not fire me without doing the decent thing of explaining to my wife why such a move was necessary. The old boy thought like that; a wife was entitled to the courtesy, and Walter Mountain operated with Jeffersonian nicety in these matters. I explained this to Joby, whose expression became even bleaker.

We dressed in silence and foreboding. Rafe, sensing the family depression and unable to do anything about it, kept up a quiet, almost inaudible whimpering.

"Want a cup of coffee before we leave?" Joby asked, giving me a brave smile. She was dressed in her very best town suit, an affair of smart grays and blacks. No jewelry except a small gilt clip which I had given her on one of our anniversaries. I remember that we had driven out to Laurel, for some odd reason or other, since neither of us is especially horse-happy, and had placed a two-dollar bet on a very long shot which had shaken its owner by winning handily. Our winnings had paid for a spectacular anniversary lunch, and Joby had declared that her gilt clip was her official good-luck piece. Seeing her wearing it now. . . .

"Steady the Buffs," I said, raising my cup and trying to match her smile.

"Steady the Buffs," replied my Jobiana softly, and her eyes were definitely wet. I would have downed my cup and taken her in my arms for a long, hard kiss, but this was no time to be smearing make-up that her hand would not be steady enough to repair. "Let's go," I said instead.

We left the house with Rafe's mournful baying in our ears. He frequently howls when we leave him alone, but today his deep, hoarse belling seemed to carry an unbearable sadness.

Bang the drum slowly; play the fife lowly,
For they're hangin' Danny Deever in the morning . . .

But you get the picture, I'm sure.

Purely coincidentally, as it turned out, the reception hall at Youth House was empty when we arrived, and the echoing hollowness was as yet another portent of doom. Again as luck would have it, the elevator operator was a new man, and his greeting was as impassive as that of an Ethiopian nobleman receiving a delegation of minor chiefs.

In silence we rose to the third floor and stepped out into the thickly carpeted solemnity of the executive suite. Mrs. Strangeways, the editor's receptionist, arose from behind the broad, glossy expanse of her scrupulously tidy desk and approached us with a face devoid of expression.

"Mrs. Strangeways, my wife," I said, feeling that some sort of introduction was in order. The ladies acknowledged each other with polite nods.

"Will you go right in, please. They're waiting for you."

They! Had Mountain assembled the entire editorial staff to witness my disgrace? Would we be marched to the center of a hollow square while the Accounting Department Glee Club hummed "The Rogue's March"? And there stand to attention while Samuel K. Nurney ripped off my buttons and broke my ball point pen over his knee? For a wild, rebellious moment I felt like forbidding Joby to accompany me; I would not tolerate such treatment of my wife. But then reason prevailed. I took Joby's arm and together we marched to face the end of my career, through the tall, heavy oaken doors that led to the Editor's inner office.

Even in the happiest of circumstances, the inner office of Dr. Walter Van Meter Mountain is a chamber to inspire awe in all but chiefs of state and museum curators. Massive oak beams span the ceiling of the vast room, dominated at one end by a towering green marble fireplace in which stand tall, black fire-dogs salvaged from the ruins of some ancient Scottish castle. Along one wall are ranged several superb Queen Anne cabinets, housing the incredibly detailed British Admiralty ship models which are the pride of Dr. Mountain's famed collection of marine antiquities. On the oak-paneled walls hang naval dirks and cutlasses representing every period in the development of the Royal and United States Navies, while the end of the room opposite the fireplace is almost completely occupied by an enormous oil painting depicting the closing stages of the Battle of Lake Erie. Tall, leaded windows supply a diffused, ecclesiastical light over all.

I felt Joby tense as she caught her first glimpse of this weighty splendor, and now, as we entered, I saw Dr. Mountain rise from behind the graceful mahogany table which had for a time accommodated Samuel Pepys when the diarist was serving as clerk to their lordships of the Admiralty. He was rising! Joby's hand tightened on my arm, and I was conscious that there were, indeed, others present, seated in the tall-backed leather armchairs flanking the editorial desk. I stared at the round, ruddy face of my liege lord, trying to catch the expression in the ice-blue, amazingly youthful eyes behind the old-fashioned steel-rimmed spectacles, or the first flicker of movement by the lips beneath the toothbrush mustache which has for years been the delight of his caricaturists. And then I saw him begin to smile.

"Welcome home, Frederick," he said. "Welcome to Youth House, Mrs. Lazenby. Won't you both sit down?"

Now the Senior Ass was rising to show Joby to a chair, and I was having difficulty seeing because my eyes were all fouled up and my throat was at full choke, and fantastically, it was Nat Walsingham who was guiding me to a chair.

"I ask you to accept my apologies, Fred," Nat said, and all I could do was nod numbly and take his hand.

Well, sir, it was the damnedest third-act curtain any boy could desire; Andy Baxter was undone, and Captain Putnam had cleared Dick Rover of the accusations falsely laid against the sturdy youth; Tom Swift's Steam Dirigible would fly again! I might have broken out in maudlin sobs if Mountain hadn't taken charge.

Youth House, he declared, acknowledged no master save the law of the land, and if the law found me guiltless, not all the outraged subscribers in Christendom could force Walter Van Meter Mountain to find otherwise. I had served, as it were, as an undercover agent in the war against crime, alone and at great and unknown hazards and on behalf of a great philanthropic organization. Nat Walsingham had done only his citizen's duty in reporting that I was probably the George Burnley wanted by the police, and he had now openly and sincerely expressed his regrets for his hasty action.

"Although," Mountain went on, casting a stern gaze in Nat's direction, "it might be wished that Nathaniel had first come to Frederick, frankly and in friendship, and asked what the true situation was. However, all that is past and best forgotten; apologies have been tendered and accepted in the best spirit of Youth House, and I am certain that the two of you will continue to work together in fellowship and amity.

"The Senior Associate has explained the unfortunate mix-up in the matter of the address to your young librarian friends, and I am more than happy to say that their senior advisors have indicated their complete understanding, as I was certain they would once the facts were made known to them. And I may add that a similar attitude prevails among the members of the President's Commission on Juvenile Correction. Indeed, Mr. Julius—er, Julian, that is, tells me he is aware of Doctor Savoury's work and feels that it is a project of the utmost value.

"And now, Mrs. Lazenby," Mountain turned his spectacles on Joby, "I have to ask your permission in a matter of some importance. As you probably do not know, I have for some time been considering the establishment of a foreign bureau for *Youth Outlook* in either Rome or Paris. I have now to ask you whether you would find yourself willing to exchange your home here in Washington for one in Paris?"

Joby's eyes went saucer-wide.

"I can conceive of no better training for a senior editorial position on this magazine than a tour of duty as chief of the first European bureau of *Youth Outlook*," the Old Man concluded archly. "But I always insist that it must be the wife who chooses."

At which point my Jobiana went to pieces as her husband staggered to his feet and toward the editorial desk to accept the outstretched hand of Walter Van Meter Mountain and, in turn, that of the Senior Ass. "Youth House stands by its own, Frederick," murmured SKN.

Talk about a love feast!

So here we are amid the rustic comforts of the Swiss Chalet Mountain Inn, which nestles its absurd balconies and verandahs among the slopes of the Blue Ridge Mountains some miles to the south of the thriving little community of Front Royal, Virginia. Joby and I have taken one of the mock-sweitzer cabins which dot the establishment's extensive grounds, "Edelweiss Cottage." This enables us to be independent of the inn's dining schedules as well as of the attentions of the Recreation Director, and were it not for the occasional passage of a group of guests off on a bird-watching hike or a small-scale cavalry exercise, we might be a hundred miles from civilization. It is an ideal place to take a breather before we essay the monumental task of packing up the household goods in preparation for the move to the City of Light.

Both of us are well aware that while the European Bureau job is a spectacular break, it is also Dr. Mountain's tactful way of getting me out of Washington for a couple of years, by which time my adventures in the pornography trade will have become dimmed in the public memory.

Oh, yes. About Eleanor Alice Horvath. Just before we left on this brief vacation, I was summoned to the office of Davis Carter Powers. I won't bother you with my instantly rekindled worries, for the fact is that all Davis did was to hold out his hand and say, "Thank you for your discretion, Lazenby."

"And yours," I replied.

"During your—ah, er, difficulties, it occurred to me that it might be wise to rearrange certain of my personal affairs," Powers added, dead-pan. "Among other things I arranged for our mutual acquaintance to accept a secretarial position with another firm, an airline as it happens, in which I have a fairly considerable interest. She will be working in Mexico City in our offices there at, naturally, a pleasant increase in salary.

"As a matter of fact," the old goat concluded casually, "I have decided to devote more of my time to my other business investments and Mrs. Powers and I are thinking seriously of retiring to Mexico. I understand the climate is delightful. If you and Mrs. Lazenby ever get down that way, I hope you'll come and see us."

And thus we parted, with much unsaid and everything understood. It wasn't more than a week after this conversation that Powers announced his withdrawal from Youth House. I shall not be at all surprised to learn that Diana Powers has sued for a divorce, and I look forward to drinking a *fine* at some sidewalk café to her complete success and a whopping alimony. Diana deserves better of the world. I doubt not that Eleanor Alice will find a sufficiency of outlets for her natural exuberance in the Mexican capital, and I would give much to have heard her explanations of her removal to her widowed mother.

The Savoury Papers, seized by the police immediately following my arrest, were turned over, thank God, to the safekeeping of the Heppinstall Foundation against Dumbo's return from Europe, and there remains little now to be done but to inhale the salubrious mountain airs and restore the soul to its accustomed serenity. Joby has bought a stack of those records which teach you French by ear, and so far we have learned how to locate the crayon of this one, my uncle, on the table of that one, my aunt, and the boat train to Paris, whereon we will be expected to defend against fuming.

As proof that the soul has been fully restored, an incident occurred just last evening which gave me comfortable reassurance.

I had strolled down to the inn to secure a bottle of soda in order to prepare a couple of postprandial highballs for Joby and myself. There is nothing like sitting out on the porch of your cottage, holding hands and communing with the evening stars to the gentle tinkle of ice cubes. As I prepared to leave the small, determinedly quaint bar parlor, I heard through its open door the sounds of distant song, coming from somewhere higher on the mountainside.

"There is a fountain filled with blood," sang the nocturnal choristers from afar, "drawn from Emanuel's veins. . . ."

My expression signaled my question, and the barman shrugged and looked disdainful. "Damnedest noise in the world," he said bitterly, drawing a moist bar towel along his already highly polished counter. "Some bunch of religious nuts got a old house futher up the hill, past where the hotel road ends. Baptists, I think. Call themselves the Blue Ridge Encampment, or some such name. All the time singing them goddam hymns, you'd think they'd go crazy."

"Perhaps," I murmured inscrutably as I moved out into the night, "they are."

In the cool darkness I listened to the dying strains of the hymn. Was Eleanor Alice out there, enjoying one last riotous fling before she left for Mexico? I had but to stash my bottle and stroll up the trail to find out; Joby would think that I had been drawn into some idle conversation at the bar. It was probably less than a mile. . . . A gust of girlish laughter was wafted down the mountain as the revels continued.

"As I walked in the garden of pray-yer," the faraway singing resumed, and now it was possible to catch the note of ribaldry in the voices as they parodied the sanctimonious words. Would they, perhaps, conclude the evening's fun with a celebration of the Black Mass?

I turned and began walking swiftly back toward my own cabin and my own gentle, calm, lovely Jobiana. And then I began to run.